An Unlikely Friendship

by

Jann Rowland

One Good Sonnet Publishing

This is a work of fiction, based on the works of Jane Austen. All of the characters and events portrayed in this novel are products of Jane Austen's original novel, the author's imagination, or are used fictitiously.

AN UNLIKELY FRIENDSHIP

Published by One Good Sonnet Publishing

ISBN: 1987929284
ISBN-13: 978-1987929287

To my family who have, as always, shown
their unconditional love and encouragement.

ACKNOWLEDGEMENTS

Creating these works is
Always lots of fun.
Refining them is a lot of work.
Of course, my
Labors are supported
Implicitly by my family and friends too
Numerous to mention.
Energetic thanks to all for their support.

Chapter I

*I*t was a magical night. The musicians played, the delicate strains wafting over the assembled, providing a quality of music not often seen in this backwards town, the decorations created a night of mystery and romance, and the refreshments served were nothing but the best. It was a night to remember. It was the culmination of almost a month's worth of painstaking preparation. It only required the presence of . . .

Caroline shied away from the thought and decided she would not consider such matters that only tested and tried her endurance. That particular situation would be resolved shortly — she was only required to be patient.

As the dancers moved in the middle of the ballroom floor, Caroline Bingley looked out over those assembled with satisfaction. Meryton was literally nothing more than a speck on the map, and as Netherfield — by far the largest estate in the neighborhood — had remained uninhabited for some time, she doubted that most of these people had seen such an elegant ball in many a year. Certainly none of the other manor houses she had visited seemed capable of hosting such an event. And though she felt confined and at times ill at ease in the company of these people, it was only proper that Charles make a good impression upon his new neighbors. Caroline would prefer not to socialize with most of them, but it was required, and she would not shirk from performing her duties.

It was not so very bad, she mused. She had not kept her disdain for many of these people from those in her party—though carefully not allowing anyone from the neighborhood to overhear her comments—but they were not all bad. Miss Jane Bennet in particular was all that was good, and if she was a little naïve, Caroline could easily forgive that as a fault.

The problem was, of course, Charles's fascination with the young woman.

The Bingleys were a new family. Their fortune came from trade. It was unfortunate, but in a society where status was everything and where those who made their fortunes from the movement of goods were looked down upon, it took much effort to move beyond those origins. The Bingley family's longstanding connection with the Darcy family helped, of course, as did Louisa's marriage to a gentleman (though Hurst was really only a gentleman in name). But their success in society could only be improved by impeccable behavior, connections to others of higher society, and distance from their roots in trade.

Though Jane Bennet was all that was good, and she *was* a gentleman's daughter, she did not possess the kind of connections which would assist the Bingley family in society. From what Caroline understood, she also did not possess a dowry which would help make up for the evil of the lack of connections. It was unfortunate, as she truly was a likeable young woman, and Caroline could very easily accept her as a sister for that reason alone. Of course, if Charles truly did love her . . . .

And that was the true question. Charles was clearly infatuated with the woman, and unlike his previous paramours, his interest seemed to be more . . . focused than any she had seen in him before. It did not appear that he would lose interest in Miss Bennet. And Caroline could readily acknowledge there was something more about the young woman which was not present in so many others she had seen, something undefinable but pleasing.

"Miss Bingley!" came a voice, and Caroline grimaced before turning and regarding the woman who had addressed her, her countenance carefully devoid of her previous annoyance.

"Mrs. Bennet," said Caroline. Though she was polite, she could hear in her own voice a distinct lack of enthusiasm.

Luckily, the woman in question was not precisely perceptive, and she completely missed Caroline's tone.

"I must commend you, Miss Bingley," said the other woman with an enthusiastic shiver of delight. "Your arrangements are as fine as any I have seen. We are so happy you have invited us to attend!"

Of course my arrangements are fine, thought Caroline. *I have been educated in all the accomplishments of polite society. And it is not as if you would know if the quality was not the best anyway.*

Out loud, she merely smiled and nodded to accept the compliment. "Thank you, Mrs. Bennet. I am happy to have performed this service for the neighborhood."

"And we are very happy to have you! In fact, I cannot remember such a wondrous night as tonight, and I have been to all the finest gatherings of the neighborhood. You are very much to be commended. The romantic nature of the decorations you have chosen are perfect, especially given the . . . current state of affairs. I for one could not be more pleased!"

The woman prattled on, but Caroline allowed her thoughts to drift, knowing as she did so that when Mrs. Bennet started to speak in such an excited manner she would not require a response.

It was a sad fact that Mrs. Bennet was a large drawback to any alliance between Charles and Miss Bennet, and the youngest Bennets were no better. Mrs. Bennet was loud, obnoxious, mean of understanding, and as determined a fortune hunter as any woman Caroline had ever met. She would be an embarrassment to have as a relation. The younger girls were loud, brash, and fearless, and they did not possess the most basic concept of proper behavior. Caroline knew that if they were included in any events in London, they would immediately upset the Bingley family's attempts to gain acceptance, likely never to recover. If Charles *was* seriously considering Jane Bennet as a prospective wife, the mother and sisters would need much seasoning before they could be admitted to London society. Either that or they would need to be held at arm's length, a difficulty, considering the fact that Jane obviously loved her family despite their less than proper behavior.

But then again, every family had less than desirable members; the current family in residence was ample proof of that fact. Why Louisa had ever married such a dull bore as Hurst was beyond Caroline. She had attempted to convince her sister to refuse the proposal, but it had all been for naught as Louisa would have him regardless of Caroline's counsel. And of course there was Uncle Edward . . .

Caroline shuddered. It was fortunate that Uncle Edward was content to remain in York and run the family business, for he was coarse and unrefined and swore like a midshipman! He would never receive any notice from polite society, and as he openly disdained the higher classes, it was fortunate that he and society were mutually exclusive.

"And I am certain that it will be a most excellent match, for as much as I would wish for my daughter to be happy, I am sure you would wish the same for your brother."

The piercing voice next to her once again pierced Caroline's thoughts, and she turned and smiled at Mrs. Bennet. "Perhaps it is as you say, Mrs. Bennet. But I believe we should allow the principals to determine that matter themselves."

A hasty nod met Caroline's statement, amusing her as to the speed at which Mrs. Bennet agreed with her. The woman then said:

"You are quite right. I am certain they will come to a resolution agreeable to all."

"Indeed," said Caroline. "Now, if you will excuse me . . ."

"Of course, Miss Bingley. I am certain you have much to do."

In fact, it was a dance with a local man which called Caroline away. And though Caroline might have preferred not to dance at all this evening, as the hostess, she was obliged to stand up and act in a gracious manner to those in attendance. So when the man—his name escaped Caroline at the moment—arrived to escort her to the dance floor, Caroline assumed an air or polite attentiveness and allowed herself to be led away.

It was no great burden to dance, she mused as the music started and the dancers began their intricate steps. The man with whom she was paired, while perhaps not exactly light on his feet, was still competent. He was no Mr. Darcy, but then again, few were. And as he did not speak, it meant Caroline was allowed to sink once more into her thoughts.

The crux of the matter was as Mrs. Bennet stated, loath though Caroline was to acknowledge any sense whatsoever in the woman's words. Caroline *did* wish for Charles to be happy. The question was: did Charles's happiness depend upon having Jane Bennet for a wife? Though Caroline could not be certain at this stage, he was showing signs of an enduring regard for Miss Bennet which was quite beyond any regard he had held for any other woman. Caroline could not be certain, but she felt that he was becoming attached to Jane Bennet.

Could Caroline welcome her into the family if that was what Charles wished? If Miss Bennet was essential to Charles's future happiness, then Caroline would swallow her objections and welcome the young woman into the family, no matter what she thought of the matter herself. Miss Bennet was well-mannered and self-effacing, and other than being looked down on as a newcomer—something with which Caroline was familiar herself—she would ultimately be accepted into society with little resistance.

When the music came to an end, Caroline curtseyed to her partner for the dance and allowed him to lead her off the floor. The man smiled at her in farewell and moved off, and Caroline was able to look around the ballroom. But before she was able to take any impressions of the night's amusement, Louisa bustled up to her, an exasperated huff of annoyance escaping her lips.

"What is it, sister?" asked Caroline.

"Mr. Hurst," was her sister's short reply. "He is well on his way to being soused yet again and we have not even reached the dinner hour."

Caroline shook her head. She had known what Mr. Hurst was from the moment she met him—for that matter, so had Louisa! But her sister had been determined to have the man, as she had felt that since she had a proposal in hand, it would be best to take it; there would be no guarantee of another, after all. Hurst's status as a gentleman would help raise their family from obscurity, in Louisa's mind, though she never considered that their name was already becoming known due to their connection with the Darcy family. Louisa was not the most beautiful, accomplished, or intelligent woman, but Caroline knew that she could have done so much better than to settle for Hurst. Alas, it was much too late for that.

"Is Charles dancing again with Miss Bennet?"

Shaking her head at the fact that Louisa was once again choosing to ignore her husband's behavior, Caroline turned to look where her sister was pointing. Charles was indeed on the dance floor, again paired with the lovely Miss Bennet, who was laughing at something he said. Caroline had already known of her brother's plans, so it did not come as a surprise, as this was now the supper set. It *was*, however, an overt mark of favor and attention. In such a small society as this, some might consider Charles's honor to be engaged. Yet nothing Caroline said had dissuaded him from his purpose.

"He is enamored yet again," said Louisa, gesturing at the dancing couple with disgust. "How long will this one last?"

"His interest actually appears to be much more serious than any I have seen before."

Louisa scowled. "It cannot be allowed. After all *I* have sacrificed to ensure our rise in society, he cannot simply throw it away."

"Marrying Jane Bennet would not be 'throwing it away,' as you say. She *is* the daughter of a gentleman."

"With an improper family and ties to trade."

Caroline nodded, reflecting that Louisa's concerns were only what she had considered herself.

"The question is, does Miss Bennet hold Charles in the same esteem which he holds her?" mused Caroline aloud.

"It is immaterial," said Louisa. "We must find some way to deflect him. He may yet lose interest."

Caroline looked at her sister, waiting for her to continue.

"If we can persuade him to leave for town before his fascination becomes fixed, he may yet lose interest," explained Louisa.

"Not from what I am seeing. I have never seen him this attentive toward a woman."

"Still, it may induce him to think the matter over rather than make an impulsive decision based on a moment of infatuation."

Caroline merely shrugged; she knew that Louisa, with her distaste for her own marriage, would expect Charles and even Caroline herself to make similar sacrifices for their family name, though Caroline herself had no need to do such a thing. Louisa might even be feeling a hint of misery loves company mixed in with her desire to further their family name. While Caroline did not hold with such a sentiment, she would understand her sister's concern.

As Caroline turned her attention back to the assembled dancers, she noticed something she had not before. At the end of the line of dancers, moving gracefully across the floor as if he was floating in air, was Mr. Fitzwilliam Darcy. But that was not what had caught her eye, for though William did not often choose to dance, he excelled at the activity as he did at most of those pastimes he to which chose to apply himself. It was the woman with whom he was dancing which focused Caroline's attention on the man.

It was no secret that Caroline had never held much esteem for Miss Elizabeth Bennet. To Caroline, a woman who, though born to a tradesman, had been given the benefit of the finest finishing school and the best society had to offer, Miss Elizabeth's manners were not of the fashionable set. Some of that could be attributed to the confined society in which the young woman had been brought up, but that did not make her any more estimable a character, in Caroline's opinion. Furthermore, though she was not as overt in her behavior as her mother, Caroline felt the woman to be a fortune hunter.

More to the point, however, Caroline had seen how William had reacted to Miss Elizabeth, and the knowledge she had gleaned from watching their interactions had not pleased her in the slightest. William was obviously intrigued by the young woman, yet he seemed to be blind to the fact that she did not like him in the slightest. It was an odd combination for one who was an excellent judge of character and manners otherwise.

As Caroline watched them dance, she noted how Miss Elizabeth's eyebrow rose several times, how William's countenance became even more severe as she spoke, and how that voluble oaf Sir William approached them as they were dancing. William did not show much reaction to anything, but Caroline, who knew him as well as anyone, could see enough to concern her for the man's sake.

No, this will not do, thought Caroline to herself. *I cannot allow this to continue.*

There was nothing as mortifying as a buffoon who could not—or would not—accept a rational woman's refusal of his proposal of marriage.

Due to the lateness of the previous night, Elizabeth Bennet had woken the morning after the ball at Netherfield feeling out of sorts. The wish for a quiet day spent in reflection and solitary pursuits had been usurped by the ridiculous proposal of her equally ridiculous cousin, and now the halls of Longbourn literally rang with the displeased screeching of her mother.

Mr. Collins was even now in the sitting-room commiserating with her mother, and though his thoughts on the subject were not as vociferous, still Elizabeth could almost feel his injured silence from where she sat. Since Elizabeth was situated in a back parlor, away from where her mother usually held court in their family sitting-room, at least she could be out of her mother's presence, if not out of the range of her hearing.

As she was content where she was and expected an interruption to her solitude only if her mother decided to ty once again to persuade her, Elizabeth was thus surprised when the door opened, and one of the maids stepped into the room, leading the last person Elizabeth had expected to see. She rose, uncertain as to why this particular woman would be here on this of all mornings.

"Miss Bingley," greeted Elizabeth. "What a . . . surprise it is to see you."

"Miss Bennet," said the other woman, the insolence of her tone making it clear that she took no pleasure in visiting.

"I am not sure why the maid has directed you to this room," said Elizabeth, wishing to spend as little time in Miss Bingley's company as she could manage. "Shall I conduct you to the family sitting-room? I am certain Jane would be happy to receive you."

"That will not be necessary," said Miss Bingley. "In fact, I requested an audience with you and when I learned that you were alone, I asked the maid not to betray my presence to the rest of your family."

"And audience with me?" Elizabeth gazed at the other woman with wonder. Unless Miss Bingley meant to warn Elizabeth away from her precious Mr. Darcy, Elizabeth could not imagine what the other woman wished to say.

And if that was indeed her purpose, Miss Bingley had wasted her time in coming to Longbourn that morning. Elizabeth could not imagine Mr. Darcy — of all people — condescending to request the hand of such a lowly country maiden as herself. And furthermore, she could not imagine accepting such an application should it ever be extended, as she could not fathom the thought of living with Mr. Darcy's silent and condemning stare for the rest of her life.

At that moment a loud shriek rang through the house. "That child shall be the death of me yet! How dare she refuse such an eligible offer which would have secured our futures!"

Her face blooming in sudden mortification, Elizabeth sat rather abruptly on the edge of the sofa, her eyes looking anywhere but where Miss Caroline Bingley stood. She could almost feel the disdain from her position on the sofa, though the woman had not said anything. Elizabeth was in general a courageous sort of person who was not at all inclined to allow anyone to intimidate her, but the thought of Miss Bingley discovering the inanities of the morning and the indignity she had suffered at the hands of William Collins was almost more than Elizabeth could bear.

In silence, she gazed at the floor, not daring to look up. The other woman did not move for several moments, and Elizabeth almost held her breath, waiting to see what she would do. At length, however, Elizabeth heard the rustle of her skirts, as Miss Bingley moved to a nearby chair and sat.

"I hope you do not mind if I sit," said Miss Bingley.

Elizabeth looked up in shock. Miss Bingley's words had been colored with a slight hint of censure; it was deserved, Elizabeth had to acknowledge ruefully, as she had not thought to invite her guest to sit. It was evident on a glance that Miss Bingley's manner was more thoughtful than contemptuous.

Shaking herself from her reverie, Elizabeth apologized for her neglect and offered to send for refreshments. This offer was refused with alacrity.

"I cannot stay long," explained Miss Bingley. "My visit is due to a particular matter about which I wished to speak with you.

"Before I delve into that matter, however, I find that I am curious. Am I to understand that you have refused an offer from your cousin?"

"And what business is it of yours?" demanded Elizabeth, her resentment flaring.

"It is not," replied Miss Bingley, her tone of voice entirely reasonable. "But I would ask you to please oblige me. It may have a bearing on my errand here this morning."

Her anger spent as quickly as it had blossomed, Elizabeth passed a tired hand over her eyes. "I cannot account for your presence at all, Miss Bingley. But if it will bring you to the point, I will answer your question. Mr. Collins did indeed make me an offer this morning, and I have refused him."

"May I ask why?"

Elizabeth glanced up and regarded Miss Bingley with no little suspicion, only to find, to her annoyance, that the woman was not displaying the expected haughty superiority that Elizabeth had come to expect. Rather, Miss Bingley was watching Elizabeth intently, as if she was trying to understand something. The sight mollified Elizabeth a little, and she was able to sigh and respond:

"Because he and I do not suit each other. In fact, I cannot imagine a man who is less suited to be my husband than William Collins."

"That is a consideration," said Miss Bingley. "But at the same time, should you not consider the entail? I understand Mr. Collins to be the heir to Longbourn. Though I have no direct knowledge, I assume that your dowry is not substantial. If you should become homeless when your father passes, how will you support yourself?"

"Miss Bingley," said Elizabeth, directing a stern glare at the other woman, "I can think of no greater misfortune than to be tied for the rest of my life to a man whom I do not love and cannot respect, especially one so irksome as Mr. Collins. I would prefer to make my own way in the world and be forced to earn my daily bread than to suffer a life of mortification and regret as Mr. Collins's wife."

"Some might call such a position to be the height of selfishness."

Elizabeth gazed at the woman, trying to see her purpose, but Miss Bingley's expression was carefully neutral. As her manner did not appear to be mocking, Elizabeth allowed herself to relax slightly and to respond in a like manner.

"Perhaps it is. But I cannot repine my decision. I have not lived in a home in which there exists a harmony between man and wife, and I am witness to the effects of such a union on a daily basis. Though you may call me selfish and warn me of my ultimate fate should I fail to marry, I find that I would much rather live a life of genteel poverty than the life my parents live."

Miss Bingley sat back, gazing at Elizabeth with a frankness which was a little unnerving. Elizabeth had never seen such behavior from the woman before, and she found that she could not make her out.

"You surprise me, Miss Bennet," said Miss Bingley after a moment's pause. "I was not certain what to expect today, but it certainly was not this."

"I believe you should explain your purpose," said Elizabeth. "I am in no mood for games."

"That is understandable." Miss Bingley paused again before she shrugged and spoke: "Very well. I shall come to the point. I have come today to ask what your intentions are with respect to Mr. Darcy."

Astonished, Elizabeth could not help but gape at the other woman. "And you have appointed yourself to be Mr. Darcy's protector?"

"No. But I am an acquaintance of longstanding, and as such, I am interested in his concerns."

"I cannot imagine that Mr. Darcy requires assistance," said Elizabeth with no little disdain. "I hardly think he needs a nursemaid."

Miss Bingley's eyes narrowed and she glared at Elizabeth. "He does not. Yet he has shown a disturbing amount of interest in you, and I cannot in good conscience stand aside and do nothing. Before I came this morning, I was most concerned about your intentions, though your refusal of Mr. Collins—while foolish in some respects—has spoken well to your convictions.

"But I must be certain. So I ask you again: what are your intentions toward Mr. Darcy?"

Though Elizabeth would have liked nothing better than to refuse to answer such an impertinent question, she could only respond, saying: "I have no intentions toward Mr. Darcy and I cannot believe he has any toward me. He is a proud, disagreeable, severe sort of man, and I wish you well with him should you happen to induce him to ask for your hand."

At that, Miss Bingley descended into laughter. Elizabeth looked at her with shock, wondering what the woman could find so amusing.

"You believe I have set my cap at Mr. Darcy?"

"Can you deny it? I have seen how you attempt to attract his attention, how you admire his handwriting and praise his sister and his estate. In short, you behave much as a predator which has set its eyes on its next juicy meal, though I imagine Mr. Darcy to be much more wolf than deer."

Miss Bingley's laughter grew apace, and in a moment, Elizabeth heard the delighted tones of true amusement issuing forth from the woman. It was a sound that she had not heard previously and that she might not have believed the woman capable of making. Offended, Elizabeth glared at her guest and began to rise to insist upon the woman's immediate removal from Longbourn.

"I apologize for my unseemly outburst," said Miss Bingley, wiping tears of laughter from her eyes. "But I must own that I am excessively diverted at the thought that you think I wish to elicit a proposal from Mr. Darcy."

"You do not?" asked Elizabeth, her tone laced with skepticism.

"No, indeed, for I have no need of such a thing. I am already engaged, and it is not to Mr. Darcy."

Starting, Elizabeth watched Miss Bingley through wide eyes, but though she doubted what she was being told, she was silent.

At length, Miss Bingley's mirth ran its course and she once again spoke. "May I ask what led you to believe that I would wish to marry Mr. Darcy?"

"Do you mean beyond the fact that you agree with every word which proceeds forth from Mr. Darcy's mouth? Or perhaps the way you seem to hang from his arm at times. The way you size him up as a fox might size up a fat rabbit?"

Perhaps her frustration induced her to respond in a fashion which was more than a little insulting, but Miss Bingley seemed to take no notice of her tone. Instead, the other woman colored a little, and favored Elizabeth with a rueful look.

"Mr. Darcy has told me that my overly familiar manner and teasing gives the impression of admiration."

Elizabeth was skeptical. "And what of your request for me to 'take a turn about the room' with you? Was that not a blatant attempt to garner his notice?"

Shaking her head, Miss Bingley responded: "I was attempting to determine his interest in *you*. I knew that he would never give *me* a second glance, but I thought to test him to see if he would watch you. His attraction for you was amply proven in that instance, but I was still uncertain as to his true level of interest. My brother's ball heightened my suspicions."

"If that is so, why come here to confront me about it?" asked Elizabeth plaintively. "Do you expect me to throw myself at him? And why do you take such an interest in him if not for the purpose of marriage?"

With a sigh, Miss Bingley leaned back in her seat, considering Elizabeth, sizing her up, unless Elizabeth missed her guess. Gone was the woman's typical supercilious air, to be replaced by a sort of pensive introspection.

"To answer your first question," said Miss Bingley, "I have never thought you were the sort to throw yourself at a man, but I have wondered about your family in general. You must concede that your mother makes no attempt to disguise her intention of marrying you all off to the highest bidder."

A loud lamentation pierced the walls of the room, punctuating Miss Bingley's words, and Elizabeth ducked her head in embarrassment. Then her courage reasserted itself; she met the woman's eyes and said:

"It does not necessarily follow that any of us fall in with her schemes. I would never accept a man for reasons of prudence only."

"I am glad to hear it. But I could not have known that before." Miss Bingley paused for a brief moment. "What of Jane?"

"What of her?"

"Can I assume she would also not behave in such a manner?"

Elizabeth almost sighed with exasperation. "If you are asking about Jane's feelings for your brother, I assure you esteems him greatly. If she did not, she would never accept a proposal from him."

Nodding, Caroline said: "I thank you for confirming it, Miss Bennet. I shall not scruple to assert that Jane's serenity makes it difficult to understand."

It was only the truth, Elizabeth was forced to acknowledge, and she nodded her head. Miss Bingley was silent for a moment and after a moment's reflection, continued to speak, one single elegant finger tapping her lips in thought

"As for your latter question, I believe it is necessary to relate the full story of my family's acquaintance with the Darcy family in order for you to understand."

Though she was not certain she wished to hear what Miss Bingley had to say, her curiosity was roused and she agreed and settled in to listen to her tale.

"The Darcys and the Bingleys are connected from the time our fathers were alive. In short, my father and Mr. Darcy's father were close friends who attended Cambridge together." Caroline paused and released a short laugh. "In those days, even more than now, it was not fashionable for a member of the gentry to have a close acquaintance who was a tradesman, and my father was not even attempting to rise from his status in life. He was happy in trade, and as it was the world he knew—his father and grandfather both having built the family business before him—he was content to stay within that sphere."

Miss Bingley's expression became mischievous. "In fact, the rumored extent of Mr. Darcy's wealth is *only* that which comes from Pemberley, and not even including the other, smaller estates owned by the Darcy family. In fact, a large portion of Mr. Darcy's wealth is due to investments he made in partnership with my father. His wealth is much greater than it is rumored, though many of society would scoff as it comes from trade."

By the way Miss Bingley was watching her, Elizabeth assumed that she was testing her to see if the actuality of Mr. Darcy's much greater wealth would affect her. Elizabeth maintained her bland expression— knowing the man was much wealthier than she had heard did not make up for his utter lack of amiability and tendency to look down on others.

Seemingly satisfied, Miss Bingley resumed her tale. "I apologize, Miss Bennet. Perhaps I should be more trusting of your integrity. I have learned that there are few who would not be moved by such wealth as I describe. I assure you that I do not know the full extent of it, but I do know that Mr. Darcy is an uncommonly wealthy man.

"My father died when I was but six years of age." Emotion seemed to be getting the better of Miss Bingley, though she remained stoic and continued on with her tale. "I remember my father as an affectionate man and one who delighted in his children. His younger brother, though a good man of business who was intimately involved with my father's company, was rough and coarse, prone to womanizing and hard living. My father feared that his children would suffer under his brother's supervision. My mother died in childbirth—my birth. Thus, when my father fell ill, he begged Mr. Darcy's father to take us in and care for us. Mr. Darcy agreed."

That piece of information surprised Elizabeth. "So you have lived with the Darcys since that time?"

"Yes. Mr. Darcy and his wife took us in and cared for us, treated us like his own. When Mrs. Darcy passed away, Mr. Darcy largely withdrew from society. Then my own coming out was delayed by a year, as Mr. Darcy passed away when I was eighteen years of age. Since then, it has been the son who has supported us and assisted our entrance into society.

"That, Miss Bennet, is why I take such an eager interest in Mr. Darcy. I care for him as much as I care for the brother of my own blood."

It was not easy for Elizabeth to digest what she had been told, but she attempted to look at it with a clear mind, untainted by her impressions of the past. That Miss Bingley had appeared to have set her cap at Mr. Darcy was unmistakable; the woman had given all the impression of a woman on a mission to secure a wealthy husband at any cost. And yet, she did not think Miss Bingley had any reason to invent such a history or to invent an engagement with someone else. It must be true, she decided.

But to think that Mr. Darcy held Elizabeth in esteem — that was the most difficult thing for her to credit. The man's every look at her was filled with censure and disdain, and she could not imagine Mr. Darcy looking upon any woman without expecting to see some flaw which he could use to prove his own superiority!

"As for myself," continued Miss Bingley, "I am to be married after Christmas — in fact, we shall be leaving the neighborhood on the morrow. Charles, when he returns, will not be back until at least the New Year. I shall not return at all, unless Charles takes ownership of Netherfield and I visit him in the future."

Elizabeth glanced up at that bit of intelligence, concerned for Jane's heart.

Miss Bingley noticed the glance, and she sighed. "I assume you are concerned for your sister."

When Elizabeth allowed it to be so, Miss Bingley shook her head. "I have told Charles before that he should be more guarded in his behavior so as to avoid raising expectations, but he is open and friendly and he cannot help himself."

A feeling of incredulous anger welling up within her, Elizabeth glared at Miss Bingley. "Are you telling me that your brother is a flirt who goes about breaking young maidens' hearts?"

"No Miss Bennet. Charles is not deliberately malicious, only a little thoughtless at times. He has often fallen in and out of love, and though there have been many young ladies who wished to catch him for pecuniary reasons, his own propensity to become quickly enamored by the next young lady has protected him to a certain extent.

"Or at least, until now."

Elizabeth regarded the other woman with suspicion. "What do you mean?"

"His interest in your sister is far greater than anything I have witnessed before," replied Miss Bingley, her face an odd mixture of intensity and hesitation. "I do not know for certain, but I believe his feelings are lasting. Still, I think a bit of distance would be best for them both, do you not agree? I would not wish Jane's heart to be further hurt should Charles follow his usual pattern, but by the same token, I would not wish them to rush into marriage either. A little time away from Jane will allow Charles to recognize his own feelings, and he will be more prepared to act upon them."

Though the residual dislike of this woman urged her to disagree— that Miss Bingley was merely attempting to put the best face on her attempts to separate them—Elizabeth could only concede that her suggestion was sensible. Jane would be disappointed as it was if Mr. Bingley was not in love enough to take their courtship to its natural conclusion. If it continued much longer and still Mr. Bingley proved fickle, it would break her heart. Besides, Elizabeth could not abide the thought of Jane actually marrying a man whose head would be turned by the next pretty face.

Once Elizabeth had given her grudging agreement, Caroline smiled. "I am not an enemy of your sister's interest in my brother, Miss Bennet. I cannot deny that I had perhaps hoped for someone of status with a large dowry, but against Jane herself there can be no complaint. She is goodness personified."

"I am glad you agree."

"Now, as for yourself and Mr. Darcy—"

"There is nothing between us," exclaimed Elizabeth.

"There is nothing from *your side*, Miss Bennet, but I am convinced of Mr. Darcy's interest. Whether he ever acts on that interest I cannot say. I do not know the reason why you hold him with such contempt, but I assure you that a steadier man than Darcy cannot be found."

Elizabeth scoffed at such a description. "Is that steadiness what prompts such a paragon of virtue to cast off the friend of his youth and destroy all that friend's hopes for the future?"

"I presume you speak of Wickham?"

Miss Bingley's voice was carefully neutral, but Elizabeth thought she sensed an undercurrent of displeasure beneath her even tone. What was not in dispute was the contempt with which Miss Bingley spoke the name.

"I am," replied Elizabeth, scowling over the woman's lack of respect. "*Mr.* Wickham told me of his misfortunes at the hands of Mr. Darcy. Mr. Darcy's actions in that matter do not speak well of his virtue."

"Miss Bennet, since I have lived with the Darcys since I was a girl, do you acknowledge me as one who has knowledge of this matter? Or more particularly one who has knowledge of Mr. Wickham himself?"

Frowning, Elizabeth was forced to agree that she was.

"I cannot speak to it all—I do not know all the particulars, and certain parts are for others to tell. But before I leave today, let me acquaint you with a few truths concerning George Wickham.

"Mr. Wickham, as you know, grew up at Pemberley, the son of old Mr. Darcy's steward. What he likely avoided telling you was that he was not cut from the same cloth as his father. Of his exploits with the maids and the young women of Lambton and Kympton, anyone who has lived in the area can tell you. I myself was forced to tell him in no uncertain terms that he would lose more than just his position at Pemberley if he ever attempted to lay his hands on me. You should not allow your sisters to have any sort of association with Mr. Wickham, Miss Bennet, as he is completely without morals.

"Can I also assume he told you of the living which was cheated him?"

Elizabeth nodded, albeit reluctantly.

"He is nothing but predictable," said Miss Bingley with a sigh. "The living was left conditionally, and when he denied all interest in becoming a member of the clergy, he was compensated with an amount that totaled several thousand pounds. But that was apparently not enough for Mr. Wickham, as I am aware of several establishments in Lambton at which he owed substantial debts when he finally quit the area. I understand that he has behaved in a like manner not only in Cambridge, where he attended school to Mr. Darcy's largesse, but also in other places he has visited. The debts in Lambton and Cambridge I know for a fact Mr. Darcy paid in order to save the shopkeepers from hardship."

About to open her mouth and declare Miss Bingley's words as nothing more than the grossest of falsehoods, the words died on Elizabeth's tongue. She had nothing but the man's own words as proof of his assertions, and now that she thought of it, ample evidence that he had related the particulars to her in a most improper manner to a new acquaintance. Furthermore, Miss Bingley had lived at the estate herself when the events had taken place—was her knowledge to be discounted so readily?

"I can see that you do not fully believe me, Miss Bennet," said Miss Bingley. "All I ask is that you think on the matter, weigh what you know of both gentleman, and then make a decision on the merits of both." Miss Bingley's gaze turned stern. "But make sure that you are careful when it comes to that man, or you may regret it later."

Miss Bingley rose, bringing Elizabeth up with her. "I thank you for the time you have given me, Miss Bennet. Especially given the trying morning you have had. I will bid you farewell, though I suspect that our acquaintance is not at an end. If you would convey me to your sister, I would like to take my leave of her."

Mystified and still a little befuddled at the conversation she had just had with a woman she had disliked so vehemently, Elizabeth could only consent, and she led Miss Bingley from the room. The house had quieted considerably since they had been ensconced in the parlor, and a quick query of a nearby maid revealed that Mrs. Bennet had retired to her room. Elizabeth was thankful for small miracles; Miss Bingley had already been a witness to her family's poor behavior that morning and she was glad she would not be required to suffer Mrs. Bennet's effusions.

Upon entering the parlor, several things became immediately clear to Caroline: Mr. Collins was still present, and his pride was injured if the reproachful glances he cast at Elizabeth were anything to go by; the youngest Bennet daughters were amused by the whole episode, and their laughter, though muted, could be heard; finally, Miss Elizabeth, though she was obviously uncomfortable in the company of the parson, had marshalled her courage to meet his glares with indifference. As for Miss Mary, she appeared to be looking on the entire scene with an air which Caroline could not quite make out. Mr. Collins, after greeting them in an almost perfunctory manner, quit the room directly, though not without another injured glance at Elizabeth.

"Miss Bingley," said Jane Bennet in her typically serene manner. "I was not aware that you were visiting."

"Dear Jane," said Caroline, stepping forward to embrace Jane. She truly was a sweet girl, and in temperament very well suited to be Charles's wife. "I have actually come to take my leave."

A hint of distress crossed Jane's countenance before it was replaced with the placid manner which was so much a part of her character. It seemed to confirm Miss Elizabeth's assertions — Miss Bennet admired Charles.

"Indeed I am," said Caroline out loud, determining in that instant that her brother would not break this gentle creature's heart if she had anything to say about it. "I am afraid I have been holding back from you. I am, in fact, engaged to be married, and shall marry after Christmas."

A warm smile came over Jane's face. "I offer my congratulations, Miss Bingley. I wish you every happiness."

Caroline smiled at the girl and sat down for a few moments with her, speaking to her of her thoughts and expectations for the marriage state. Caroline noticed that Miss Elizabeth sat close by to listen to their conversation, though she did not say much.

At length, however, Caroline rose to take her leave. "I am afraid that we shall not see each other before my wedding. Therefore, I wish you all well in this Christmas season. Once Charles's obligations with respect to my wedding have been completed, I expect that he will wish to once again seek out the society of all the pleasant people we have met in Hertfordshire. I hope we shall all meet again very soon."

It was evident that Jane understood Caroline's reference, for her cheeks were instantly suffused with a rosiness which Caroline could not have imagined had her heart been only slightly touched. Yes, Caroline would have to ensure that Charles did not forget this woman.

With a few moments, she had said farewell to those in the house and left to go to her carriage. There, she was met with the sight of Mr. Collins standing out in the entrance, looking out over the landscape, a fierce frown piercing everything within range of his displeasure — or it was as stern an expression as could ever appear on the face of such a silly man.

Thinking about what she had witnessed inside — and considering what she could do to ease the situation for Miss Elizabeth, Caroline greeted him pleasantly. For once, he did not seem inclined to reply to her with the flowery phrases and pompous platitudes which so frequently pervaded his speech.

"I understand that Miss Elizabeth has refused your offer, Mr. Collins."

The scowl on his face deepened, but he succinctly allowed it to be so.

"Then I congratulate you on the good fortune of your escape," said Caroline. Then she turned to enter her carriage.

"Pardon me?" asked Mr. Collins in an incredulous exclamation. "I have not the pleasure of understanding you, madam."

Turning, Caroline smiled at the man. "Just that I have met Lady Catherine and I cannot imagine the great lady would approve of a woman as decided in her opinions and as outspoken as Miss Elizabeth."

Mr. Collins's mouth worked, but no sound came out of it. Miss Bingley noted this and, suppressing a grin of triumph, played her final card:

"I believe that Lady Catherine would prefer a quieter, more respectful sort of girl, one who possesses all the social grace, but is not overly forceful in expressing her opinions. Furthermore, I believe that as a parson, you would do well to search for one who is intimately familiar with the Holy Bible, who knows what is expected of a young woman who marries a parson, one who cares for her reputation is if it was her most precious possession. Knowledge of Fordyce would also not go amiss. I wish you well in your search, Mr. Collins, as I suspect that Lady Catherine would only be happy with just such a woman as I have described."

With that, Caroline nodded at the man and entered the carriage. The order was given and the carriage soon departed. But before they had pulled away, Caroline was witness to the sudden light of understanding coming over Mr. Collins's face and his hasty entrance into the house.

Grinning, Caroline congratulated herself on a well-played hand.

Chapter II

$\mathcal{U}$pon Miss Bingley's departure, Elizabeth sank back onto the sofa, at a loss to understand what had just happened. This entire morning—from Mr. Collins's mortifying proposal, to Miss Bingley's arrival and the revelations she imparted—had upset Elizabeth's equilibrium. The pride she had always taken in her judgment appeared to have been upended by their short tête-à-tête, and it would take some time for Elizabeth to right herself. It was vexing indeed!

"It was good of Miss Bingley to come and inform us of her party's departure," said Jane, startling Elizabeth from her thoughts. She had forgotten there was anyone else in the room.

"It certainly was," said Elizabeth, shying away from informing Jane of Miss Bingley's true errand. It would be some time before she was ready to reveal to anyone what she had heard that morning.

"Had you any notion of Miss Bingley's engagement?" asked Jane, apparently insensible to Elizabeth's inattentiveness.

Sighing, Elizabeth forcibly pushed her ruminations aside, and concentrated on Jane.

"I had not, Jane. It was as much a surprise to me as it was to you."

"To have kept it a secret all this time . . ." Jane trailed off and turned to look at Elizabeth. "Have you any notion why she did not acknowledge it openly when she arrived? Or perhaps when we became friendly at the very least."

Jane appeared to be a little uncertain, as if she was questioning the level of Miss Bingley's affection for her. It was all Elizabeth could do not to laugh at the irony. Only an hour earlier Elizabeth would have urged Jane to question Miss Bingley's friendship, and now it appeared like the woman had been genuine all along. "I suspect that she is simply wary of people with whom she is newly acquainted," said Elizabeth. "I have heard she possesses a substantial dowry, and with that and her connection to the Darcys—who I understand are an influential family—she must be cautious making friends."

The clouds in Jane's countenance lifted, and she smiled tentatively at Elizabeth. "Yes, that must be the case. And she did say her brother would be returning and that she thought we would meet again."

"Exactly," said Elizabeth. Though she was still uncertain of the matter herself, Elizabeth knew that she had to put her own doubts aside and support her sister. Otherwise Jane would convince herself that Mr. Bingley was leaving with no intention of returning. "I will own that I have been Miss Bingley's severest critic in the past, but she betrayed no hint of duplicity this morning. The final decision must lie with Mr. Bingley, but of him I have no doubt. His manner toward you is unmistakable. I cannot imagine that he would not see you again."

Jane smiled with pleasure, but before she could respond, the door to the sitting-room opened and Mr. Collins rushed in. His appearance was more than usually ridiculous, as he was looking about the room with wild eyes, his unkempt hair standing upon his head as if he had been running his hands though it with violent motions. He stopped once he had entered and looked at Mary, who appeared to be engrossed in her book, and a slow smile came over his features. But when he started to move toward her, his progress was arrested upon espying Elizabeth and Jane, and he lurched to the side to approach them instead.

"My dear Miss Elizabeth," said he, his manner as animated as Elizabeth had ever seen, "I am delighted to say that I have come to a most remarkable understanding concerning the reason you refused my proposal. I must say that I am astonished and humbled that you, a mere slip of a girl, have seen to the heart of the matter where I, a man of the world, have apparently been rendered incapable of seeing a most fundamental truth. You are to be commended for apprehending our unsuitability as a couple, and though I flatter myself that you would have had no hesitation in accepting me should the situation have been different, I can only thank you for your sagacity, and for your patience in bearing with me while I fervently — though misguidedly! — pursued the wrong sister."

Though bewildered, Elizabeth attempted to respond to the parson, who stood there gazing at her with a pathetic expression of hope directed at her. "Of course, Mr. Collins. I hold you no ill will. I am happy that you have come to this realization yourself."

"Very good, indeed," said Mr. Collins. His ever-present handkerchief appeared in his hand from his pocket, and he ineffectually swiped at the beads of sweat which had gathered on his forehead. "I must also ask for your indulgence, Miss Elizabeth. For you see, I have been struck by an important realization, and I now know who I should pursue with the intention of making her my partner in life. If I do not make haste, I shall lose the opportunity. As my gracious patroness herself has condescended to allow me this time to find I wife, I must not return to her empty-handed. So I beg for your forgiveness in pursuing another so soon after so recently bestowing my attentions on you."

"Do as you feel you must, Mr. Collins," said Elizabeth, now even more mystified. Of what could the silly man be speaking?

"I thank you, cousin, for your benevolent forgiveness. I can only cordially wish you well in your future, and hope that you will find someone who can make you happy."

And then bowing low several times, Mr. Collins retreated, only to approach Mary and sit next to her on the couch. "Miss Mary, I have been struck by the most startling, and indeed a most humbling realization. It appears to me that I have misled myself to a certain extent, when I should have been looking for one who was in fact well suited to be the wife of a parson. As such, I would ask for your permission to rectify this oversight and attempt to come to know you better, if you are willing."

Watching Mary's countenance as Mr. Collins's speech continued, Elizabeth saw several emotions run over her face, and though Mary's countenance showed her to be equal parts flattered, embarrassed, and awed, she was of no mind to put the man off. Instead, she smiled at the parson in a shy manner, and nodded her head, without replying.

"Excellent!" enthused Mr. Collins. Then, gesturing to her book, he said: "I believe that I have observed some similarity of mind when it comes to our taste in reading material. Will you share with me what you are reading?"

As the two began to speak in quiet voices Elizabeth turned to look at

Jane, only to see her own astonishment mirrored on her sister's face.

"What just happened, Jane?" asked Elizabeth, the beginnings of a laugh bubbling up within her throat.

"I must own that I am not certain, Lizzy, but Mary does not seem averse to Mr. Collins's attentions."

"At least he did not tell her that he ignored her because he was enraptured by our beauty," muttered Elizabeth as he she looked on the pair who were now engrossed in their discussion.

"Surely even Mr. Collins could not be that . . ."

"Daft?" asked Elizabeth with a wry smile. "Perhaps not, but I almost thought he was going to offend Mary with such language. If she is happy receiving his attentions, I certainly shall not stand in the way."

"Not when you are freed from said attentions," said Jane.

"Too true," said Elizabeth with a laugh.

As diverting as Elizabeth found Mr. Collins's sudden defection to Mary, the true measure of amusement was reserved for later that afternoon when Mrs. Bennet once again made an appearance. Elizabeth had always possessed the highest respect for her mother's instincts when it came to any hint of interest from a single young man toward her daughters; not only could she ferret out information regarding their situation in life and level of income within moments of hearing of them, but she possessed an almost supernatural instinct which told her almost instantly when a young man looked on one of her daughters with favor.

However, for the first time in Elizabeth's remembrance, Mrs. Bennet's perceptiveness failed her, no doubt due to the fact that she was still quite put out with Elizabeth. Upon entering the room, her eyes were immediately caught by Elizabeth, and she stared with considerable anger. Unfortunately Elizabeth, who had been thinking on all that had been revealed to her that morning, was slow to understand that her mother had once again targeted her to receive her displeasure.

"Elizabeth!" screeched her mother when she entered the room. "What do you mean by sitting there as if you did not have a care in the world? I insist that you come to your senses and accept Mr. Collins's proposal directly, or I shall never speak to you again!"

Startled from her thoughts, Elizabeth was about to respond with a scathing retort when Mr. Collins jumped to her defense.

"Mrs. Bennet," said he, his tone typically ponderous, "I would ask you to forgive your daughter and cease to importune her on this subject. Miss Elizabeth has shown a remarkable greatness of mind in the course of these events, and I would not have her made uncomfortable by a repeat of any of those words which were spoken in anger this morning."

All color drained from Mrs. Bennet's face, and she gaped at Mr. Collins with horror. It was clear to Elizabeth that her mother thought that Mr. Collins had given up all possibility of persuading Elizabeth to accept, and that she had thus lost all opportunity of seeing a daughter married.

Mr. Collins said nothing further; he only smiled at her and turned back to Mary, seating himself beside the middle Bennet daughter and engrossing himself in the conversation once again.

Now, it is not to be said that Mrs. Bennet's instincts were in any way deficient or that she could not adapt to changing circumstances. Though her initial reaction had been one of horror, she quickly took note as to where Mr. Collins had seated himself and how he was interacting with Mary. And though she did not seem to be able to fathom how such a change had come about, neither was she about to question the man when all seemed to be — unaccountably — proceeding so well. However, she did require a little confirmation.

"Lizzy," said Mrs. Bennet as she approached, keeping her voice low so as to avoid interrupting Mr. Collins and Mary, "has Mr. Collins turned his attentions to Mary?"

Incredulous surprise was positively oozing from her voice, and Elizabeth had to own that she had been more than surprised herself.

"It seems to be so," said Elizabeth. "He even asked me for my approval, given he had been so recently been paying his attentions to me."

Mrs. Bennet appeared to be more confused than she had been previously, but she nodded with acceptance, and left to sit in her usual chair. Elizabeth noted that she watched the new couple with some interest, but though understanding never came to her, she seemed to accept the matter after a few moments, and Elizabeth almost laughed to see the resolve come over her. Apparently one daughter married was as good as the next!

Within a few days, all was settled, which was fortunate for Mr. Collins. As the ball at Netherfield had taken place on Tuesday, and Mr. Collins had been obliged to return to Kent on Saturday, he had been left with a limited opportunity to make himself agreeable to Longbourn's middle daughter. And he did not waste an instant of that time.

It almost seemed like he was glued to Mary's side, as Mr. Bennet had laughingly told Elizabeth when he had emerged from his bookroom later that day. Not that Mr. Bennet had been upset to see the man paying attention to one of his other daughters.

"I would refuse consent to any of my daughters who did not wish for the attentions of a man," said he to Elizabeth in a low voice that evening when they were all sitting together. "But for Mary, I almost think that Mr. Collins will do well indeed. They are both of the same serious frame of mind, the same pompous self-importance that I declare they shall do very well together. I do not doubt that their days shall be filled with lofty thoughts and ponderous tomes, and I dare say that they will be alike in opinion more often than not, and that their decisions will be made in perfect harmony. Or at least these decisions will be unanimous once they have managed state the copious number of words each of them feels is necessary to say anything of substance."

Elizabeth peered at her father with a disapproving scowl, the effect of which was of course negated by the laugh that escaped her lips. Mr. Bennet, however, was unrepentant. He merely grinned at Elizabeth and turned his attention back to a book which he had brought with him from his bookroom. Elizabeth could not help but note that his eyes kept flicking to where the couple was sitting talking together, and she witnessed his frequent descent into quiet laughter.

On Friday, Mr. Collins came to the point and made his proposals, and this time the answer was more favorable than the last. The previous days of his courting of Mary so assiduously rendered his company much more tolerable, and the entire family was able to wish the happy couple the best in their future marriage, though it was not without some giggling from the youngest Bennets.

Unfortunately, there was one item of concern which did much to disrupt the harmony of the home in those days before Mr. Collins proposed. For Mrs. Bennet became aware of the departure of Mr. Bingley and his party the night Caroline had visited, and her lamentations were loud and long.

"No!" cried she, as he fell back into her chair upon hearing of the matter. "How can Mr. Bingley—such an amiable and charming man who appeared to be in love—do such a thing as to leave my dearest Jane without making his proposal? Oh, it is more than I can bear!"

"Mama!" exclaimed Jane. "Miss Bingley merely repairs to London to see to the final preparations for her upcoming wedding, and Mr. Bingley goes with her. I am certain that we shall see Mr. Bingley before more than a day or two has passed after her marriage."

"Indeed you should listen to Jane," added Elizabeth. "Miss Bingley was quite emphatic on this point. And who would know the man's mind better than his beloved sister?"

But Mrs. Bennet was not to be consoled. She lamented and cried for her salts, complaining of the unfairness of the world and how they would all be destitute upon her husband's death. It truly was a pitiable sight, though most of the residents of the house were more irritated than compassionate by the time her lamentations had continued for more than a day.

It was finally Mr. Collins who was able induce her to cease her wailings.

"Mrs. Bennet," said he, "you should cease to fear for your fate. I have every hope that matters shall proceed to everyone's satisfaction, and I furthermore promise you in the most animated fashion that I am not the sort of man who would cast a grieving widow from her home to live in destitution. You will be provided for, I assure you."

That more than anything else, served to quiet the Bennet matriarch, and by the time he proposed to Mary, Mrs. Bennet was quite reconciled to the new match. In fact, her effusions upon the proposal being offered were second in silliness only to that of the parson himself. The household was in such uproar with the grave pronouncements of the parson and the excited proclamations of Longbourn's mistress that the estate's master even emerged from his bookroom for a time to enjoy the spectacle. But even such great sources of diversion could not overcome Mr. Bennet's aversion for such loud tumult, and he quickly retreated back to his private room where the exclamations would at least be somewhat muted.

With Mary's new courtship and subsequent proposal accomplished, Elizabeth was largely left to her own devices, and she welcomed the opportunity to consider what Caroline Bingley had told her that fateful day she had visited Longbourn. Subsequent thought on the matter had rendered Miss Bingley's account all the more sensible, and though Elizabeth had originally thought that the woman might be making up her story of having lived with the Darcys, she was forced to discard the very notion; such a thing was too easy to disprove, and Miss Bingley would never wish to be branded a liar.

Thus it also followed that had Miss Bingley lived with Mr. Darcy, then she would know Mr. Wickham and be familiar with his character. Mr. Wickham's actions toward young ladies must also be well known to Miss Bingley, and her portrayal of the man was troubling. In all fairness, Elizabeth reflected that she had not seen any hint of such behavior; Mr. Wickham, though friendly and charming, had always behaved with the utmost in propriety and decorum when in Elizabeth's company. His behavior toward her sisters had not been any different, from what Elizabeth had been able to determine. But it would be prudent to be on her guard, Elizabeth decided, as regardless of her lack of proof in the matter, Kitty and Lydia were in no way equipped to question the man's motives. In fact, Elizabeth had no doubt that either would fall in with his schemes if asked, and would no doubt disgrace the entire family as a result.

A few days after the departure of the Netherfield party—and after Mr. Collins had returned to Kent amid promises to return again to attend his betrothed as soon as possible—Elizabeth was presented with the opportunity to test Mr. Wickham.

The Lucases and a few other families of the area had been invited to dine with the Bennets to celebrate Mary's new engagement, and to this gathering a certain number of officers had also been invited. Among their number was the object of Elizabeth's recent thoughts and confusion, and it was not long before Mr. Wickham graced Elizabeth with his presence, though Elizabeth could see that many young ladies in the party were jealous of his attention to her.

"Miss Bennet," greeted Mr. Wickham with a cheerful smile. "I am very happy to see you, indeed. I have been longing for your delightful conversation."

Elizabeth received him with feigned pleasure, but underneath she was considering his words. Perhaps more importantly, she wondered at how she might test him and prove Miss Bingley's assertions.

"I must own to some surprise at hearing you say such a thing, Mr. Wickham."

Puzzled, the man regarded her. "I assure you, Miss Bennet, that I speak nothing but the truth. I hope that I have never given you cause to doubt my constancy."

"Oh, it is nothing," said Elizabeth with an exaggerated nonchalance. "I merely refer to the fact that you were not present at Mr. Bingley's ball. I seem to remember you saying that nothing would keep you from Meryton society, and I was anticipating the opportunity to dance with you."

A slow smile crept over Mr. Wickham's face, and it contained a quality which Elizabeth could not define and did not like in the slightest.

"I wished for it myself. Unfortunately, however, you are well aware of my history with a certain gentleman who at the time resided at Netherfield. If I had attended Mr. Bingley's ball, it is possible that some unpleasantness might have occurred, given that man's capacity for resentment, and I would not bring disruption to such a fine event. I decided it was better not to tempt fate."

"I assume you mean that you had a history with several of those who resided at Netherfield."

Again, Mr. Wickham's brows furrowed. "Who do you mean?"

"Why, Mr. Bingley and his sisters. I understand they resided at Mr. Darcy's estate in Derbyshire for many years. Since you also grew up on the estate, you must be acquainted with them also."

An uncomfortable grimace overset Mr. Wickham's features, and in a short and clipped sentence, he declared that he was acquainted with the Bingleys. "However," continued he, "my primary connection is with Darcy, not Mr. Bingley and his sisters, though I do know them. Bingley is a happy and engaging sort, but his sister's manners are far different. In fact, they are more like Darcy, though I suppose that the fact that they were raised in the same house has something to do with that."

A week earlier and Elizabeth would have agreed wholeheartedly with Mr. Wickham's assessment. In a certain way, Elizabeth believed it to be true; though Miss Bingley had been far friendlier and open the day of her visit, Elizabeth still knew her to be proud and had likely deemed herself to be above her company. And Mr. Darcy was no different himself.

And yet Mr. Wickham still decried her as a proud sort of woman, when he should have known better. It bespoke a lack of true familiarity with the woman, though it could also betray an intentional design to mislead.

Either way, Elizabeth now knew that it was not true, and she was not afraid to let him know.

"Miss Bingley's manners may at first give such an impression," said Elizabeth, "but I believe that her disposition is better understood when one knows her better, and perhaps even more importantly, when she bestows her trust. There are many people in this world who are branded as aloof when they are guilty of nothing more than reticence with new acquaintances."

The fact that he was made uncomfortable by the observation was evident in his sudden fidget, but Mr. Wickham allowed it to be so. He also did not seem to miss the double meaning of Elizabeth's words, and that they could be accurate when speaking of Mr. Darcy as well. It appeared that he was not about to allow Elizabeth to gain a better opinion of Mr. Darcy, and he quickly spoke to forestall it:

"While I am certain that is certainly the case in many instances, there are others who are *exactly* as they seem."

Elizabeth raised an eyebrow at Mr. Wickham's vehement statement, and the gentleman grimaced, seeming to realize that he might have pushed too hard.

"I apologize, Miss Bennet," said he, "but you, of all people, must understand to what I refer. While I would hope that my old friend is not beyond amendment, I am afraid that he is firmly set in his ways. You and I are nothing more than insects to him, and I do not expect that to ever change."

Though she watched the man impassively, it did not escape Elizabeth's attention that Mr. Wickham had attempted to utilize the full measure of his charm, which, she was forced to acknowledge, was not inconsiderable. He smiled at her in a dazzling fashion as he spoke, and he shifted slightly, moving a little closer to her. It was clear that he expected to be believed by nothing more than the force of his pretty words. In his eyes there shone a gleam of some other, more nefarious purpose, and she was almost unable to suppress a shudder at the sight. In that moment, she was certain that what Miss Bingley had told her was nothing but the truth. It appeared, moreover, that Mr. Wickham had chosen Elizabeth to be his next seduction.

Elizabeth almost laughed at the mere thought; if it was indeed Mr. Wickham's intention, then he did not know her well at all. Even if she had been enamored of the man she would never have allowed him to persuade her to any improper behavior.

"You are passionate in your opinions, Mr. Wickham," said Elizabeth, intending to disabuse him of the notion that he could ever deceive her again. "However, from my perspective, you must understand that I have nothing more than your words as to Mr. Darcy's perfidy."

"Miss Bennet—"

"Please allow me to finish, Mr. Wickham." The man subsided but not without a bit of a sulk, which Elizabeth actually found humorous. "As I was saying, you have portrayed Mr. Darcy in a negative light, which seems to confirm his character, given his less than amiable behavior. However, I have seen nothing of any unchristian tendencies from the man, and I have excellent references as to the uprightness of his character."

"And who might that be?" asked Mr. Wickham with a frown.

"Why, Mr. Bingley and his sisters, of course. In fact, though I cannot betray any particular knowledge of the matter, I believe there was some talk of compensation in regard to the living which was promised on a *conditional* basis to you in Mr. Darcy's father's will."

At that the blood drained from Mr. Wickham's face and he almost appeared to take ill. "You have . . . That is to say . . . I am not certain where you might have heard such a thing, but . . . Well, I can only declare—"

"You do not need to declare anything, Mr. Wickham," said Elizabeth in a soothing tone. Inside, she was relived at having had her suspicions confirmed. "As I said, this matter is all nothing more than hearsay and it is not really my business at all. Would you not agree?"

Though Mr. Wickham appeared to wish to be gone from Elizabeth's presence—and equally desirous to avoid being be required to endure it ever again—he nodded his agreement, accompanied with a few unintelligible words.

"I am happy that we have come to an understanding, Mr. Wickham," said Elizabeth in a cheerful tone. "And as the matter of your dispute with Mr. Darcy is not my business, I hope that you will understand that it also does not concern anyone else from Meryton either. Your discretion would be very much appreciated. I expect that once his duties with respect to Miss Bingley's wedding are complete, Mr. Bingley will return to Hertfordshire to continue his acquaintance with us. I imagine he will be happy to greet you again as an old friend, as he had not the opportunity to do so before his sister's wedding necessitated his departure."

Mr. Wickham was certainly not bereft of wit; he understood the thrust of Elizabeth's words immediately. "I would not dream of repeating such a thing."

Then Mr. Wickham went away, and Elizabeth had all the satisfaction of seeing the man put in his place. With his avenue of abusing Mr. Darcy curtailed, Elizabeth could only hope that Mr. Wickham would rein in his other proclivities in anticipation of Mr. Bingley's return. Regardless, Elizabeth knew that she would need to discuss the matter with her father. Something would need to be done to protect the citizens of Meryton should Mr. Wickham decide he could act as he normally would.

Chapter III

$\mathcal{M}$r. Bennet was an intelligent man, discerning and capable. What he was not, was a sociable man.

A chance encounter had recommended a young girl to him, and the appearance of good humor and an abundance of physical beauty had captivated him, resulting in a marriage which had taken place long before he had taken the opportunity to truly know the woman who would become his wife. Bennet had regretted that decision ever since as, with the discovery of his wife's less than impressive intellectual capabilities, the love that he thought he felt for her had been revealed as nothing more than infatuation, and lacking any respect for the woman, his feelings soon settled into indifference.

All this Bennet knew of himself. He knew that his wife was a silly woman whose behavior was more often embarrassing than not, but he had long ago decided that it would be far healthier for him to feel amusement than embarrassing. That he should have behaved better and taken her in hand was not in question. But the fact of the matter was that he was also an indolent man, and the extent of her silliness meant that correcting her behavior would require much more effort than he felt himself willing to expend.

The lack of an heir to the estate had also affected Bennet's outlook. By the time the Bennets had given up the dream of producing an heir,

Bennet had decided, with a philosophical bent, that as his own progeny would not benefit from any increase of his estate, that the effort to improve Longbourn was a waste of his time. And as for his daughters, they were silly and ignorant like all other girls, and he simply could not be bothered with them.

That is, except for his Lizzy, of course. For a time when she had been a young girl, Bennet had thought the fates perverse that his favorite daughter had not been born male, for she certainly had the quickness of mind and fortitude necessary to be the future proprietor of the estate. But as she had grown, Bennet had come to the conclusion that she would not have been the same—would not have been *his* Lizzy—had she been anything other than what she was. In truth, Bennet thought that his daughter was a remarkable woman, and he fully expected that she would be as successful in her life as she wished to be. Jane, though everything that was good and beautiful, had not the drive that Elizabeth possessed, and thus, though she was a good sort of girl, could never match up to the fiery Elizabeth. And as for the younger girls . . . Well, the less said about them, the better.

Again, it must be stated that Bennet was well aware of his faults— he should have taken his wife in hand, he should have educated *all* his daughters, and he should have ensured that the estate produced to its maximum potential, and taken care of his family in preparation for his demise. But knowledge and action do not always travel hand in hand; it was easier to concentrate on matters which brought one pleasure than deal with unpleasant realities.

Elizabeth, for all that she was the bright light of his life, was not perfect. For one, though she imitated his study of character, she was prone to hasty conclusions based on emotion rather than close observation. Her judgment of Mr. Collins was accurate, of course, but the parson was so simple that even the most novice studier of character must understand the man's character within five minutes of being in his company.

No, what Bennet found far more amusing was Elizabeth's judgment of Mr. Darcy and Mr. Wickham. The entirety of her opinions of the two men was based entirely upon Mr. Darcy's unfortunate comment the evening of their first meeting, and all subsequent belief hinged upon that event. Even her estimation of Mr. Wickham's character had its origins in her opinion of Mr. Darcy—for if Mr. Darcy was the villain that Wickham portrayed him to be, then Wickham, for his part, must be good.

For Bennet's part, he had immediately perceived that Mr. Darcy was uncomfortable in company, and though he undoubtedly possessed more than his share of pride, more of his aloofness was due to the former quality than the latter. In actuality, Bennet suspected that Mr. Darcy was a good sort of man—better than Bennet was himself, he had to confess. By all accounts the man was a conscientious manager of his estate and a loyal friend.

By contrast, Wickham's smoothness, the cunning looks which he seemed to believe were hidden beneath the veneer of his charming manners, the lascivious looks Bennet saw directed at his own daughters—especially Elizabeth—told a very different story. Bennet did not doubt that the man was a womanizer of the first order, and likely possessed other, equally distasteful habits. Since Bennet knew that Elizabeth was of such moral fiber that she would not succumb to seduction, he contented himself with amusement at the man's ineffectual attempts, while watching him closely when in company so that he did not ingratiate himself with Bennet's other, less intelligent daughters.

In Bennet's experience, Elizabeth's passionate nature would not allow her to change her opinion unless forced to do so. Elizabeth would not suddenly see Mr. Wickham for what he was unless the man somehow betrayed himself to her, or the knowledge was imparted to her by someone else. He eventually meant to do so himself, when he satisfied himself with the knowledge that his favorite daughter could be as silly as her sisters. Thus, it was a surprise when his most intelligent daughter appeared in his bookroom to discuss that selfsame matter.

"Papa, I have come to ask your advice," stated Elizabeth when she had been allowed admittance into his sanctuary. Generally speaking, she was the only one who was afforded that privilege, though Jane sometimes sat with her father as well. He did not remember the last time Kitty or Lydia had been found within the confines of these walls.

At his prompting Elizabeth made her case, telling him of her suspicions and conjectures concerning Mr. Wickham's activities. Mr. Darcy she did not mention at all, but in reading between the lines Bennet was able to discern the fact that her opinion regarding that gentleman was undergoing a revision as well.

But Bennet was curious. How could she have come to such knowledge? When he asked the question, she appeared to be uncomfortable, but she gathered her courage and said:

"Miss Bingley visited just before the Bingley party returned to London. She explained Mr. Wickham's history with the Darcy family.

Then when the militia was here last night, I took the opportunity to speak with Mr. Wickham and determine the truthfulness of the matter myself."

"And what was your success?"

Sighing, Elizabeth said in a quiet voice: "More successful than I would have imagined."

Then she proceeded to detail her conversation with the man, including her conjectures regarding his behavior and his intentions while in Meryton. As Bennet listened to her tale, he reflected fondly on the fact that his daughter, though blinded by her prejudice for one man and preference for the other, had been able to accept what she heard with untainted attention, and had managed to see the truthfulness of the matter. She truly was exceptional. It was only because of her sheer passion that she was sometimes led astray, though Bennet had attempted to regulate that passion and turn it to her benefit. But he would not change a thing about her, and he suspected that her eventual husband would relish such passion as well, even when it was directed at him in anger.

"It seems that your opinions have been turned upside down, Lizzy," said Bennet once her tale had wound down to its conclusion. "But I must own that I am curious; what does Miss Bingley have to do with the matter and why would she choose to involve herself?"

The blush which spread down Elizabeth's checks and to her neck was amusing in the extreme, and Bennet was forced to suppress a smirk while he waited for Elizabeth to speak. When the story finally came out amid stops and starts and pauses while his daughter collected her thoughts, Bennet sat back to consider what he had heard.

Mr. Darcy's interest Bennet had detected almost immediately; why, the poor man was hardly able to take his eyes from Elizabeth when they were in company! His somber expression and seemingly haughty disapproval were irrelevant—no man looked upon a woman in such a manner if he was only trying to criticize. Bennet had never thought Darcy would act upon his fascination, and whether he ever would still remained to be seen.

In the matter of Miss Bingley, however, Bennet found himself quite interested, as he had not detected this person which Lizzy now claimed existed. In fact, Mr. Bennet had paid no further attention to either Bingley sister after a cursory look, convinced that both sisters were nothing more than haughty social climbers. It appeared like he had been wrong.

But what is life but to make mistakes and learn from them? thought

Bennet with some amusement.

The more he considered the matter, the more he became convinced that these new revelations were nothing but the truth. And Mr. Darcy, though he was a taciturn sort of man, he was also a man who was quite well-suited to be Elizabeth's husband. Not only was he by all accounts a clever man, but he was also the sort of man who demanded respect. Elizabeth could never be happy with a man unless she respected him. Furthermore, her liveliness would only soften Mr. Darcy's manners, and in turn his knowledge of the world would direct and hone her passionate nature. Such a marriage would be the making of them both.

"This is all very interesting indeed, Elizabeth," said Bennet out loud. "Given the fact that you have arrived at my door, it seems evident that you have given credence to these revelations and revised your opinion, not only of both gentlemen, but also of Miss Bingley, who I must confess I misjudged myself."

"I have, sir."

Bennet smiled, knowing how difficult it was for her to alter cherished beliefs. "Then can I assume you have some specific goal in mind for approaching me with this information?"

"I do. I believe it would be wise to warn the shopkeepers of Meryton of Mr. Wickham's propensity to accrue debts. I also think it would be wise to warn everyone as to his behavior with respect to young ladies."

"And we should simply go through the main street of Meryton, announcing to all and sundry what we know of Mr. Wickham's misdeeds?"

Elizabeth's eyes flashed with fire and displeasure. "I am certain there is some more tactful way of achieving this, father."

"Indeed, there is," replied Bennet, enjoying himself thoroughly. "In fact, I am pleased you brought this matter to my attention, for I am now further justified in doing just that."

A measure of shock fell over Elizabeth's face, and Bennet smiled in, what he had to confess, was a rather smug manner. The ability to surprise his intelligent daughter was a triumph to be savored.

"You have already spoken with the shopkeepers?" demanded Elizabeth.

"I have indeed," replied Mr. Bennet. "I have also had words with the gentlemen of the area to watch their daughters with the militia in residence."

"But how . . . ?"

"Lizzy," began Bennet, speaking softly, yet firmly, "you have a tendency to be a little too emotional."

Rising, Bennet stepped around his desk and sat in the chair next to Elizabeth's, taking her hand in his.

"Mr. Wickham is all that is charming and affable, but the way he looks at you and your sisters, and the speed in which he divulged his supposed woes at the hands of Mr. Darcy do not speak well of the man. It appears to me that he has a grudge against Mr. Darcy, and he played upon your avowed dislike for the man in order to ingratiate himself with you. I can only think of one end he might have been hoping to achieve, and as an intelligent young woman, I am certain you are aware of it yourself."

Huffing, Elizabeth glared at her father. "No matter what he *intended* to do, he would never have succeeded with me."

"I am well aware of your morality, Elizabeth. But Mr. Wickham does not know you as I do. He strikes me as a practiced deceiver, and one who has not failed often. And when he fails, I imagine that he invents excuses and claims to himself that he did not really take the trouble to succeed."

Elizabeth nodded to acknowledge the point, but she then turned a stern eye upon Bennet. "But what of the matter of the shopkeepers and the daughters of the area?"

"That was accomplished upon the militia's arrival in the area." At Elizabeth's questioning glance, Bennet explained: "I am sure that you are aware of your mother's propensity for speaking with great fondness for the regiment which was quartered in the area when she was a girl." Elizabeth nodded. "Though I was a young man at the time and I was still not the master of Longbourn, I remember it well myself. I also remember several young ladies being sent away in disgrace and several shopkeepers petitioning the landowners to cover debts left behind by members of the militia. Such behavior as this Wickham fellow engages in is not singular, and I am certain that he is not the only bad apple in this current crop of officers.

"Thus, when the news of the regiment's posting was made official, the gentlemen of the area conferred with one another and we agreed on the need for vigilance. Furthermore, we approached the businessmen and warned them of the dangers of trusting unknown officers, informing them that we would not cover any unpaid expenses for those foolish enough to extend an excessive amount of credit. The fact of the matter is that it was not truly required, as several of the shopkeepers remember the days of Colonel Archer's regiment well themselves, and had already warned the rest.

"However, given the specific threat that Mr. Wickham poses, I will consult with Sir William and we will ensure warnings are issued to all. Until he leaves the area, an unscrupulous man such as Mr. Wickham must be watched carefully. I shall see to it that if he tries anything with any of the young ladies he will be met with the hounds of hell, baying for his blood with pitchforks and torches!"

"Thank you, Papa," said Elizabeth, her eyes shining with relief. "I am happy that you have taken care of us so well."

Bennet grinned in response. "Your sisters are at times ill-mannered and silly and I have often been an indifferent father, but I would not have any one of you hurt by my neglect. You may be assured of that."

A kiss on the cheek was the only reply Bennet was to receive, and he rose with his daughter and returned to his desk while she opened the door.

"And Lizzy," said Mr. Bennet as he picked up his book. "Should this Darcy fellow ever come to his senses and offer for you, you may be assured of my blessing. I dare say you would suit well indeed. But do not tell him—you must send him to me so that I may intimidate him. It is a time-honored tradition, you know, and we must uphold tradition."

Bennet then waved Elizabeth from the room, chuckling to himself at the sight of her incredulous stare.

Life settled after Elizabeth's conversation with her father, and her sense of relief was acute. Subsequent meetings with the members of the regiment were undertaken with more reserve on Elizabeth's part than was her previous wont, but no comments were made within her hearing as to any change in her behavior.

What she did witness—and what gave her great satisfaction—was a rather marked change in Mr. Wickham. In short, the man seemed to be disgruntled about some matter, and Elizabeth could not help but suppose that he was learning that he would not be able to descend to his typical behavior in Meryton. And when the local landowners seemed to begin to watch him in particular, his reaction was to retreat to his manners, and attempt to charm everyone within reach of his smile. Unfortunately for the lieutenant, his charm affected no one other than the youngest and silliest ladies, among whom numbered Elizabeth's youngest two sisters.

It was not long before the lack of his normal activities became too much for Mr. Wickham, and one day it was reported throughout Meryton that the man had disappeared and was now wanted for being a deserter. Elizabeth was relieved and happy that Wickham was gone, and fervently wished to never lay eyes upon him again.

The preparations for Mary's upcoming wedding were undertaken with a zeal Elizabeth had rarely seen from her mother. It seemed like the realization of her life-long ambition to have a daughter disposed of in marriage—and perhaps more importantly the fact that the marriage to Longbourn's heir would save the family—had made Mrs. Bennet determined to host a celebration which would not soon be forgotten by anyone in Meryton. The rest of the family was pulled along with her enthusiasm, Mary somewhat reluctantly—pious as she was, Mary was far more focused on the religious significance of marriage—Elizabeth and Jane with resignation, and Lydia and Kitty with avoidance, whenever possible. Mr. Bennet took the simple expedient of ensconcing himself in his library whenever talk of lace and traditional wedding breakfast foods became too much for him.

Before the second week of December had passed by, an event occurred which, though perhaps she should have expected it, still astonished Elizabeth exceedingly. For a letter arrived in the post from Miss Caroline Bingley.

It is not the purpose of this narrative to recite word for word the messages contained in Miss Bingley's missive. However, it is important to note that the letter had a significant effect on the fortunes of several of members of the family.

"It was good of Miss Bingley to write, was it not?" inquired Jane after she had shown the letter to Elizabeth.

Elizabeth had to allow that it was indeed. "And such specific language concerning Mr. Bingley's anticipation for his return to Hertfordshire can be left to no interpretation."

"I am anticipating it very much myself," said Jane shyly. "I have never met a man with such happy manners, and I would not be averse to knowing him better."

"The mistress of understatement, as always!" said Elizabeth with a laugh. "I am certain that your desires shall be gratified, dearest Jane. I have never believed anything else."

For the most part Miss Bingley's letter detailed the preparations for her wedding, and her excitement and hope for her future felicity. She did include a few words for Elizabeth herself, and with this bit of civility, Elizabeth found herself convinced that Miss Bingley's words had been genuine. Though she was still not sure she really even liked the woman, Elizabeth was grateful to have confirmation of the woman's friendship with Jane.

The fact of Miss Bingley's continued desire to correspond with Jane also had a positive effect upon Mrs. Bennet. Her wailing about Mr. Bingley's desertion had already lessened with the advent of Mary's engagement, but after she had seen the evidence of what she considered to be Mr. Bingley's continued regard, her former good opinion of the man was restored.

Just before Christmas the Gardiners arrived at Longbourn, and with the return of Mr. Collins, they made a merry party over the holiday. And then three days after Christmas, Mary was joined in holy matrimony with Mr. Collins. The relief and ecstasy felt by Mrs. Bennet at the event was only equaled by that of Elizabeth, who was grateful that the man's efforts had been turned in the proper direction.

When the wedding was accomplished and the newlyweds had embarked on their journey to Kent, the Gardiners left again to return to London, this time taking Jane with her. Jane had hesitated to accept the invitation, but had finally been persuaded to accept.

"But Mr. Bingley has made it clear that he shall return to Netherfield," protested Jane.

Elizabeth, who had been attempting to convince her sister to accept the invitation, could only smile and respond: "Then send a letter to Miss Bingley indicating your arrival in town. I am certain she will share it with her brother.

"And you must concede," continued Elizabeth with a sly grin, "that there are certain . . . benefits to being courted in town, rather than at Longbourn. If nothing else, there would be much less interference, would there not?"

"Oh Lizzy!" exclaimed Jane.

Her exasperation did not prevent her from following Elizabeth's advice and dispatching the missive with alacrity. Though Elizabeth was sad to see her sister go, she was heartened by the thought that Jane would almost certainly return to Longbourn as an engaged woman.

This suspicion was borne out in two letters which arrived within a day of each other in early January. The first detailed that Jane had indeed seen Mr. Bingley, and the second that he had proposed and they were engaged. The reaction of the Bennet family to such good news was loud and excited—especially by the matriarch—and the entirety of the family was happy for their most deserving member. The neighborhood joined in the good wishes, and it was the general opinion that the Bennets had been marked out in some manner for good fortune. Elizabeth was content—her dearest sister would be happy, and whatever happened in the future, the family would have a means of support.

*   *   *

Caroline Powell returned to London after her wedding trip blissfully happy. Her new husband David, who was a friend to both her brother and William from their Cambridge days, was attentive and delightedly in love with her. Caroline, who had grown up believing that it was the match that was important rather than the relationship, was pleased to have been proven incorrect, and had enjoyed the attentions of her husband, while ensuring that he knew that he was loved in return. It was a match made in heaven, in Caroline's opinion.

If Caroline was honest with herself, she knew that the attractions of the season, though still welcome, were not as important to her as they had been previously. Caroline was well aware of her character—she was a little vain, she was fond of fine clothing and finer company, and though her vanity had never been excessive in her own opinion, she was well aware of the fact that she was quite happy to see and be seen, especially when she could be seen by those of the first tiers of society.

A new outlook had replaced her girlish desires, however, and she knew it was because of her marriage. Now, though she still enjoyed society and all the trappings of wealth, Caroline was more concerned with happiness, both that of her husband and her immediate family. David was well able to hold his own in society, and he enjoyed it in a limited measure—a kind of a mixture of Charles and William. He also enjoyed his estate and was well able to leave society behind for quieter pursuits. That he was more sociable than William was welcome; Caroline did not know how she would have dealt with William's unsociable tendencies had she ever seriously looked upon the man with any interest in matrimony.

The first bit of news she received upon returning, delivered by a grinning Charles, was that her brother was engaged to be married, and that the bride was none other than Jane Bennet.

"That is good news indeed," replied Caroline to her brother, amused at the way he was nearly bouncing up and down in excitement. "I am glad you have found someone so well suited to you. I am certain Miss Bennet will be a very good wife."

"Thank you, Caroline," replied her brother happily. "I am grateful you informed me of her presence in town. It has been wonderful seeing her in town, and I am certain you will like her relations as well. Mr. and Mrs. Gardiner are all that is intelligent, obliging, and elegant."

Privately, Caroline could not imagine how a brother of Mrs. Bennet's could be anything other than a masculine version of his sister, but she avoided making such a statement and asked when the introductions could take place.

Grinning, Charles replied: "Actually, that is one reason for my visit today."

"And visiting your favorite sister was not enough of an inducement?"

If anything Charles's grin only widened. "Not when the happiness of my beloved is at stake."

Caroline swatted at him, but his expression did not alter a jot. "Then you had best tell me what you would like as I cannot abide your teasing."

"It is good to have you back, Caroline," replied Charles. "Hurst is a bore and Louisa does nothing but bemoan her fate, when her husband is not likely to hear, of course. You are much better company indeed.

"I wish to host a dinner to which Jane and the Gardiners will be invited, not only to introduce her to some of my closest friends, but also in order for her to tour the townhouse. Would you be willing to act as my hostess for the evening?"

"Of course I will," replied Caroline warmly. "Please inform me of the date and I will ensure our calendar is clear of any other engagements."

It turned out that Charles's proposed dinner was to be held a week after he requested her assistance. And so it was that Caroline, along with David and Charles, welcomed his guests to his townhouse on the designated evening, and was able to greet Jane Bennet and her aunt and uncle with pleasure.

"Jane, my dear!" exclaimed Caroline when she caught sight of the young woman. "I cannot tell you how pleased I am that you have come, not to mention the happiness you have brought my brother. I shall be very pleased to call you my sister!"

"Thank you, Mrs. Powell," said Jane. Though she was as reserved as Caroline remembered, the sparkling of her eyes told the story of her contentedness.

"Please, call me Caroline. We shall be sisters before long, shall we not?"

"Indeed, we shall," said the young woman in return.

Once her duty of greeting her guests had been completed, Caroline took upon herself the task of introducing Jane to all of Charles's friends, along with the Gardiners, who were everything that Charles had said they were. By and large, Jane's introduction to their group of friends was a success, though there were a few young ladies who appeared to be a little jealous of her good fortune. Still, nothing was said to make her uncomfortable, and since Caroline was well aware of how vicious the young ladies of society could be, she was happy she was not required to intervene.

There was one in attendance who did not appear to greet the news of Charles's engagement with any pleasure, and though Caroline had the highest opinion of this person's judgment, she thought she knew of another reason why he would not wish for his friend to be connected to the Bennets. But as Caroline had other plans, she knew it behooved her to ensure he overcame his displeasure in as expedient a manner as possible.

Her opportunity came later that evening in the drawing-room after dinner was complete and the gentlemen had rejoined the ladies. Charles was engrossed with Jane as usual, and David had gathered with some of the other young men and was speaking of sport or some such nonsense. William, however, was separated from the rest of the group, standing beside the fireplace and gazing moodily into the flames. As there was no one else close enough to overhear their conversation, it was the perfect time to have a frank conversation.

"Hello, Mr. Darcy," said Caroline as she approached him. "You appear to be less sociable than usual tonight."

The use of his formal moniker was twofold: first, Caroline generally used it when in company to avoid any misunderstanding as to the state of their relationship, and second, she often used it to inform him that she was annoyed with him. In private, she almost always called him "William" as most of his family did, and at times, she had even been able to get away with "Fitzy," though he understandably was not happy with that particularly nickname.

"Mrs. Powell," said he, turning a slightly softer smile upon her. "How are you finding married life?"

"I am enjoying it very well indeed," replied Caroline. "David is a wonderful man, as you are well aware. We are happy together, though I would imagine our habits will eventually generate some measure of friction."

William nodded. "As one would expect in any marriage. I would suggest that the manner in which a married couple handles their disagreements and differences of habit to be the true determining factor which decides their ultimate happiness."

"And to what do I owe this bit of philosophy, Mr. Darcy?" asked Caroline, amused at his words. "For, unless you have kept it a secret, I do not think that you have ever been a member of a marriage."

"It does not follow that I do not understand what constitutes a happy marriage. It would appear to be common sense."

"Of that I must agree." Caroline paused and looked at him, noting his distracted air and his frequent glances at where Charles was sitting in deep conversation with Jane.

"Come, Mr. Darcy. I have known you long enough to understand when you are not happy about something. Will you not share whatever troubles you?"

Her words drew a pointed look from the man and he huffed a little in exasperation. "I cannot imagine why *you* are so sanguine about this matter, Caroline. I know we all hoped for something better in a prospective marriage partner than Miss Bennet. She is a good sort of girl, but she will not add to his status in society."

"Perhaps you are correct, Mr. Darcy. But surely you would not wish to deny Charles what I have found in my partner in marriage, or that which your parents shared. For that matter, I would think that you would wish to follow your dearly departed parents' examples as well and form a connection of the same sort with the woman you will eventually marry."

"But surely he could have found such a connection with a more suitable woman," replied William with another glance at Charles.

"The heart is a mysterious organ, Mr. Darcy. You are well aware of Charles's open and affectionate disposition. It is possible he might have found someone with greater standing in society and a splendid fortune. But for him to be tied to someone who did not return his affection would have ruined him. There is no danger of that misfortune happening with Miss Bennet."

"And how do you know that?"

"I have watched her, Mr. Darcy. Can you honestly look at her and not see the affection with which she holds my brother?"

Though with obvious reluctance, William *did* look at Jane Bennet closely. At that moment, the young woman laughed at something Charles said, and though her actions were ever proper, she reached forward and touched his hand. It was as Caroline had said; her countenance spoke to her joy and her pleasure in Charles's attentions, leaving no doubt of the state of her feelings to anyone with even a hint of wit.

It was clear from William's expression that he saw it too and was forced to recognize it, little though he appreciated the necessity.

"It appears as if you are correct."

"A fine concession, Mr. Darcy," said Caroline. "As a woman, I am much better equipped to determine the contents of another woman's heart. Charles shall be very happy with Jane Bennet as his wife, and I could not be happier for him."

A grunt was all the answer Caroline was to receive, and William turned and began to stare into the fire again, apparently his poor mood from before having returned.

"Is there something else the matter, Mr. Darcy?" asked Caroline, while hiding a grin. "Maybe there is some other reason for you to feel less than happy concerning Charles's choice? Might it not be a pretty, lively reason, possessed of fine eyes?"

William turned and scowled at her. "You should not go fishing, Mrs. Powell. You are not likely to catch anything."

With that, he sketched a slight bow and departed, moving across the room to stand with David and the rest of the men, though he did not seem to add anything to the conversation.

On the contrary, my dear William, thought Caroline, *I believe I have learned all I need to know.*

And Caroline knew exactly what to do about it.

Chapter IV

Winter and early spring that year seemed to pass in the blink of an eye, and soon early April had arrived and with it, the time for Jane's wedding to Mr. Bingley. Jane herself had returned to Longbourn by the end of February at Mrs. Bennet's demand; with a daughter engaged to be so advantageously married, Mrs. Bennet would not allow the opportunity to show her daughter off before all the neighborhood. And Mr. Bingley also returned at the same time, happily foregoing the delights of the season for the frenetic pace of visiting and accepting congratulations, basking in the affection of his beloved, and preparing the estate to receive its new mistress.

His sisters and his friend had, however, not accompanied him on his journey from London, presumably as there was much attraction still in residing in town. Elizabeth did not regret their absence—her feelings regarding both Mrs. Powell, as she was now known, and Mr. Darcy were unsettled and she did not feel herself equal to meeting with either of them.

Unfortunately, her avoidance was not to last, as two weeks before the wedding, both Mr. Bingley's sisters arrived in preparation, not only for the wedding, but also for an engagement ball which would be held at Netherfield three days prior. Mrs. Powell and Mrs. Hurst visited Longbourn the very next day, but Elizabeth's meeting with the former

Miss Bingley was brief and very little was said between them.

The days before the engagement ball saw an influx of visitors to Netherfield, presumably those who had been invited to witness Mr. Bingley's marriage. Jane visited on more than one occasion, and as Elizabeth did not, she had nothing more than the report of her sister to go on when Jane said that everyone she met was pleasing and well mannered. That she had already met many of these same people when lately in London allowed Jane to relax and not fret about meeting so many strangers. For that Elizabeth was grateful.

When the night of the engagement ball arrived, Elizabeth and her family boarded the Bennet carriage for the short journey to Netherfield, and they soon arrived. Though the ball held the previous November had been all that was elegant and tasteful, Elizabeth entered Netherfield that night thinking that this time Mrs. Powell had completely outdone herself. The setting was somehow more intimate, from the navy and silver decorations which hung from the walls of the ballroom, to the vivid red of the roses which liberally festooned the entire estate. It appeared that no expense had been spared to celebrate the upcoming marriage.

"What a complement to you, dear Jane!" said Mrs. Bennet when they had entered the room, but whereas Elizabeth would have expected some loud outcry when her mother first laid eyes upon the finery, her tone was subdued; she was obviously in awe.

"It certainly is," said Mr. Bingley, as he approached with a smile. "I would do all this and more for your daughter, Mrs. Bennet."

"Thank you, Mr. Bingley," said Jane with a shy smile.

Elizabeth was once again thankful that her mother seemed too stunned to reply yet again, but the sensation was soon forgotten, as Elizabeth witnessed Mr. Darcy step up behind his friend and bow to the Bennets.

It was the first time since Elizabeth had seen the man since the previous ball at Netherfield, and perhaps more important to her at present, the first time she had seen him since Caroline Bingley had made her surprising assertions. As he rose from his bow and greeted the Bennets with perfect civility, Elizabeth studied him, looking for some hint of what Mrs. Powell claimed she saw in his behavior. But Mr. Darcy may have been a stone wall for all Elizabeth could read in the man's face. In fact, though he did meet Elizabeth's eyes for an instant, he immediately turned his attention to Jane and Elizabeth's mother, complimenting and congratulating them on Jane's upcoming marriage. In fact, Mr. Darcy did not so much as glance at Elizabeth again; his attention to Jane, however, contained a searching quality that raised Elizabeth's ire, though she stamped it down with ruthless annoyance.

"Shall we all move into the ballroom?" suggested Mr. Bingley as he extended his arms to Jane and Mrs. Bennet to escort them.

For her part, Elizabeth entered on the arm of her father, but when she met his glance, he grinned at her and then flicked his eyes in a suggestive manner at Mr. Darcy, then showed her an exaggerated rolling of his eyes.

"It appears that Mr. Darcy has determined to resist the lure of Longbourn's second eldest and now most eligible daughter," whispered Mr. Bennet. "Shall we wager as to how long he is successful?"

Elizabeth scowled at her father. "I have seen nothing of admiration in Mr. Darcy's manners or in his looks."

"And yet it is there, nonetheless."

With a smirk and a kiss on Elizabeth's cheek, Mr. Bennet left her in the company of Charlotte Lucas. Elizabeth glared at his back, but soon Charlotte's questioning look brought her emotions under good regulation and she began to speak with her friend, firmly putting the matter out of her mind.

It was a wonderful night, and Elizabeth had the pleasure of seeing her sister display her love for Mr. Bingley in a far more open fashion than she ever had before. Mr. Bingley's affections had never been in question, and on that night they were more marked than ever. If incivility is truly the hallmark of love, then Mr. Bingley and Jane displayed it for all to see that evening, as neither seemed to have eyes for anyone but the other.

As for Elizabeth herself, she was rarely without a partner for the entire evening, and though many of the men she danced with were local men she had known all her life, many more were friends of Mr. Bingley's come from town to witness his wedding. There were several with whom she conversed in an amiable and animated fashion, but none of them were anything other than interesting new acquaintances. Whether the fact of her meager dowry warned them away or something else was at work Elizabeth did not know, but though interesting conversation was abundant, there was nothing deeper in any of her interactions that evening.

Mr. Darcy was much in evidence, but he danced very little as was his wont. He danced the obligatory sets with Mrs. Powell and Mrs. Hurst, and there were one or two more ladies with whom he stood up, for the rest of the evening he stood to the side talking with others, or simply standing by himself and watching the dancers. He said no words to Elizabeth, and he did not ask her to dance.

For the first part of the evening it appeared that his attention was largely on Jane, as though he was attempting to puzzle something out. Elizabeth could not make any sense of his behavior, as Jane was no more and no less than she ever was, though her countenance shone with a joy Elizabeth had rarely seen. Whatever he was looking for seemed satisfied, as his attention soon shifted and more than once Elizabeth thought she caught a glimpse of him watching her, but she could never quite be certain. Even if he was looking at her from time to time, Elizabeth could see nothing of admiration and everything of censure in his glares, and she resolved to put the man out of her mind and not think of him.

The evening progressed to the supper hour, and the revelers gathered to partake of the meal, when Elizabeth was once again afforded the opportunity to speak with Mrs. Powell. Though Elizabeth was not quite certain how it had happened, somehow she ended up seated next to the woman, and though she was still a little ambivalent about her, she greeted Mrs. Powell with civility as propriety dictated.

"Again, congratulations on your recent marriage," said Elizabeth, feeling obliged to make some attempt at conversation.

"Thank you, Miss Bennet."

The woman snuck a look at her husband who was speaking with Mr. Darcy, an action which spoke more to her feelings than any words could have. Mr. Powell Elizabeth had been introduced to briefly earlier that evening, and though she could not say that five minutes in his company gave her any great insight into his character, he impressed her as a kind and friendly sort of man.

"I must own that I find the marriage state to be agreeable indeed."

Elizabeth smiled warmly at the woman for perhaps the first time. Though their marriage was new, the Powells seemed to be besotted with each other, which bespoke the greatest potential for lasting felicity. Elizabeth wanted such for herself, even while she sometimes despaired of ever finding it.

"I understand that there has been another marriage in your family recently," said Mrs. Powell in a conversational tone.

"Yes, there was," replied Elizabeth. "A few days after your party quit Netherfield, Mr. Collins proposed to my sister Mary."

"That must have been a great relief for you in particular."

Elizabeth looked sharply at the woman, but she betrayed nothing but friendly interest in her expression. Elizabeth had often wondered at Mr. Collins's sudden change of heart, but she had never been able to come to a conclusion as to what had prompted the man to suddenly realize that Mary was much better suited to be his wife. Surely Mrs. Powell could not have had something to do with the matter.

"Surprised would be closer to the truth," said Elizabeth, thinking to try to provoke a response. "As you are well aware, he had just proposed to me only that morning, and then suddenly, not long after you left, he entered the house and apologized to me for his change of heart, and for burdening me with his attentions in the first place. I still cannot account for his behavior."

Mrs. Powell smiled at Elizabeth. "I suppose we must credit him with a measure of insight which was not apparent before."

Though she was not satisfied with the answer, Elizabeth could only agree with the woman's words, and the conversation proceeded to touch on other subjects. It was largely desultory for several moments, consisting primarily of Mrs. Powell's observations concerning married life, while Elizabeth some mention of minor events in her own life the previous months. It was some time later before their words once again covered a serious subject.

"I believe I must extend my thanks to you, Mrs. Powell," said Elizabeth in a grave tone.

Mrs. Powell regarded her evenly. "To what are you referring, Miss Bennet?"

"Your warning concerning Mr. Wickham. I must confess that I was mistaken in my judgment of the man. He turned out to everything deceitful, immoral, and false, and without your words I no doubt would not have seen through his façade until it was too late."

"Did Mr. Wickham hurt you, Miss Bennet?" Mrs. Powell's manner was concerned, something Elizabeth had not seen from her in the past.

"He did not." Elizabeth chuckled. "Unless you consider my gullibility and the injury to my pride to be laid at Mr. Wickham's feet."

"Mr. Wickham is well able to convince even those who possess a discriminating eye of his goodness, Miss Bennet. I hardly think that you can be held accountable for believing in his words."

Elizabeth sighed. "You can if you consider the fact that I was willing to believe the worst about Mr. Darcy without the benefit of any proof."

"Perhaps you did not show the best judgment in Mr. Wickham's case, but you are only one among many. Mr. Darcy's own father, who was as keen a judge of character as I have ever met, was fooled by Mr. Wickham's manners. We tried to tell him on a number of occasions what his godson had become, but he shrugged it off, saying it was nothing more than the exuberance of youth."

"I did not know that he was Mr. Darcy's godson," said Elizabeth.

"It was done as a favor to his steward, who had been Mr. Darcy's faithful employee for many years." Mrs. Powell sighed, and passed her hand over her eyes, a weary motion. "The son, unfortunately, did not take after his father. Rather, he favored his mother, who always overspent and behaved as if she were the lady of the manor. It was truly unfortunate."

Then Mrs. Powell seemed to shake off her melancholy, and she turned to Elizabeth with a shrewd look in her eye. "Will you not share what has happened with respect to Mr. Wickham?"

The compassion in Mrs. Powell's eyes almost proved to be Elizabeth's undoing. But she controlled her emotions, reminding herself that no matter what the incident had done to her confidence, she was uninjured by the man. Perhaps even more importantly, Wickham was gone and the danger to her sisters had gone with him, and as such, she could breathe easier.

Thus, Elizabeth relayed to Mrs. Powell the pertinent events concerning Wickham's exposure and ultimate flight, including her conversation with the man, her warning to her father and his revelations, and her thoughts after his departure.

"I am impressed, Miss Bennet," said Mrs. Powell when she had completed her narration. "When informed of the truth of the matter, you did not attempt to rationalize or minimize what you heard. Instead, you confronted the man and with skill and subtlety you led him to contradict his words and prove for your own peace of mind just exactly what kind of man he was. I dare say that his flight necessitates his absence from Meryton on a permanent basis. He would face transportation at the very least for the crime of desertion."

"That was my thought as well," replied Elizabeth, though inside she was warmed by Mrs. Powell's approbation. "But I cannot claim any great measure of insight or triumph in this matter. But I do thank you for your warning."

"It was given with a desire to help you and your family, Miss Bennet," said Mrs. Powell. "I am happy Wickham is no longer present, and hope that none of us shall ever be required to lay eyes upon him again."

Elizabeth nodded and smiled, and the subject was dropped. Her equilibrium was further upset, however, when Mrs. Powell addressed her at the close of the meal with a proposal which was unlooked for and astonishing.

"Miss Bennet," said she, "I would like to invite you to visit me at my husband's estate in Northamptonshire. When we depart Hertfordshire, we are not to return to town, as he desires to make for our estate in order to oversee the spring planning."

Shocked, Elizabeth only caught herself from staring at the woman with incredulity, and responded, with a surprised: "Visit your estate? But surely as a newly married couple you would wish for your privacy with your new husband."

"We had more than two months in one another's exclusive company," said Mrs. Powell with a smile. "And with such dry subjects as planting and drainage—though I know them to be important—I find that I would prefer the company of another woman.

"And your sister and my brother are to join us at the conclusion of their wedding tour, so there would be a familiar face there before much time passed."

Mrs. Powell moved closer to Elizabeth and grasped her hands, gazing into her eyes with an earnestness which could not be feigned. "Please say you will, Miss Bennet. I would love the company and the opportunity to come to know you better. David's estate is beautiful, and I know that an excellent walker such as yourself with find much delight in it."

Laughing, Elizabeth was convinced to accept, and she promised to apply to her father for permission, while acknowledging with a wry grin that Mr. Bennet was not likely to deny her.

"Excellent!" said Mrs. Powell. "I shall look forward to your coming."

"And I shall anticipate it keenly, I assure you. Thank you for the invitation, Mrs. Powell."

The woman smiled and said, "I think that is enough of formalities, do you not agree? I would be pleased if you would call me 'Caroline.'"

Wondering at how she had suddenly seemed to have become friends with this woman, Elizabeth agreed happily, insisting that her new friend return the favor. And so it was set. As Elizabeth walked away with her partner for the first dance after supper, she wondered at the changes which had occurred in her life. She was actually anticipating visiting Northamptonshire. In fact, she anticipated it very much indeed.

Caroline Powell smiled at the retreating back of Miss Elizabeth Bennet, happy that her plans appeared to be bearing fruit.

Yes, Miss Bennet, I have you right where I want you, thought she, and the knowledge filled her with hope for the future. Or specifically for the future of one who was dear to her.

As dinner had ended and the ball was about to begin again, Caroline made her way back to the ballroom, and after ensuring a few items for the comfort of her guests, Caroline gave the signal and the music for the next dance began. As she was not engaged for this set, Caroline stood to the side watching the dancers, though in reality she was consumed with thoughts of Miss Bennet, planning how she could bring about the changes necessary to ensure the happiness of two important people.

"You seem to be deep in thought."

Smiling, Caroline turned to regard her husband, noting the amusement with which he was watching her.

"I assume that Miss Bennet has accepted your invitation?"

"She did," replied Caroline. "To be honest, I had expected more reluctance than I encountered. She has changed her views remarkably quickly for one who is so stubborn."

"The inducement was worth it, I am sure."

"It is indeed," murmured Caroline as she turned back to once again watch Miss Bennet.

The woman was surely a bright light, at ease in any situation and full of sparkling, intelligent discourse and pert opinions. Caroline's opinion was so different from her first impression, in which she had labeled the girl a flirt or a fortune hunter, such as her mother was. Happy that she had taken the time to know her better, Caroline anticipated the time she would spend in her company.

Of course, had Caroline been inclined to Mr. Darcy, she did not imagine that she would have felt so favorably disposed to the other woman. For she was well aware of the fact that in Miss Bennet, Darcy had met his match. The two had started off on such a bad footing that it was now up to Caroline to ensure they saw how perfect they were for each other.

"I had not thought I married such a matchmaker." Her husband's voice penetrated Caroline's consciousness, and she looked up at him, amused to see his mischievous expression directed at her. "Mayhap there are other things about my lovely wife that I have yet to discover?"

"I am sure there are," said Caroline with a happy laugh. "But I shall promise you that this will be my only foray into matchmaking. And I would not even be required to involve myself if the two in question were not so infuriatingly obtuse about each other."

"This *is* Darcy we are talking about." David's expression and tone were all amusement. "When it comes to women, the man cannot see past the fortune hunters enough to understand that there are good young women in the world." David gazed at her with an intensity that took Caroline's breath away. "It is to my advantage, to be sure. For otherwise he might have discovered for himself what a gem he was passing up before it was too late for him.

"Come, Caroline, I believe I wish to dance with my wife."

Caroline allowed herself to be led to the floor, and all thoughts of others fled from her mind. There would be enough time when Miss Bennet came to devote herself to her and Darcy's happiness. At present, it was time to focus on her own.

Chapter V

The days after the departure of the Bingleys and their wedding guests were difficult for Elizabeth. Not only had she lost her best friend and confidante to marriage, but with Jane now married and gone, Mrs. Bennet's thoughts and hopes for marriage turned to Elizabeth. Her mother's efforts had lost that slightly manic and desperate quality that had previously characterized them, but the constant stream of advice, excited speculations, and reproaches—regardless of Mary's marriage to Mr. Collins, Elizabeth *had* refused a proposal—grated on Elizabeth's nerves to the point where Elizabeth would absent herself from the house whenever possible so as to avoid Mrs. Bennet's officious attempts to instruct her.

It did not help that Elizabeth's own thoughts were turned to matrimony with great frequency in those days. The fact of the matter was that both her elder and younger sisters had married, and though Elizabeth had often stated that she would be maiden aunt to Jane's children, more and more as she had watched Mr. Bingley interact with her sister, Elizabeth realized that she wished to be loved like Mr. Bingley loved Jane.

Marriage had always been something to be considered in the future. As she had matured and become aware of her family's situation, Elizabeth had known of the difficulties they might face and understood the desirability of a good marriage. But having been witness to the contrast in marriages between those of her mother and father and her aunt and uncle Gardiner, she had become convinced that if she did not manage to find one similar to the latter, it would be best if she did not settle for the former.

She would not find a husband in Meryton; she had known that almost from the time she had entered society. But she also did not move in any other society, meaning that her options were limited to those who either moved into the area—such as Mr. Bingley—or perhaps those who occasionally visited. It was possible that if she should spend time in Jane's company moving in Mr. Bingley's society that a prospective husband might emerge, but there was no guarantee of that either. Now, however, Elizabeth had something to look forward to, and that was the invitation to join Mrs. Powell on her estate for the remainder of the spring.

To be truthful, though Elizabeth was now experiencing much friendlier feelings toward the woman than she had ever expected, a part of her still wondered exactly how they had managed to change their relationship. This of course led to thoughts of ambivalence and second-thoughts as to the wisdom of accepting her invitation. But then she remembered how warmly they had spoken, and how eager the woman was to have her visit, and she realized that Caroline's behavior was such that she could do nothing but respond in like fashion and give the woman every opportunity to prove that she was the friend she claimed to be. And perhaps a new society was just what Elizabeth needed to improve her prospects. Perhaps the one man she could love forever would be found at a neighboring estate. Stranger things had been known to happen.

Mr. Darcy's behavior at Jane's wedding, however, had solidified in Elizabeth's mind that *he*, at least, would not be her one true love. Regardless of what Caroline and her father had said, Elizabeth had seen nothing in the man's manner to indicate that he was in any way interested in her as a prospective marriage partner. And while Elizabeth's opinion of the man was in no way as ill as it had once been, she remained convinced that he was not, at heart, amiable, and that he would never condescend to make an offer to Miss Elizabeth Bennet, she of no connections and little dowry. And with that Elizabeth was content.

Though there were trying moments, the time quickly passed away, and soon the time had arrived for Elizabeth to depart. She prepared, packing her trunks and taking her leave of her neighbors. And through it all, Elizabeth was affected by some indefinable sense of loss, though she could not state exactly why. Nothing seemed different to her from any of the other times she had left home, other than the fact she never visited Northamptonshire before. But the walks in her home's vicinity, the faces of family and friends, and the familiar rooms of Longbourn were all somehow dearer to her in those weeks than they had ever seemed before.

A particularly poignant parting was shared with her dearest and oldest friend, Charlotte Lucas. Charlotte had not been much in evidence that month—in fact, Elizabeth had only seen her a few times, and when she had, a despondent gloom seemed to hover over Charlotte like the distant threat of rain. Elizabeth could not account for her friend's behavior; Charlotte had never been a boisterous sort of person, but she had always been quiet and content with her life. The day before she left, Elizabeth discovered the reason.

A morning call to Lucas Lodge to officially take leave of her friend was the setting for their parting. When Elizabeth arrived she was shown into the parlor of Lucas Lodge where she was greeted by Lady Lucas. A few moments were spent in conversation with the lady; Charlotte had been sent for upon Elizabeth's arrival, but it was some time before she appeared. When she did, Elizabeth greeted her with pleasure and asked after her. The conversation was somewhat desultory for several moments, until Lady Lucas left the room. It was then that Elizabeth discovered what had been bothering her friend.

"Have you any notion of when you will return?"

Elizabeth smiled and shook her head. "The duration of my visit has not been determined. "Jane is not expected until the end of May, and I would imagine that I will stay at least some weeks after she and Mr. Bingley arrive. After that, I cannot say, but I think it likely that I shall return with Jane when she returns to Netherfield."

Shaking her head with amusement, Charlotte said: "It seems that you have made a very good friend, Lizzy. After your initial impression of the woman, I cannot but say that I am surprised."

"No more than I am myself," said Elizabeth, considering those days in the previous autumn with rueful embarrassment. "Though I will not scruple to assert she was not friendly and welcoming when she first arrived, subsequent interactions with her seem to suggest that I was mistaken about her."

"I was not impressed either," said Charlotte. "But I am glad you have found such a good friend who may assist you in society."

Charlotte fell silent, and Elizabeth regarded her friend with some concern; the sadness appeared to be back, and Elizabeth was unable to account for it.

"Is there something wrong, Charlotte?" asked Elizabeth. "You have not seemed yourself these last weeks. Is there aught I can do for you?"

A ghost of a smile flitted across Charlottes features before it slipped away. "Not unless you can conjure me a husband."

Elizabeth looked at her friend, shocked, but Charlotte only sighed with exasperation. "I am seven and twenty, Elizabeth, and I have no prospects. I fear being a burden on my parents, and then on my brother when he inherits. I believe that I am entitled a little melancholy for the unfairness of life."

"I am sorry, Charlotte. I had no idea you were weighed down by such things."

"It is not to be wondered at," replied Charlotte. "You are still young and have the chance of obtaining a husband, and you are setting off on a grand adventure. I am afraid my time has come and gone."

"Surely not," protested Elizabeth. "Surely if you remain faithful for a little longer something will change."

"Thank you for your optimism, but I fear it is too late." A sudden smile came over Charlotte's face, though it was colored with the same unhappiness which had characterized her behavior the entire visit. "I will own, I had harbored hopes that when you rejected Mr. Collins's suit as I knew you must, that he might turn his attention on me."

Elizabeth felt her eyes might escape their sockets at the mere thought. "Mr. C-Collins . . . ?"

Her stuttering did not amuse Charlotte. "Lizzy, I have never been romantic like you are. Mr. Collins cannot be considered anything but tolerable for his position in life alone. As he is the next heir to Longbourn, I would have been the estate's next mistress, and that is not something to be laughed at."

"B-But . . . Mr. Collins . . . ? Are you telling me that you would marry such a buffoon, trade your self-respectability for the sake of a comfortable situation?"

A hard stare met Elizabeth's incredulity, and for a moment Elizabeth felt like a child being scolded by her mother. They had been friendly for so long that it was easy to dismiss the fact that Charlotte was indeed seven years older than Elizabeth, but it was only at times like this when the difference became apparent.

"Your sister married Mr. Collins, did she not?" Charlotte only waited a brief moment for Elizabeth's nod before she continued. "I understand your aversion to Mr. Collins—he is a silly man, his hygiene is suspect, and he has no room in his head for an original thought. However, he is a good-hearted man, not prone to violence, and in possession of a good living from a respectable woman. Furthermore, he is heir to your father's estate which, though not large, is comfortable and well able to support a gentle family. There are many circumstances which are highly in Mr. Collins's favor."

Elizabeth was struck by Charlotte's words which, as she recalled, echoed Mr. Collins's own statements during his ill-fated proposal to Elizabeth herself. And she realized that what Charlotte was saying was only the truth; Elizabeth had never been tempted by the man, knowing that his very character would condemn her to a life of misery. But for another woman—Mary, who was proper and pious, or Charlotte who was not romantic and only wished for a good home—what Mr. Collins offered would be tempting indeed.

"I see you understand now," said Charlotte, a shrewd and knowing smile affixed on Elizabeth. "Yes, Mr. Collins, though living with him would have been irksome, would at least have provided a good home, with the promise of being the mistress of an estate in the future. And really, I believe that your sister, being sensible, though perhaps slightly pompous herself, will have great success in moderating his manners. He will never be a clever man, but with her patient tutelage, he may one day be at least tolerable."

Nodding slowly, Elizabeth said: "I see your point, Charlotte. These are details I had never before considered."

"That is because you are a romantic at heart," said Charlotte. "You would have been miserable married to Mr. Collins, as your heart yearns for a loving relationship with your spouse. But not all women are like that. For myself, I have not a high opinion of either men, or matrimony. We have not many sterling examples of marriage to guide us. I believe that we both know what to avoid, but what is acceptable to us is different. If I should ever be blessed with a man who would treat me well and provide for me, I would be well pleased indeed. You require more than that. Either way has its advantages and disadvantages. But what is abhorrent to you would be perfectly acceptable to me."

Nodding, Elizabeth pushed her thoughts to the side for a moment and concentrated on her friend. Charlotte had always been there to support her, from the time she had been a young girl just entering society, to the present where they were so close that they rarely kept anything from each other. Yet Elizabeth had known none of this, and the possible reason for her exclusion was troubling to say the least.

"Was I so blind that I never knew you felt this way?"

Charlotte looked away and it was several moments before she spoke. "You have intended no neglect, Lizzy, and I do not hold anything against you. I have particularly attempted to keep my troubles from you, mostly because I was not ready to discuss them with anyone.

"However, you do have a tendency to be . . . firm in your beliefs. I am aware that you knew of my opinions, but at the same time, I believe you had never truly considered them. I can only conjecture it was because they were so dissimilar to your own."

"I am very sorry, Charlotte," said Elizabeth, moaning with mortification. "I have been blind it seems, and I have never been the friend to you I thought I was."

"Nonsense, Lizzy. I know your ways. I never attempted to impose my feelings upon you."

"No, but I should have known nonetheless. I have realized in the past few weeks that though it is beneficial to be of decided opinions, a little compassion for other viewpoints and an ability to be persuaded is not amiss."

Silence settled between the two friends, and for the first time in some time, Elizabeth felt that closeness between Charlotte and herself. A part of her, however, was a little angry. Charlotte was a true gem—sensible, intelligent, attractive, and in possession of a fine disposition and the ability to make any man proud. And yet no one had noticed what a wonderful woman she was. And now she faced an uncertain future without prospects for marriage and lacking a fortune with which to support herself. In a moment of clarity Elizabeth understood that had Charlotte been in possession of such a fortune, she would have been quite content to remain in her single status for her whole life. Her words concerning both men and matrimony proved it.

By contrast, though Elizabeth had always remained adamant that she would not marry unless she found a deep love with a man, she actually did wish to marry. In fact, Elizabeth longed to be loved by a man, to commit her life to his and accept his commitment in return, and to have children that she might raise in happiness and joy. Even if Elizabeth had been provided a dowry, she would always have wished for it.

Perhaps she had been hasty in decrying the benefits of a practical marriage. Nothing would induce her to accept a marriage to a fool such as Mr. Collins, a marriage which would be bereft of respect, both her for her spouse and her spouse for her, but maybe the deep love she wished for could be overlooked should the situation demand it. Once again, Elizabeth felt her cherished beliefs being overturned, and she was given much on which to think.

But the time for that would come later. For now, she wished to comfort her friend, to show her that she understood her position and empathized with her fears. And in furtherance of that goal, Elizabeth scooted toward Charlotte and, taking her hands, said:

"I understand, Charlotte. I had not thought of how much this must weigh on your mind.

"But I believe that we must hope for the best." Elizabeth directed a wry smile at her friend. "You must have faith. I must believe that there exists somewhere in this world a man who will recognize your true worth. Otherwise, I must have no more hope for humanity."

Charlotte smiled with true pleasure. "Thank you, Lizzy. I will own that I have little faith for myself, knowing that you do lifts my heart."

"Then I must have faith for us both," said Elizabeth, embracing Charlotte with great affection. "Leave it to me, Charlotte. I will carry the entire load of our faith. You will see; there must be one man on this earth who has some modicum of intelligence. I mean to find that man."

Though she truly did not appear to be in the mood for frivolity, Charlotte laughed and laid her head down on Elizabeth's shoulder. She would have faith for Charlotte. Her friend deserved everything wonderful life could give her.

Elizabeth went home that day to her final preparations for her journey. Charlotte's revelations had been upsetting for more than one reason, but she attempted to see the good in the situation. Intellectually Elizabeth was aware that Charlotte was indeed at the age where her marriage prospects were dimmed to the point that she was considered "on the shelf." But she refused to believe that no man could see the worth of her friend. It was inconceivable.

Her return to the estate was characterized by the same silliness which was almost always present in the Bennet home. Mrs. Bennet, though seeing the possibilities of having another daughter attached to a rich man, nevertheless was vocal in complaining that it was *Elizabeth* who had been invited to another estate.

"I cannot understand why my dear Lydia should not have been invited as well," lamented Mrs. Bennet. "For she is as agreeable in company as Elizabeth, and more handsome by far. She would come home with a suitor in tow at the very least, while we cannot trust Elizabeth not to scare them all away."

This last was said with a stern glance at Elizabeth, which was cheerfully ignored.

"Oh la, Mama!" exclaimed Lydia. "I much prefer to stay in Meryton with the officers, than visit the estate of stuffy Mrs. Caroline Powell."

"And if anyone else should be invited it should be me," added Kitty, her voice a petulant whine. "After all, I am two years older."

"It matters little, as it was Lizzy who was invited," said Mr. Bennet, "though I must own that I am not certain why she would accept such an invitation."

"She accepted it because there is a chance to be introduced to Mr. Powell's other wealthy friends," said Mrs. Bennet. "For Lizzy realizes now after she has missed an opportunity with Mr. Collins, that she had best not discourage any other potential suitors. Is it not so, Lizzy?"

Elizabeth shared an amused glance with her father. "I am certain that there will be no opportunities for marriage, Mama. By all accounts, I shall be in residence with Mr. and Mrs. Powell alone until Jane and Mr. Bingley arrive."

"No, Mrs. Powell has invited you so that you may find a husband. Of that I am utterly certain. Now that her brother has married our dearest Jane, she understands that it is her duty to assist you in finding a husband. And even if they have not invited potential suitors—of which I am not at all convinced—there will still be assemblies and dinners and all manner of society to attend. In fact, I should not wonder if Mrs. Powell has some particular man of the area in mind to match you with. We married women must think of these things, you know, since those who are unmarried cannot bother to do so themselves."

It was all Elizabeth could do not to roll her eyes. But she remained silent, knowing that once her mother had begun to speak of such matters she would not be gainsaid. Of course, there might be a tiny grain of truth in her words; surely Caroline would prefer that her brother not shoulder the burden of caring for Mrs. Bennet and three unmarried daughters. But to suggest that she had invited Elizabeth to visit for the sole purpose of marrying her off was patently absurd!

After some time of listening to Mrs. Bennet's pontificating on the matter, Mr. Bennet excused himself to his bookroom with a wink at Elizabeth who envied his ability to escape. It was some time before Mrs. Bennet's words ran dry, and soon after Elizabeth excused herself under the pretext that she needed to be away early the following morning.

"I am sure you can have your friend Mrs. Powell," said Lydia, as the three girls climbed the stairs to their rooms. "Though she has become more affable with you, she is still a superior sort of woman. I am sure I should be bored to tears if I was to go to Northamptonshire."

"I would be too," said Kitty, not to be outdone by her sister.

Elizabeth suppressed a weary sigh. With an insensible mother and a father who could not be bothered to control his offspring, Elizabeth did not doubt that with her departure, all restraint would fall from Kitty and Lydia's shoulders, and they would be sillier, louder, and more brazen than ever before. The only reason Elizabeth had any hope at all was because the regiment had been reposted to Brighton, and were to depart from Meryton within a matter of weeks. Kitty and Lydia, along with their mother, both had hope that Mr. Bennet could be induced to take them to Brighton on a holiday, but Elizabeth knew their ambitions had no chance whatsoever of ever coming to fruition. But she could not leave them behind without on final admonition in in the vain hope that they would behave themselves.

"Kitty, Lydia, you must take care," said Elizabeth, turning to face them. "Remember Mr. Wickham and the scoundrel he turned out to be. You must be vigilant as there may be other such men in the regiment."

"Lizzy, you are so dull," exclaimed Lydia. "And I am not convinced that Mr. Wickham was so very bad. He had all the appearance of goodness—"

"And none of the substance," replied Elizabeth. "I have it on very good authority that the man is a libertine and a debtor. Most of the other men seem to be respectable, but you cannot be certain. Use your heads and do not be tempted by pretty words."

"We shall be fine, I am sure," said Lydia, and with an almost perfunctory wave she and Kitty entered her room.

Shaking her head, Elizabeth returned to her own room and prepared to retire. She could not look after her youngest sisters forever—sooner or later they would be required to gain a little judgment for themselves. But Elizabeth could not help but worry about them. At least the regiment would soon be gone.

Thus Elizabeth left for Northamptonshire the next morning. Her parting with the remainder of her family left at Longbourn was typical, though her father made his usual comments concerning the lack of sensible conversation to be found with both Elizabeth and Jane absent. None of them seemed to feel the same sense of . . . finality which had beset Elizabeth. She did not know why, or what situation she would be stepping into, but life at Longbourn had changed so much in the previous months, and she held the distinct impression that it was about the change even more.

The carriage which conveyed Elizabeth to her destination had been sent by Caroline Powell for her comfort, and though the distance was not great, it was further than could be conveniently travelled in one day. Elizabeth spent the night in a small inn south of city of Northampton in the company of the maid who had been sent for her chaperonage. The next morning, Elizabeth once again boarded the carriage and they set out, this time with a very easy distance to be covered that day.

The coach skirted the city of Northampton and continued on north into the heart of the county. The estate of Hollyfield, the home of the Powell's, was situated near to the town of Brixworth, of which Elizabeth saw a little as the carriage passed through. It seemed to be a small market town, with one major road on which most of the village's commerce rested, surrounded by the homes of its inhabitants. In short, it was much like Meryton.

They passed by the town and before a half an hour had passed, they were entering the estate and pulling up in front of the manor house. Hollyfield was a goodly sized estate, likely akin to Pemberley in size, but not in grandeur, given what Elizabeth had heard of it. The house was situated on flat ground in the center of a large meadow, with a large forest in the distance to the north, while to the east there was a lake of some prominence. It was handsome house built of reddish stone, easily three times the size of Longbourn, and from what Elizabeth could see, much larger than even Netherfield. The woods and the meadow promised delightful hours of uninterrupted rambling, and she thought that she might even walk out to the shore of the lake if she was so inclined.

The carriage stopped in front of the manor and the door opened, allowing Elizabeth to descend from the carriage, handed down by a smiling Mr. David Powell.

"Welcome to Hollyfield, Miss Bennet," said he with good humor. "I am glad you accepted our invitation to visit."

"Thank you, Mr. Powell. I am very happy indeed to be here."

"And *I* am happy to hear it," said Caroline as she stepped forward.

But rather than curtsey to each other, Caroline enveloped Elizabeth in a warm embrace, which Elizabeth after a moment's hesitation returned with increasing pleasure.

"I can see that you are looking very well indeed," said Elizabeth as she drew back from her hostess. "It is evident that married life agrees with you."

"I dare say it does indeed," replied Mr. Powell with a laugh. "I must confess that I am quite enjoying it myself."

Caroline levelled a pointed look at her husband, and with mock severity said: "Do you not have some estate business to concern yourself with?"

"I believe that I completed everything required this morning," said Mr. Powell with a grin. "But for you, I shall relent and leave you ladies to your reunion. I have no doubt that I should only be in the way should I insist upon staying."

"You have him well-trained already," said Elizabeth *sotto voce*. "That is impressive, given the brief nature of your marriage."

A guffaw revealed more of Mr. Powell's amiable nature, and he bowed to her with a mischievous flourish. "I can see life here will not be dull with you present, Miss Bennet. Though of course it was not tedious with only my dear wife for company," amended he when he saw his wife's stern glare. "For now, however, I shall bid you farewell and leave you in the company of my capable wife."

And with that, Mr. Powell turned and departed, leaving Elizabeth with Caroline.

"Thank you for coming, Elizabeth," said Caroline. "My husband is a dear man and very attentive, but I am happy to have another woman with whom to converse. Louisa is in the north with her husband's family, and I suspect that she shall be there for some time. But you shall be a welcome substitute, as will Jane when she arrives."

"I thank you for the invitation," said Elizabeth with some feeling. "The estate is charming and the park seems to offer ample opportunities to indulge in my favorite pastime."

Caroline laughed. "Yes, of course—your penchant for wandering with impunity. I shall warn you, Miss Bennet," said Caroline with mock severity, "that I am not the excellent walker that you are, and I shall depend upon you sitting with me from time to time, rather than wearing out every pair of shoes you brought with you."

"And I shall be happy to oblige," said Elizabeth with pleasure. "I promise that I shall only wear out *one* pair of shoes walking your estate."

A shaken head met her statement. "Come, let us see that you are settled. I believe that a tour of the house can wait until after you have rested and refreshed yourself. And I am not so deficient in walking that I cannot take you to see the formal gardens in the back of the house. In fact, I have assigned you rooms that overlook them, and I expect you will find the view to be very fine indeed."

"I have no doubt I shall," said Elizabeth, and she followed her hostess up the staircase and to the second floor.

As they walked, Caroline pointed out several locations of interest to Elizabeth, taking care to ensure that Elizabeth would be able to find her way back downstairs to the rooms which were in more common use by the family. It was as fine a house from the inside as it had been from the outside, and though Elizabeth knew that Caroline was still too newly married to have made many changes, that fact did not make it appear to any less advantage. The décor was fine, though muted, and though it spoke to the wealth of its proprietor, it was tasteful and fashionable.

When Elizabeth made some comment to that effect, Caroline said: "My husband's parents both passed away some two years ago very suddenly. Before that, his mother had made a great many changes, updating the rooms to the latest fashions. As such, I have very little to do in decorating; as you can see, she had excellent taste."

Elizabeth made the appropriate comments of condolence, which prompted Caroline to inform her that she had not known her husband's parents, as they had passed before she had become attached to him. The subject was then dropped, and they moved on to other conversation of a more lively variety.

The room to which Miss Bingley led Elizabeth was a handsome room. The entrance from the hallway led into a small, but well-appointed sitting room, with a comfortable sofa and a pair of chairs situated by a large fireplace. The room was decorated in Elizabeth's favorite muted yellow and trimmed in a light blue shade which was delightful. And when the adjoining door was opened, it revealed a bedroom with the same general décor, but with the blue being the more prominent color. On the large bed was a beautiful comforter of a deeper blue. The bed and the vanity on the far wall were constructed of sturdy oak, which had been lacquered and polished until they both gleamed in the afternoon sunlight.

And as Caroline had promised, the window on the opposite wall of the room looked out onto the back of the house, were she could see several walks laid out through bounteous beds of flowers, shrubs, grass, all laid out exquisitely and cared for with a meticulous hand. And beyond the gardens, she could see the first strands of the wood which abutted the edge of the lake in the distance. For its part, the lake rippled in the slight breeze and sparkled, speaking of promised diversions during the course of her stay.

"You have a very lovely home, Mrs. Powell," said Elizabeth, turning to face her hostess. "And the room is simply delightful. Thank you again for inviting me."

"You are very welcome, but do you not recall that we had agreed to dispense with 'Mrs. Powell' and 'Miss Bennet?'"

The smile on the woman's face belied her stern words, and Elizabeth laughed lightly. "Indeed we did."

"Excellent. Now I believe that you would like to rest from your journey, and I have a few matters to see to."

Caroline turned and called out, and in a few moments a young woman, approximately Elizabeth's age, stepped into the room and curtseyed. She was pretty with honey blond hair, and was dressed in the livery Elizabeth had seen adorning the manor's servants.

"This is Maria. I have assigned her to be your maid during your stay with us."

"I have always been quite capable of taking care of myself," protested Elizabeth.

"While I am sure that is the case, there will be times when we will go into society, and I would have you attended by someone so that you will not have to worry about your appearance. Maria has served in this capacity before, and she is very skilled in styling a woman's hair."

There was nothing Elizabeth could say to such attention, so she smiled and assented, and after a few more moments, Caroline went away, leaving Elizabeth in Maria's company.

"One of the footmen is bringing some water for you to wash with, miss," said the maid. "If you would like to nap until dinner, I will busy myself with putting your dresses away."

Smiling, Elizabeth thanked the girl, and then said: "My belongings can wait for the time being. Come and tell me about yourself."

Surprised, Maria was nevertheless loquacious once she began speaking and Elizabeth passed a pleasant fifteen minutes conversing with her until the water arrived. After washing she found that she was indeed fatigued, and she succumbed to sleep with the instructions that she should be woken in an hour. As she drifted off, the thought that she would enjoy her stay very much crossed Elizabeth's mind.

Chapter VI

$\mathcal{T}$he first days of Elizabeth's stay were quiet and comfortable. Though she might not have been able to imagine it only a few short months before, Caroline was a good conversationalist with a rather dry wit, and Elizabeth found that sitting with her was in no way dull. And as for Mr. Powell, well he was also intelligent and kind, and clearly besotted with his wife. On more than one occasion, Elizabeth found it necessary to quietly attend to her needlework or open a book, as the happy couple would become so engrossed with each other that they forgot she was even in the room. Of course they attempted to apologize the first time it happened, but Elizabeth, amused at their behavior and happy that they had each managed to find someone so dear to them, insisted that no apology was required.

It became a habit in those days for Elizabeth to spend a certain amount of each day alone, so as to give the couple time to themselves. They were conscientious in doing everything they could to see to her comfort, but as she laughingly told them, they *were* still newlyweds, and as Elizabeth was well accustomed to walking out with no more company than the birds in the trees and the animals who roamed the landscape, it was no hardship to do so in order to allow them their privacy. In fact, she informed them, she rather looked forward to it, as there were many new paths to explore.

The formal gardens she had walked several times, mostly in the company of the estate's mistress, and while she was forced to concede that the Powells' tastes ran to a more formal style than Elizabeth herself preferred, still they were delightful. The forest she had seen that first day was littered with trails, and she did not doubt that it would take more time than she would be staying to explore them all. And finally, the lake itself turned out to be delightful, as the breeze which would often blow over the water tended to cool her on the hottest days. Furthermore, having lived in a location where the largest body of water was a small pond on the outskirts of Longbourn's park, Elizabeth found the lake to be a novelty. If she walked close to the shore, she could see small fishes flitting here and there beneath the surface, and the lake was home to all manner of fowl.

That was not to say that Elizabeth only walked out alone. Though she had herself alluded to the fact that she was not one to walk for hours, Caroline did walk out often, even if she did not range as far as Elizabeth was wont to go herself. It was on one of these walks that they engaged in a discussion which allowed Elizabeth to explain more of her upbringing.

"You live on a very beautiful estate," said Elizabeth as they walked in amongst the trees. "It is little different from Hertfordshire, yet I still sense that it is a little . . . wilder, almost."

"The further north one goes, the less tamed the land," said Caroline. "Mr. Darcy's estate is the epitome of this. The park is very large, and the land has largely been put to use, but where nature has been left to reign, it is quite wild indeed. The beauty of the peaks is quite beyond description, and very close to Pemberley."

Curious, Elizabeth turned to her companion. "Has it been in Mr. Darcy's family for long?"

"Centuries," replied Mrs. Powell. "The Darcy family has never been large, but it is an unbroken line from the first Darcy to hold the land. Mr. Darcy is prodigiously proud of his estate, and he cares for it a great deal."

The fact that he was proud of his estate Elizabeth could well imagine—she had always known of the man's great pride, and if some of that pride was excessive, she had no doubt that in this instance it was warranted. And she could also believe that he took great care in how his estate was managed. He was the type of man who took duty very seriously.

"And how does it compare to Hollyfield?" asked Elizabeth with a hint of mischievousness. "By now, I must assume that you are firmly on your husband's side in the matter."

Caroline smiled. "While you would be correct, even David recognizes Pemberley's matchless beauty. I have never seen its' like. I am certain when you see it, you will have no choice but to agree with me."

"*When* I see it?" asked Elizabeth, raising an eyebrow at her friend. "My viewing Pemberley is a fait accompli, is it?"

"I should think you will eventually have the chance to do so. After all, your dearest sister is now my brother's wife. As Charles visits Pemberley quite often, I would not be surprised should you accompany him at some point."

While Caroline's words were delivered in a casual manner, Elizabeth could not help but wonder if she intended some other meaning.

"I am sure you must be anticipating your reunion with your sister keenly," said Caroline, interrupting Elizabeth's thoughts.

Filing her previous words away for further contemplation at a later time, Elizabeth nodded. "I confess, I am. Jane and I have always been the closest of sisters, and though I love all my family dearly and share a special relationship with my father, I have never shared a bond with anyone in my life like that which I have with Jane. I am lucky to have been given such a wonderful sister."

"You make me quite envious," said Caroline, her tone slightly wistful. "Louisa and I have never been precisely close. We appear to an outside viewer to be one another's closest confidant, but in truth, Louisa is a little shallow and more than a little selfish. I love my sister, but I cannot call her a close friend."

Elizabeth regarded Caroline with surprise. "Then you have certainly fooled those of us who witness you together. I always thought you were as thick as thieves."

"And yet we are very dissimilar," replied Caroline.

Caroline said nothing further, and they walked on for several more moments. The strands of trees through which they roamed thinned out and they found themselves at the back of the park, close to the formal gardens behind the house. Floral scents, mixed with the earthier scents of the trees and shrubs drifted along the currents, teasing Elizabeth's senses, filling her with a feeling of contentment.

"And what of your other sisters?" asked Caroline.

Elizabeth turned to her friend, and her questioning expression prompted Caroline to add: "What I mean is that you and Jane are poised, confident, proper, and filled with every social grace, while your younger sisters . . . I do not mean to offend, but let us just say that the contrast between you is striking."

Cheeks warm, Elizabeth turned away, not quite able to find the words to respond.

"I apologize, Elizabeth. I should not have brought it up."

"It is understandable," said Elizabeth, turning back to Caroline and favoring her with a rueful smile. "It is quite odd, do you not think, that Jane and I can be so different from our siblings? The answer lies primarily with my aunt and uncle."

"They had a hand in your upbringing?"

"When we were girls, Jane and I spent a great deal of time with my aunt and uncle and we both benefitted from their instruction. Unfortunately, with his time consumed more and more by his business, and with the births of their own children, the Gardiners have not been able to devote as much time to their younger nieces, and as such, my younger sisters have not received the benefit of their wisdom."

"Then that is unfortunate. Against you and Jane nothing can be said in censure. You both carry yourselves very well indeed."

Thanking her, Elizabeth continued to walk, but inside she was wondering about Caroline's words. The censure against her younger sisters had been felt, but what Caroline had said was not in question. To those of Meryton society, accustomed to Kitty and Lydia's behavior as they were, little was ever said concerning their exuberance. And yet, to a newcomer, used to the finest of society, it must have been grating indeed. It was a wonder Caroline had chosen to overlook it, regardless of how pure Jane's behavior, or lively Elizabeth's.

It spoke to Caroline's goodness, Elizabeth decided. She was showing herself to be a true friend. And given what Elizabeth had thought of Caroline when they had first met, she now realized that she could not have been more wrong. She thought she had been able to move past this error in judgment, but apparently she was not yet past the feelings of shame and humility.

As they had reached the house, they entered and separated to refresh themselves. Then Elizabeth made her way back down to the sitting-room where a tea service and some cakes had already been ordered for their refreshment. They ate largely in silence, Elizabeth contemplating her recent errors, wondering if she would ever feel confident in her judgment again.

"You appear to be pensive, Elizabeth," said Caroline. "Is there aught amiss?"

Directing a rueful glance at her hostess, Elizabeth sighed. "I have simply been wondering at my lack of perception, and wondering if I should ever feel confident in it again."

Caroline tilted her head and she regarded Elizabeth, curiosity written all over her face. "You speak of something specific?"

"Yes," said Elizabeth, coloring at the thought. "I was just remembering how very wrong I was about your character, and that of Mr. Wickham too, of course. I have always prided myself in my ability to read the disposition of others, and to find that it has failed me so spectacularly has been humbling. I rather wonder if I can trust myself again."

Smiling, Caroline reached forward and patted Elizabeth's hand. "And I was not mistaken about you?"

"Perhaps," conceded Elizabeth. "But the fact that you have made a mistake in judgment does not lessen my own."

"It does not. But I believe that your judgment cannot be held to be faulty because of this one error. And as for Mr. Wickham," Caroline's lip curled up in disgust, "the man is a practiced deceiver who has been blessed with happy manners. He has no compunction whatsoever to use his gifts for ill. I think you should allow yourself to forget the matter. Mr. Darcy did not show himself to best advantage either, which must certainly have confused you."

"But—"

"Elizabeth, do not censure yourself so. We, all of us, make mistakes. In the end, your error was not egregious. Let us decide to live in the future, rather than ruing the past."

"Remember the past only as it brings you pleasure?"

"Exactly."

With a nod and a smile, Elizabeth agreed and the matter was dropped. Their conversation soon turned to other matters.

Elizabeth's first taste of local society came more than a week after she had arrived at Hollyfield, and she quickly learned that it was not much different from society in Meryton. The Powells were one of the more prominent of the local landowners, not only for the extent of the estate, but also for a reputation of fairness and activity in the community. There were about the same number of families present in the general area, and like the society of Meryton, there were often dinners, assemblies, card parties, and all manner of other functions to be had. For her first foray into local society, the dinner party was hosted at Hollyfield.

"You do not need to go to this trouble for me," protested Elizabeth when she was told of the dinner party and the reason for it. "I am quite content, I assure you."

"It is not only to introduce you," said Caroline. "I have not actually held an event myself since my marriage. So it is equally important that I entertain the neighborhood so that I may solidify my position in local society."

"As you know, we spent the first months of our marriage on our wedding tour and in London," added Mr. Powell. "And once we finally returned to the area, I was much more interested in keeping my wife to myself, than introducing her to the stuffed shirts of the neighborhood."

This last was said with a wink at his wife, and Elizabeth had to laugh at the sight. For her part, Caroline swatted at him in protest, though she was clearly so pleased at his newest betrayal of his besotted state that she was truly not angry.

"Regardless, it shall not be a large event," said Caroline with a final glare at her husband. "I have invited only five families—those who are closest to us in age and friendliest to my husband. I believe that we shall be a merry party indeed."

And so Elizabeth was forced to relent, and if she was honest with herself, she was curious to meet those with whom the Powells associated. Though Elizabeth was at times a solitary creature, enjoying nature and her walks, she was also a woman who delighted in society. It was no hardship whatsoever for her to be introduced to new acquaintances, and she knew there would be many more objects for her to study. Maybe this time she would even be able to correctly take the measure of those to whom she would be introduced!

The appointed day arrived, and Elizabeth provided whatever assistance she could in the preparations. Though assigned a certain subset of Caroline's tasks, Elizabeth was well aware that the woman did so in gratitude for her willingness to help and to allow her to feel like she was being of use. In actuality, Caroline needed no help. She was a consummate hostess, a fact that Elizabeth had never doubted, even when her opinion of the woman had been at its lowest.

She retired to her room early in order to dress for the evening, thankful that she had possessed the foresight to see the possibility of attending functions while visiting. Maria spent, in Elizabeth's opinion, and inordinate amount of time on her hair, making sure that every curl was in place, and though Elizabeth, unused to taking such time with her appearance, chafed a little at the delay, she had to allow the girl's efforts were well worth the final result. Elizabeth had never felt so pretty in her entire life.

Descending the stairs, Elizabeth was greeted by her hosts, who were dressed in similarly fine fashion. Mr. Powell with light-hearted gallantry, took her hand and assisted her the final few steps to the floor, saying:

"I must say that you look simply ravishing tonight, Miss Bennet." He peered over at Caroline, who was regarding him through narrowed eyes, and amended: "Though not as ravishing as my dear Caroline, of course."

Elizabeth laughed at the sight of Caroline's mock annoyance. "Very smooth, Mr. Powell. You must certainly take care not to offend your wife on my account. I would not have poor Maria's efforts ruined should your wife become annoyed enough to pull my locks from their pins."

"I assure you, Elizabeth, that should I become offended, it would be with my scoundrel of a husband, and not with you."

"That is a relief indeed," said Elizabeth through her laughing.

"If it is your intent to provide Miss Bennet with a suitor or three, then I dare say you might be gratified," said Mr. Powell. "I dare say her appearance is enchanting enough tonight, that when combined with her vivacity, there will be very few who can resist."

"Oh please," groaned Elizabeth. "I have enough matchmaking from my mother, thank you very much. I had hoped that I would be able to escape such schemes here."

Caroline only smiled in a mysterious—and to Elizabeth, alarming—fashion, before turning to greet the first guests who arrived at that moment.

Though she was not a member of the family, Elizabeth stood with her friends greeting the visitors and being introduced to them.

By and large, those with whom Mr. Powell was close were a friendly group, and Elizabeth was pleased to know them. The first family to arrive was the Trents, close neighbors to Mr. Powell, living on an estate just to the north. With the married couple came Mr. Trent's younger brother, John; he was a tall man, dark of hair and eyes, and though not in any way ill-favored, he was not especially handsome either. During their introduction, Elizabeth learned that the younger Mr. Trent was a Major in the army, and that he was recuperating from a battlefield injury he had sustained some months earlier. Mr. Trent was friendly and agreeable, and Elizabeth thought would be an interesting acquaintance.

The following families were a succession of names and faces, from the Middletons, accompanied by Mrs. Middleton's brother Mr. Johnson, to the Fredericks, who brought a pair of male cousins and their sister, all within a few years of Elizabeth's age, to the Hancocks, who were also accompanied by house guests of theirs, a Mr. and Miss Graves. By the time the Hancocks and Mr. Graves had been escorted into the sitting-room, Elizabeth was looking pointedly at Caroline, her expression promising retribution. Caroline merely smiled and shrugged, while turning to greet the last arrivals.

When they walked in Elizabeth, was arrested by the sight of a handsome couple, about the same age as the Powells, accompanied by a young man, likely the brother of the husband, unless Elizabeth's eyes were misleading her. They were all tall, possessed of blond hair and blue eyes, and in Elizabeth's estimation, were all handsome people.

"Powell," greeted the man, stepping forward with an extended hand. At the same time, the young lady had greeted Caroline in a familiar manner.

Greetings were exchanged, and Mr. Powel gestured to Elizabeth, saying: "Please allow me to introduce my good friends. Mr. Henry Jamison and his wife Cecilia, as well as Mr. Jamison's younger brother, Mr. Gabriel Jamison, this is my wife's good friend, Miss Elizabeth Bennet."

"Miss Bennet is the younger sister of Jane Bennet, who recently married my brother Charles," said Miss Bingley.

The greetings were exchanged and Elizabeth barely had time to rise from her curtsey before Mr. Gabriel Jamison stepped forward and, grasping her hand, bestowed a gallant kiss on it.

"Enchanted, madam," said he. "I had not expected to find such beauty at Hollyfield tonight. I must say that I am most pleasantly surprised."

"Have a care, Gabriel," said his brother, though his light expression belied the reprimand. "You would not wish to offend Mrs. Powell with such a dismissal."

"Oh stuff and nonsense!" said Mr. Jamison with an airy wave of his hand. "Given the protective nature of newly married men, I risk being called out if I am too warm with the lovely Mrs. Powell." Mr. Jamison dropped an elaborate bow at Caroline, who was eyeing him with barely concealed amusement. "Miss Bennet, however, is fair game, unless of course she is hiding a suitor or a fiancé somewhere."

Elizabeth blushed, but she refused to let the man's familiar attitude fluster her. "I am not engaged, Mr. Jamison. You, on the other hand, appear to be an incorrigible flirt."

An elegant hand went up to his breast, and Mr. Jamison cried out, "You injure me, madam! I assure you that everything I say to you is the absolute truth.

"Now, for such an offense, I must insist that you allow me to escort you into the room."

Laughing, Elizabeth took his extended arm and allowed him to guide her into the room. It already promised to be a very interesting night indeed.

The fact that there were several single young men present was a testament to Mrs. Powell's efforts to introduce Elizabeth to the young gentlemen of the neighborhood, but though Elizabeth caught the woman's eye more than once, she rather suspected that Caroline had some goal in mind other than marrying her off to one of the men present that evening. What that could be Elizabeth could not fathom.

Of more immediate import to Elizabeth's state of mind were the attentions of Mr. Gabriel Jamison. In short, Elizabeth's first impression of the man appeared to have been accurate—the man flirted and flattered, regaling her with tales of his exploits, some of which she felt bore a cursory resemblance to the truth! It would have been easy to dismiss the man as a fop had he not proved himself to be possessed of a rare intelligence and a happy disposition.

In fact, Elizabeth thought her head might have been full of him had it not been for a rather unfortunate circumstance; for when she considered the man, she realized that in essentials, he reminded her of Mr. Wickham, a factor which could not at all speak to his favor. She rather suspected that he was more harmless than that man had been, but the fact that he was smooth as honey made her wary of him.

And furthermore, while he might be of more substance than Mr. Wickham, she rather thought he was still lacking. He certainly could not measure up to Mr. Bingley, Mr. Powell, or even—though Elizabeth almost regretted conceding it—Mr. Darcy.

What he was, however, was an engaging conversationalist who spoke of a variety of topics and never allowed a moment in his company to pass in a dull manner. Elizabeth was well-entertained in his company.

When dinner was announced, there arose a minor matter of disagreement when Major Trent approached Elizabeth where she was speaking with Mr. Jamison and said:

"Miss Bennet, may I escort you into dinner?"

"I believe that I shall escort her to dinner, Trent," said Mr. Jamison.

Elizabeth could not detect an obvious animosity between the two men but it was clear that they at least did not think much of one another.

"Shall we allow the lady to decide?"

"She would not wish to be lulled to sleep by someone as dull as you."

Annoyed by the man's unkind words and presumption, Elizabeth turned toward Major Trent and said: "I would be happy if you would escort me, sir."

An appreciative smile met her words, and she took his arm to follow the others into the dining room.

"Ah, bested on the field of battle," exclaimed Mr. Jamison as he followed them, a hand going to his heart with an extravagant flourish. "But you had best beware, Trent. The battle may have been conceded, but the war is far from won."

They went in to dinner, and though Major Trent was not the flirt that Mr. Jamison had proven himself to be, he was intelligent and thoughtful, and Elizabeth found that she enjoyed his company at least as much as she had enjoyed her previous companion's.

Mr. Jamison did not approach her for the rest of the evening, but as Elizabeth mingled with the guests, she felt his gaze resting upon her several times. She did not know what the man was about, but she was determined not to be taken in. Once in a lifetime was enough, and she had already met her quota with Mr. Wickham!

"I am not sure what you meant by that performance of yours tonight."

Caroline raised an eyebrow at her husband, though inside she was feeling rather satisfied with the events of the evening. "I am sure I do not know to what you refer."

The pointed stare could not be mistaken for anything but one of some confusion, mixed with annoyance. "I had understood you wished to pair Miss Bennet with Darcy."

"I do not wish to 'pair' her with anyone, David."

Her husband's expression turned skeptical, prompting a laugh from Caroline. She stepped forward and touched his arm, reveling in the closeness between them. They had returned to their rooms after the evening with their guests and were now preparing to retire.

"Yes, it is obvious that they would suit one another very well, but I merely wish to allow them the opportunity for them to realize that fact themselves. They may then resolve the matter on their own."

"Then what prompted the parade of unmarried men tonight?"

"It will not hurt Darcy to experience a bit of competition. I rather think that it will force him to wake up and take action. Perhaps more than anything else would."

"Caroline," said David gently, "I understand your desire to see your friends happy. But do you not think that this is interfering a little too much? And if you wish Miss Bennet to be happy, why did you ever invite Gabriel Jamison? The man has the reputation of a rake, and I would not see her hurt by him."

"There is little chance of that happening," said Caroline, a little smugly. "Mr. Jamison's mannerisms bear a striking resemblance to one George Wickham, a fact which did not pass Elizabeth by unnoticed. And even if she was not disposed against him for that reason, I have great faith in her morality.

"And what's more," said David with a knowing smile, "Darcy will note the man's behavior as soon as they meet, and will undoubtedly feel protective toward Miss Bennet."

"As I said, I am confident that everything shall work out as it should."

"Very well," said David with a sigh. "But we must watch Jamison carefully. I do not like the man's reputation."

Caroline just smiled and thanked her husband for being so diligent. For herself, Caroline knew that Jamison was not a threat to Elizabeth, as she was well aware of the fact that Elizabeth was well able to care for herself. But perhaps just in case, she would have a discussion with her the following day to make sure that she was on her guard. No sense tempting fate, after all.

Chapter VII

$\mathcal{T}$he morning after the dinner party, Elizabeth descended the stairs, her head still full of the events of the evening before. In the forefront of her thoughts was the guest list from the previous evening and the preponderance of young, unattached males, and she wondered just how much Caroline intended to put her in the way of them.

The issue was, of course, that Caroline was adept at avoiding questions she did not wish to answer, and Elizabeth thought it certain that she would only smile in that superior way of hers, which, though Elizabeth now considered the woman a friend, still had the power to irritate her. And the way Elizabeth had noted her amusement when Elizabeth had been forced to bear the attentions of Gabriel Jamison almost set her to grinding her teeth in frustration. Caroline could not mean to pair her with the man, but she was not above enjoying herself when observing Elizabeth's attempts to fend him off.

Thus, when she entered the room, Elizabeth greeted Caroline and filled her plate, and then after taking her seat, tried to determine how best to broach the subject. It turned out to be unnecessary as Caroline soon spoke, addressing Elizabeth with an unusually serious air.

"How did you enjoy the evening, Elizabeth?"

"It was interesting indeed," said Elizabeth. Deciding she was not above a little dig at her hostess's designs, she commented: "It did seem like there was an overabundance of men present, but your neighbors are, for the most part, charming."

"I am glad we were able to entertain you," replied Caroline, refusing to give anything away. "If I may be so bold, I believe that you spent most of the evening in the company of two gentlemen in particular."

"Major Trent and Mr. Jamison," said Elizabeth with a nod.

"And what were your opinions of them?"

Elizabeth was a little uncomfortable; the previous impression she had of Caroline rose up in her mind, and for a brief moment she wondered if the woman meant to be severe upon her. But then she remembered the warm greeting, the conversations they had shared, the walks they had taken, and the way in which Caroline had behaved with her, and she knew that the ghost of her old opinion of this woman was still affecting her. Whatever reason Caroline had for bringing this up Elizabeth knew that it was not a malicious one.

And thus, Elizabeth responded with her honest impressions. "Major Trent is a pleasant man and he seems to me to be one who takes his duty seriously. His behavior reflects that. As for Mr. Jamison, I was not impressed. He is flirtatious, forward, and he appears to be of the opinion that as a woman, I should swoon the moment he smiles at me."

Caroline laughed. "I should not have wondered whether you had understood the man. His manners *are* blatant, after all."

"Perhaps you are right to question," said Elizabeth with a rueful smile. "I completely missed the worthlessness in Mr. Wickham, and Mr. Jamison is a similar character."

"Do not censure yourself, Elizabeth," said Caroline. "Mr. Wickham is well able to deceive and his manners are far less overt than Gabriel Jamison's, thereby lending him an ability to conceal what he truly is."

Elizabeth grimaced. "I would agree with you and say that Mr. Wickham is the more dangerous of the two. To anyone possessing any hint of discernment, Mr. Jamison is easily recognizable as a flirt and likely a philanderer. Mr. Wickham lies in wait and lulls a lady to sleep before he makes his move."

"Excellent," said Caroline with an unmistakable warmth. "I am happy that I do not need to warn you concerning Mr. Jamison. He is well known in these parts, and as he has inherited an estate from his mother's family, he is entirely at his leisure. Unfortunately, he usually chooses to use that leisure to pursue women, gamble, and carouse. I would not wish for you to be taken in by the man."

"Thank you. After Mr. Wickham, I like to think that I am a little less trusting, but I appreciate the sentiment all the same." Elizabeth paused and then directed a pointed glance at her hostess. "I would observe that it appears as if you had a specific purpose in mind when you contemplated the guest list for your dinner last night. I had thought that in leaving my mother behind I would be free of matchmaking, but perhaps I was wrong?"

Caroline only smiled. "I shall not attempt to take your mother's place, Elizabeth. I will confess that I think it a good opportunity to meet with young men who are not part of the society in which you were raised, but I shall not push you at any of them. To a large extent, last night was due to chance. As I issued a general invitation to each family, I did not know until they responded who would be attending, and there were more visitors than I had anticipated."

Though she was skeptical, Elizabeth let the matter rest. She would not allow Caroline her way when trying to pair her with someone, any more than she would allow her mother to direct her, so in the end it really did not matter. And while Caroline might have some thought that she might take a fancy to someone in the neighborhood, Elizabeth knew that she would not be push the matter.

"I do have another item to discuss with you, however," said Caroline. "We are expecting some more visitors in the next few days."

Elizabeth smiled with pleasure. "Yes, Jane and your brother will be joining us. I am very much looking forward to being reunited with my sister."

"As I am with my brother," said Caroline. "But there will be some additional visitors who will arrive a few days after. Mr. Darcy will be joining us along with his sister Georgiana and his cousin Colonel Fitzwilliam."

This bit of news was definitely a surprise, but whereas she might have been annoyed at the thought of once again being thrown into Mr. Darcy's company, she decided it was truly of no concern. The man still impressed her as proud and unapproachable, but as he was a close friend — even family — to the Bingleys, it was to be expected that he would appear from time to time. So Elizabeth focused on those with whom she did not yet share an acquaintance.

"You have told me previously of Miss Darcy, but I would like to know what kind of girl she is."

"She is sweet and shy, not lacking in the social graces, but lacking in confidence and the fear of making a mistake. She is quite talented musically, and I expect that when she reaches her true potential she will surpass my own accomplishments, which I flatter myself are not insignificant."

"You play very well indeed," said Elizabeth.

Caroline nodded her head in appreciation, but continued, saying: "She is very rarely persuaded to sing, but her skills on the pianoforte are exquisite. In fact, I believe that you and I and Georgiana should plan to do a duet — you and I can sing, accompanied by Georgiana on the pianoforte. It would be very well received."

"I would be happy to," said Elizabeth. "Do you have any suggestions concerning Miss Darcy? If she is so shy, she may have difficulty speaking with a stranger."

"Just be her friend," said Caroline. "She has had enough young ladies attempt to befriend her for the sole purpose of gaining access to her brother. If she senses that you are genuine, she will happily respond to your overtures."

Elizabeth digested that bit if information and said: "And what of Colonel Fitzwilliam?"

"The colonel is much like my brother — of a happy disposition and gentlemanly manners, though he is a little more garrulous than Charles. Do not let his amiable façade mislead you, however — he is a soldier through and through, and he has seen battle and hardship."

"Thank you," said Elizabeth. "I shall anticipate making their acquaintance. I only hope they will both feel disposed to like me in return."

"I am sure they shall," said Caroline.

A few days later the anticipated reunion took place. Elizabeth found herself restless the entire day in expectation of Jane's arrival, and her hostess was not above teasing her for her impatience.

"Relax, Elizabeth," said Caroline with a laugh. "Pacing the floor will not hasten their arrival."

"I cannot help myself," said Elizabeth, as she once again looked from the sitting-room window toward the drive. "I have been parted from Jane before, of course, but never for such a length of time. I find that I cannot wait to see her again."

Caroline looked upon her wistfully. "You are exceedingly close to Jane."

"We have always been each other's confidant." Elizabeth smiled in recollection. "In a house where peace and serenity often did not exist, we were each the one on whom the other could depend."

Elizabeth stopped pacing, lost in her thoughts. "I would not have you believe me to resent your brother or lament my sister's marriage. But it changed so much in my life and I will confess that it has been hard at times. And then I remember Jane's shining countenance on the day they married, and I can do naught but be happy she has found a man who will love her as she deserves."

"I understand your conflict, though I cannot claim the same. I have spoken of my lack of closeness with Louisa."

When Elizabeth nodded, Caroline continued: "She is my sister and I love her. I tell myself nothing matters, but then when I see you and Jane, I must admit to a little jealousy for your closeness."

"I feel the same about my younger sisters," said Elizabeth. "Mary is absorbed in her reading and her music, and if the fact that she was eager to marry a man I spurned is not enough evidence of our difference in characters, then no mere words can express it."

Caroline laughed and Elizabeth joined her. "And as for Kitty and Lydia," said Elizabeth after a moment, "well, it is obvious that they are as different from me as night is to day. My only consolation where their behavior is concerned is that the regiment has left Meryton by now."

This time it was a rueful and commiserating glance which warmed Elizabeth. Obviously, Caroline was well aware of the inappropriate behavior of Elizabeth's youngest sisters, but in supporting her brother's marriage to Jane and her friendship with Elizabeth, she had chosen to overlook what she could not change for her brother's sake. Elizabeth was well aware that many of society would not be so forgiving, especially those who had connections to the highest echelons.

"I am happy for Jane," continued Elizabeth, "but I am also eager to see what changes marriage have wrought in her life."

"As it should be. I remember being quite curious when my sister married. I expect that the changes in Jane will of a happier variety than those I witnessed in Louisa."

Elizabeth said nothing to such a statement and resumed her restless pacing. Her discussions with Caroline had revealed the unhappy nature of Louisa's marriage, and there was no reason to belabor the issue.

At length, Elizabeth was able to calm her anticipation to the point where she was able to sit and converse with Caroline, if not with perfect ease, at least with the semblance of composure. When the sound of horses' hooves and the rolling wheels of an approaching carriage were heard, however, Elizabeth was on her feet in an instant, and on her way toward the front of the house, the sound of Caroline's laughter ringing behind her.

She arrived at the entrance as the carriage was coming to a stop, and when a grinning Charles Bingley alighted and turned to help his new wife down, Elizabeth flew into her sister's arms, tears streaming down her cheeks. A flurry of greetings — some almost intelligible — proceeded from the two girls' mouths. Jane was a woman now, Elizabeth reminded herself. She had been of age for some time, but Elizabeth had to own that her sister carried herself with a confidence which had not been entirely present before. It was nothing Elizabeth could define. Rather she seemed to exude an air of maturity and contentment. Jane was more beautiful than Elizabeth remembered.

"Let us step into the house, shall we?" said Caroline, her amusement rolling from her tone in waves.

Still with teary eyes, Elizabeth let go of Jane and allowed her to greet Caroline, after which they were all escorted into the house. The new arrivals were conducted to their suite of rooms to refresh themselves, forcing Elizabeth to wait even longer before she could question her sister concerning the first months of her marriage. When Jane did appear, however, the sisters sat together discussing the events of the previous month. Elizabeth recounted the few items which would be of interest to Jane, and then sat listening as Jane described her travels.

"Charles's family is very friendly and obliging," said Jane as she described her new relations. "I was accepted with open arms."

"And what of the infamous uncle?" said Elizabeth. "I understand he is yet a bachelor and that his manners are rather rough."

"Mr. Bingley *is* rather . . . singular," said Jane. "I suspect he could not understand what the to-do was all about when Charles and I married. But he is kind-hearted and pleasant, though rather bluff in manner. I found that I liked him exceedingly."

Elizabeth had to force herself not to laugh. It was Jane at her most obliging, always making excuses for others and seeing only the good in them. Caroline, on the other hand, had painted a picture of a man who spent half the day in his cups, and the other half chasing anything that wore a skirt.

"And what of your travels? And your new husband? Is he as fine a catch as our mother seemed to think?"

Jane blushed, but she looked at Elizabeth, the happiness shining from her eyes. "Charles is everything I could have wished for," said Jane with a dreamy smile. "I could not imagine a better or more attentive husband. We spent most of our time near the sea in the vicinity of York, and the location was both beautiful and private."

"And privacy was most likely what your husband wished for most of all," said Elizabeth with a mischievous grin.

"Perhaps we should find *you* a husband, Lizzy," said Jane, returning Elizabeth's comment with a playful dig of her own. "It appears to me that now you are the eldest unmarried daughter, it has only caused you to become more impertinent than ever."

At that moment, Mr. Bingley, followed by Caroline and Mr. Powell entered the room, all smiling indulgently at the reunion between the two sisters. Mr. Bingley in particular approached them, regarding them with pleasure, though he also sported a mock-injured air.

"Ah, I see now the sisters are reunited, the charms of a mere husband are not enough to keep my wife's attention."

Jane blushed, but Elizabeth laughed at his comment.

"Surely you can occasionally spare my dear sister for a few moments, Mr. Bingley. After all, you have her for the rest of your life, while I must be content to steal her attention when you least suspect it."

"I am sure I cannot begrudge your reunions," said Mr. Bingley. "But I must take exception to the manner in which you address me. As you are the sister to my wife, I insist that you call me 'Charles.'"

Warmly Elizabeth responded that she would, as long as she was afforded the same courtesy. The rest of the evening passed in a pleasant manner, and Elizabeth enjoyed herself very well. The two couples in no way made her feel as if she was not welcome, but Elizabeth had to own to a small measure of wistfulness, due entirely that she was the only one of the party who was not a newlywed.

At length, however, after a joyful evening spent in the company of loved ones, they retired for the night, and Elizabeth entered the land of dreams thinking on the very great pleasure of once again being in the company of her beloved sister. The pleasure she had experienced in visiting with Caroline and her husband could only be enhanced with the arrival of two others so dear to her.

The next days were equally pleasant for Elizabeth, and she could not imagine any place she would rather be than at Hollyfield. Jane's presence was, of course, a pleasure, and together with Caroline, the three ladies were in the process of forming a close friendship which Elizabeth imagined would last all their lives. The gentlemen were also much in evidence, but Elizabeth was so absorbed in her sister and Caroline that at times she scarcely noticed them.

Jane was confirmed to be everything that Elizabeth noted upon first seeing her sister again after their separation. Though it was difficult to say exactly what had changed, Elizabeth was finally forced to acknowledge that it was her sister's attitude more than anything. As a calm and steady sort of character, Jane had always been rather diffident, and though she did not lack in confidence, she was also not one to put herself forward, tending to allow others to take the lead.

Regardless of whatever changes her marriage had wrought, Jane would never be an assertive person; she would never desire to be the focus of attention. But though Elizabeth understood those facets of Jane's character, it was also clear that Jane had gained a new level of confidence, and that her opinions were more grounded and more forceful because of it. Elizabeth, who had always been a more assertive sort of person, relished this change in her sister. It was as if Jane was finally becoming the person she was meant to be.

Three days after the Bingleys arrived at Hollyfield, three more guests were expected to join the party, and Elizabeth's anticipation of this event—though it was obviously looked on with a great amount of anticipation by both Mr. Bingley and the Powells—was quite different than when Jane was due to arrive.

She was interested in meeting the two whom she had never met before—Caroline's anecdotes had suggested that Miss Darcy was a pleasant young girl and had given Colonel Fitzwilliam a flaming character. Mr. Darcy was to be part of the party as well, and while Elizabeth had acquitted the man of ruining a childhood friend's prospects, she was still of the opinion that he was not an amiable man, regardless of Caroline's assertions. Her first impression of the man after his arrival at Hollyfield did nothing to disabuse her of that notion.

The party present at the estate gathered on the stairs leading to the front entrance when the carriage pulled up. Elizabeth's attention was caught by the two she had not met before.

Miss Darcy was tall—standing slightly taller than Elizabeth, though shorter than Jane—and was well formed and womanly, if rather slender and willowy in appearance. She had blond hair and pleasant features, and her downcast eyes spoke to her diffidence and lack of confidence. By contrast, Colonel Fitzwilliam was a large man, taller even than Mr. Darcy and broad of shoulder, the top of his head adorned by a mop of reddish hair. He was not a particularly handsome man—though certainly not ill-favored—and she imagined that should her youngest sisters be present and he was dressed in his regimentals, that they would be caught in a veritable swoon at the very sight of him.

Being the only one who was not acquainted with the colonel and Miss Darcy, the introductions were soon made, and Elizabeth greeted them with pleasure. Miss Darcy was overcome by shyness and her greeting was completed in an unintelligible monosyllable, a greeting Elizabeth returned in a brief fashion, in deference to the girl's discomfort. Colonel Fitzwilliam's salutation was, by contrast, bluff and friendly.

"Miss Bennet," said he with a low bow, "I am quite happy to make your acquaintance. Though we have not met before, I feel as if I already know you."

Elizabeth started, peering at the man and wondering if she had misheard him. "You feel like you already know me?"

"I have heard much of you from various sources, though I will say their words did not do you justice."

Though she might be mistaken Elizabeth thought that she caught the briefest turn of the colonel's eyes to Mr. Darcy, a glance which Elizabeth found herself mimicking. She immediately swished she had not however, as the severity of Mr. Darcy's countenance almost made her recoil in alarm. He truly was a tall and intimidating man and he was regarding his cousin with a hard and unfriendly glare. In the back of her mind Elizabeth wondered if some of his displeasure was directed at Elizabeth herself.

"Fitzwilliam, of course, exaggerates," said Mr. Darcy. "We have all made mention of our previous meetings in relation to Mrs. Bingley's marriage to my closest friend, who is, you understand, well acquainted with him."

Though she accepted such an explanation without comment, understanding immediately that the colonel was likely a man prone to such exaggeration, Elizabeth could not help but think there was something else at play here. Regardless of whatever conjecture she indulged in, it appeared irrefutable that Mr. Darcy was not happy to see her, and she wondered why he had come if her presence was so offensive to him.

"Shall we move into the house?" interrupted Caroline's voice.

The new arrivals were shown to their rooms in order to wash and refresh themselves, returning to the rest of the party before too much time had passed.

When they did make an appearance, Elizabeth, who was sitting with Jane and Caroline, immediately welcomed Miss Darcy as she diffidently approached their group.

"I *am* pleased to make your acquaintance," said Miss Darcy a few moments after she had joined them. "Mrs. Bingley, I wish you every happiness."

Elizabeth had the distinct impression that Miss Darcy was unaccustomed to making statements even half as long, but Jane merely smiled and replied: "He already has made me happy, but I thank you for your kind words nonetheless. I understand that you have been acquainted with Charles and Caroline for some time?"

"All my life," replied Miss Darcy.

The conversation continued from there, and though Miss Darcy did interject a few words from time to time, she appeared to be largely content to listen and allow others to speak. Elizabeth, seeing her reticence and understanding her sweet nature, began to try to draw her into conversation. It was only when she happened upon a topic which was of interest to the girl that the floodgates opened and Miss Darcy began to speak with less reservation.

"I understand your skills on the pianoforte are quite extraordinary," said Elizabeth.

Rather than her typical brief answer Miss Darcy blushed, but she soon looked shyly up at Elizabeth and said with a smile: "I believe that Caroline has been singing my praises again. I assure you that I am not nearly as talented as she suggests."

"But you do enjoy music."

"Yes."

"As do I." said Elizabeth.

"To me it is one of the great pleasures in life," said Miss Darcy, her tone become a little more animated. "It is one which I indulge in whenever possible. But though I play the pianoforte and the harp, I do not sing, as a rule, as I do not possess a fine singing voice."

"We cannot possess every talent," replied Elizabeth. "In fact, I have it on good authority that there are only half a dozen women in society who can be deemed truly accomplished, as only they possess all the skills necessary to lay claim to the word."

As she said this, Elizabeth directed a sly look at both Caroline and Mr. Darcy, but while the latter only regarded her with his usual severe expression, Caroline appeared amused.

"I would implore you not to reopen that argument, Elizabeth. Or perhaps you feel as if you are capable of laying claim to one of the six available titles?"

A raised eyebrow accompanied the barb, and Elizabeth could only laugh. "No, Mrs. Powell, I shall leave the procurement of such titles to those who care for such things." Elizabeth smiled at Miss Darcy and said: "I have far too many interests and far too little time to become a proficient at *everything*."

Miss Darcy giggled and nodded her head in agreement.

"Should you have the opportunity to meet our aunt, she will tell you that she would have been the most accomplished of her sex, had she only learned," said the colonel, with a mischievous smile.

Elizabeth laughed. "This would not be the infamous Lady Catherine de Bourgh, would it?"

Colonel Fitzwilliam appeared to be impressed. "Are you acquainted with the lady?"

"Only anecdotally. My cousin, Mr. Collins, who is heir to my father's estate, is the parson of Hunsford, which I believe is under Lady Catherine's purview."

"Ah, yes, the inestimable Mr. Collins." This time there was no mistaking the playful glint in the colonel's eyes. "He is a very . . . singular gentleman indeed. I suspect that if you have spent any time at all in his company, you could hardly have avoided hearing a great deal about my aunt. Mr. Collins is married to your sister, is he not?"

"She is," confirmed Elizabeth. "Theirs is . . . perhaps not a marriage I might have chosen, but I believe that it suits my sister quite well."

"Then I would inform you of your sister's health and apparent happiness with her situation. Darcy and I were recently in the company of my aunt in Kent, as we visit every year at Easter. They are quite at Lady Catherine's disposal, I dare say, though I doubt Mr. Collins would have it any other way."

"Have a care in how you speak of Lady Catherine, Fitzwilliam," said Mr. Darcy, as he glared at the colonel.

The colonel made some retort to Mr. Darcy, but Elizabeth turned her attention back to Miss Darcy. "Do you visit your aunt with your brother, Miss Darcy?"

A look of horror came over the girl's face, and her previous mask of timidity came over her when she said: "I find my aunt much too frightening." She then started and covered her mouth with chagrin.

"It is completely understandable," said Elizabeth with a kind smile. "A forceful older relative might very well seem to be difficult and severe.

Elizabeth paused, glancing at Mr. Darcy, and though she had intended to say something impertinent to the effect that Mr. Darcy was likely not nearly as intimidating as he appeared, she stayed her tongue. Though she had not passed much time in their company, she had the distinct impression that whenever he looked upon his sister, it was with great affection and indulgence, rather than severity.

Miss Darcy then said, "I understand you play as well, Miss Bennet?"

"I do play," said Elizabeth, happy to return to their conversation about music, "but I do not play well at all. If you recall, I claimed many interests only a few short minutes ago. It is those interests which prevent me from attaining the skill I might otherwise have achieved. I find that I cannot repine the loss. Let those who desire to be praised for such accomplishments and have the aptitude for them have them. I am quite happy to continue on as I have been."

"Do not let Elizabeth fool you, Georgiana," said Caroline. "Elizabeth may not play with a technical perfection, but she is quite competent. In fact, we had discussed the possibility of doing a song together—you may play while Elizabeth and I sing, if that is acceptable to you."

Apparently Miss Darcy was not accustomed to playing in front of an audience, but after a moment of seeming consternation, she appeared to reconsider and she agreed, though her composure was a little suspect.

"Thank you, my dear," said Caroline. "It is hard, but facing your fears and playing when the focus is on someone else will help you become accustomed to it. I dare say when you make your debut, you will be poised and confident."

Miss Darcy beamed and said: "Only if I have such confident ladies as you, Mrs. Bingley, and Miss Bennet to guide me."

"You perhaps attribute a little too much experience to myself," said Elizabeth cheerfully. "I have never had a season, you know."

"You have not?" asked Miss Darcy with surprise. "How can that be? You carry yourself with such composure."

"That is only because I have been out for some time, but only in the small neighborhood in which I was born. My father does not like London, so we do not go there often. I have been forced to content myself with nothing more than the society of four and twenty families in our little corner of the kingdom."

"And yet your confidence is remarkable," said Caroline. "You could do worse, Georgiana, than to emulate Miss Bennet's poise and ease in society."

"Perhaps we should not discuss such matters," interjected Mr. Darcy. "Miss Bennet is correct in that she has very little experience in London society, and would not be an ideal guide."

The way the man regarded her, Elizabeth thought that she detected a measure of contempt in his face and his tone, and she was affronted all over again. No, she, Elizabeth Bennet, daughter of a minor country squire and insignificant country miss, had not had a London season, nor had she made her curtsey before the queen. But she was not some nobody whom Mr. Darcy could regard down the length of his nose with derision. All of the old feelings of scorn for this man's proud behavior and supercilious condescension came rushing back, and Elizabeth was forced to look away lest her disdain become evident upon her countenance.

Elizabeth decided that he was not deserving of her attention. She resolved to be polite, but distant to the man. He would receive no attention from her!

That evening, Caroline felt herself becoming upset with the behavior of a certain man whose blindness astounded her. What made it even more surprising was the knowledge that William, usually as perceptive as anyone she had ever met, had taken leave of his senses in this instance. And Caroline decided that she was not about to stand for his behavior.

Caroline was very familiar with William's character, having grown up in the same house, though she was several years younger. In short, the man was reticent among company, and that reticence often came across as aloofness, or in some cases haughty superiority. He could also be accused of towering resentment when he did not get his own way. The fact that he had been warned of this by all his family more than once did not stop him from falling into the habit again from time to time.

It was these very traits which had prevented Caroline from ever considering William as a prospective husband herself. Caroline was very self-aware, and she knew that in some ways, she was not much different from William, as her behavior in Meryton, which she now looked back on with regret, had so amply displayed. She knew that William required someone who was comfortable in company, playful, open, engaging, and one who could soften the hard edges of his personality. In short, William needed Elizabeth Bennet.

Furthermore, the man was attracted to Elizabeth, drawn to her in a manner which Caroline had never seen before. But his iron control and his unbending sense of duty were getting in the way of his ultimate happiness, and Caroline was convinced that Elizabeth was the means by which he could obtain that happiness. And if the woman's performance with Georgiana—from whom it was often a trial even for Caroline to obtain more than a word or two—was any indication, Elizabeth's presence in the young girl's life on a more permanent basis would also do her a world of good.

But he could not see it. Or mayhap it was more correct to say that he refused to see it. His resentment—which Caroline could easily detect despite his iron control—suggested to Caroline that he was almost wild with attraction for her but considered her to be unsuitable, and so he was determined not to act on his feelings.

Caroline was very aware that William would almost certainly be angry with her, and she had to allow that he had every right. She had engineered this meeting between the two for the purpose of inducing them both to see how perfect the other was as a marriage partner. Caroline was not afraid of William and looked upon the possibility of his being angry with her with indifference. All he was accomplishing at present was to convince Elizabeth that *she* was the cause of his anger and worsening her opinion of him as a consequence. Whether they ever saw the truth for themselves Caroline could not predict. But there was no reason for his incivility.

After dinner the party retired to the sitting-room where Caroline was witness to more of William's poor behavior. She was sitting with Elizabeth conversing pleasantly when the woman leaned toward her, and in a whisper said:

"Is there aught amiss with my dress or my hair?"

Instantly understanding the thrust of her question, Caroline could only respond: "You are lovely as always, Elizabeth. Do not concern yourself. Mr. Darcy is often out of sorts after travelling."

The look of skepticism amply informed Caroline that her obfuscation had not been successful.

"I know that you champion Mr. Darcy as a good man, and he very well may be. But I rather think that the looks he is directing at me could curdle milk."

Caroline had to allow it to be so, though she was well aware that William's glares were equally directed at Caroline herself.

"I believe that it is time for me to retire," said Elizabeth, and before Caroline could say anything to persuade her to stay, she had bid good night to the company. Caroline's only consolation was that Georgiana stood with her and made her own excuses, and the two girls went off together.

Incensed, Caroline glared at William, but all she received in return was a heated scowl.

"It was quite ungentlemanly of you to drive the beautiful maiden from the room, Darcy," said Colonel Fitzwilliam.

Privately, Caroline felt that the colonel's typical flippancy was not welcome in this particular situation, though the sentiment was accurate.

"I have no idea of what you speak," was William's short reply.

The colonel raised an eyebrow at his cousin, but the man did not deign to reply. Instead, Caroline looked at the clock and decided it was sufficiently late that the company could retire. Or at least *most* of the company.

"Shall we all follow Elizabeth's example and retire for the evening?"

The responses were a study in contrast. Jane, ever the sweet obliging woman, appeared to be confused over the sudden tension which had fallen over the group, likely because of the fact that her attention had hardly left her husband all evening. Charles, by contrast, was well aware of William's behavior though Caroline suspected that he was not aware of the reason. Charles no doubt thought of Elizabeth as *his* sister now and thus considered himself responsible for her protection. Colonel Fitzwilliam regarded his cousin with exasperation mixed with amusement and David, who was well aware of all the particulars—including Caroline's plans—was watching all the rest, clearly expecting some sort of confrontation.

As for William himself, he appeared to be quite belligerent, though it would take someone who knew him well to detect it; his impenetrable mask was firmly in place.

Fortunately, most of the company did not appear to be disposed to linger any longer, and readily accepted Caroline's suggestion, though Charles appeared to want to have a word with William. Caroline caught his eye and shook her head slightly. Indicating that she would handle the matter, and he nodded and guided Jane from the room. The colonel clearly wished to be part of the conversation, but he too excused himself and left the room.

Finally David, though he clearly did not wish to leave Caroline alone with an angry Mr. Darcy, caught her eye, sighed, and quit the room, but not without directing a harsh glare at the man, suggesting retribution should he step out of line. William ignored this byplay, focused as he was on Caroline herself.

Once Caroline was left alone with William, the man wasted no time in making his displeasure known.

"What did you hope to accomplish by this . . . this . . . farce?"

"And what did you mean by offending a guest in my house? A guest who, I might add, is quickly becoming a dear friend, and whose company I am loath to lose."

"I have not the faintest idea of what you are speaking," replied William, though his tone was akin to a growl. "I wish to know what you mean by throwing that girl into company with me again when I have stated my position in a manner which cannot be misunderstood."

"I extend my apologies, Mr. Darcy. I was not aware that we had removed to Pemberley. I should not have presumed to invite my friend to visit your estate."

"Will you stop speaking nonsense?"

"And will you cease to presume you may control who I might invite to visit at an estate of which *I* am mistress?"

William's glare became even more forbidding and had Caroline not been intimately familiar with the man she might actually have been afraid.

"Do not believe that I do not see through these machinations of yours."

"*If* I have any machinations, they are now at an end. No such plans could survive your incivility tonight. You may rest assured that I would not dream of interfering."

"Incivility!" said William, throwing his hands up into the air and stalking toward the fireplace, where he stood looking away from her. "I have hardly said ten words to the girl all evening."

"You may not have been uncivil in word, but in your actions you most certainly were. I do not think Elizabeth was mistaken when she said to me, and I quote, 'The look Mr. Darcy is directing at me could curdle milk.' Was this not incivility on your part?"

"She has completely mistaken the reason for my discomposure. I fully understand that she could not have thrown herself at me without your complicity and support. I consider your role in this to be the more egregious."

"And yet you have offended her."

"Very well," said William, and he turned to face her. "Georgiana and I shall depart on the morrow if you would prefer not to be witness to my 'incivility.'"

"And you will prove it to Elizabeth," exclaimed Caroline. "Furthermore, how do you think it will appear to her if you suddenly depart, especially after your performance this evening?"

"We would not have come at all had you informed me in advance of her presence!"

"That is why I did not inform you," said Caroline.

William glared at her, but he said nothing, seemingly surprised that Caroline had acknowledged the matter openly.

"If you depart now," said Caroline, "not only will it be an insult to one of my guests, but she will assume that you do not wish for her to know your sister."

"I do not," said William. "She is not of Georgiana's sphere and is not a suitable companion."

Caroline glared at the man with incredulous disbelief. "Am I to infer that you now do not consider *my brother and me* to be suitable companions for your sister?"

"Do not willfully misunderstand me!"

"On the contrary, Mr. Darcy, I believe that I understand you perfectly. Or have you forgotten that the Bingley money was obtained in the despicable realm of trade? On a pure societal scale, Miss Elizabeth Bennet was above me only a few short months ago, regardless of whatever dowry she may or may not possess. The money I brought to my marriage still carries the stench of trade, and you well know it. And for that matter, as Charles still does not own an estate, he cannot be considered to be an appropriate acquaintance for your sister either. Even should he purchase one, it will be long before he or his descendants will truly be accepted."

To that William had nothing to say. Though his color was still up indicating his anger, he appeared to be considering her words, and for that Caroline could only smile grimly.

"I shall assume that you do not mean that, Mr. Darcy, so I shall discount your words as those arising from anger and frustration.

"I will, however, direct your attention toward your sister tonight. Did you not notice how Elizabeth drew her out effortlessly? I myself have little more success and I have known her all my life. Is she not a wonderful woman who would bring you much happiness?"

William's stubbornness once again made an appearance. "She is a good sort of girl, and I will concede that Georgiana seemed to take to her with little hesitation. But she is in no way suitable to be Mrs. Darcy."

Caroline sighed and conceded defeat. She had never meant to do more than put the two in company again and let them sort matters out on their own. She had known William would not be amused, but she had thought that spending a little time in Elizabeth's company would cause his resolve to crumble. She had done all she could, and if William could not see what a gem Elizabeth was, then he did not deserve her in any case.

"I will not promote a match between you, Mr. Darcy.'

A suspicious look met her declaration, but he blessedly did not say anything further.

"Yes, I intended to put you into one another's company, but that was the extent of my 'machinations' as you say. Besides, I rather think that it would be difficult to persuade her to consider you a marriage partner now."

"I am certain she would not be so foolish as to reject a proposal should I make it. I do not doubt that her mother would not allow her such freedom."

His tone was filled with such arrogant confidence it was all Caroline could do not to laugh at him. William truly was a prideful man, and though he did not behave that way in order to consciously display his superiority, it was still an intrinsic part of his character. Caroline knew that he made some attempt to suppress it, but he was not always successful.

"That very statement shows how little you know her," said Caroline.

Standing, she regarded William, who was peering at her with a dangerous glint in his eye. "I assume you are not aware, but Miss Elizabeth Bennet is so much under her mother's dominance, that she refused a proposal of marriage from her cousin Mr. Collins, though it would have secured the family's fortunes. And this she did long before her eldest sister *secured* my brother."

William's jaw dropped, likely at the mere thought that Elizabeth might have been married to that sycophantic imbecile Collins. But he recovered quickly and said:

"But the man married her sister."

"I believe *I* can take as much credit for that as anyone." A puzzled expression came over William's face, and Caroline said: "I visited Longbourn the day after the ball at Netherfield last November soon after Elizabeth refused the man's proposal. As I was leaving I had the opportunity for a brief conversation with Mr. Collins, and divining the fact that he was much better suited to the middle girl, I suggested that he redirect his attentions accordingly, though not in so many words."

This time William's expression was disapproving. "It seems like you have developed an unexpected penchant for matchmaking, Caroline. It would be best if you would restrain yourself from such activities."

"I shall not apologize for my actions. Not only did my few words result in Mrs. Collins's situation, but the Bennets were assisted and Elizabeth was freed from her mother's lamentations."

An elegant eyebrow rose in response to Caroline's statement. "I thought you had little use for the Bennets, and Mrs. Bennet in particular. In fact, I seem to remember you being quite severe on Miss Bennet herself on several occasions. Did I mistake your meaning?"

"You did not," said Caroline. "But that was only before I knew what kind of woman she was. Once I came to know Elizabeth better I realized that I had judged her without the benefit of any knowledge of her. I am quite ashamed of my behavior. Perhaps you should be ashamed of yours."

And with that, Caroline quit the room, only to be surprised at the presence of her husband waiting out in the hallway. David motioned for quiet and led her to the stairs and up toward their chambers.

"He did not sound happy," said David once they had achieved some distance from the sitting-room.

Caroline could only laugh, though it was forced. It was the understatement of the century, in her opinion.

"You did not need to wait for me. I was in no danger from Mr. Darcy."

"I am well aware of that, my dear. But I could not leave you to face the dragon alone."

"Colonel Fitzwilliam is apt to refer to his aunt with such an irreverent statement."

David only smirked. "I am also well aware of Fitzwilliam's penchant for such frivolity. But it is a more accurate description of Darcy when he gets his back up."

"Thank you," said Caroline, reaching up to touch her husband's face. "I still hope that he will come to his senses, but I cannot predict how he will react."

"Even if he does, he will have a difficult time of it. Miss Bennet is convinced that he is the most disagreeable man on the face of the earth."

"As she should," said Caroline with a dismissive shrug. "And it only serves him right. He could use a little humbling, and if I were Elizabeth, I would require him to grovel before I would forgive him."

David laughed. "If you truly wish for them to sort the matter out, then you had best hope that she is not as unforgiving as you are."

"On the contrary," said Caroline, "William needs to be knocked from his high horse. I can think of no one better than Elizabeth Bennet to take on the task."

Chapter VIII

$\mathcal{T}$owering resentment was an apt description of Darcy's mood as he left the sitting-room sometime after Caroline Powel had quit it. How dare the woman attempt to take him to task for his behavior when she had all but ambushed him with Miss Elizabeth Bennet's presence! And that after Darcy had made clear to her that he had no intention of elevating a country miss to become the next mistress of Pemberley, a position which was highly sought after among those of society.

The truth was that the woman would never fit into his life, and he would not make her miserable by subjecting her to a role for which she was wholly unsuited. In the confines of his own mind Darcy was willing to acknowledge a powerful attraction to the woman. She was playful and intelligent, confident and kind, and possession of many good attributes. But she had not been brought up to high society and she had never been taught how to behave, how to manage a house as great as Pemberley, not to mention Darcy house in town. It was in every way inconceivable.

When Darcy reached his room, he hurried his valet along — Winters had been with him for many years and he understood when it was best to leave his master to his own devices — and then flung himself into a chair near a cold fireplace, dressed in nothing but his nightshirt. It was a warm evening for late May and the fireplace had not been needed, though Darcy wished for it now. The tongues of dancing flames had always had a mesmerizing effect on Darcy, and at that moment he would prefer to have been able to lose all conscious thought while staring at the fire.

Darcy was far too enamored of Miss Elizabeth Bennet, and regardless her complete unsuitability, his fascination was weakening his resolve. If he stayed at Hollyfield, he was very much worried that he would lose himself in a pair of fine eyes and propose marriage to her. And if he did so, he would be going back on centuries of Darcy heritage and tradition. His duty was to marry the right sort of girl who would increase his holdings, bring him connections to higher levels of society, and increase the power and influence of the Darcy name. Darcy was well aware of the fact that he could easily aspire to marry the daughter of an earl as his father had done before him.

That is why Miss Bennet was so unsuitable, even though he had never met a woman who had interested him as much as she did. He could not and he would not do such a thing.

As Darcy sat on his chair, moodily glaring about the bedchamber, he was forced to remember the evening, and he had to confess, if only to himself, that Caroline had been correct about his behavior. Though he had been angry at Caroline for what she had attempted to do, his attention had largely been fixed on Miss Bennet, and though his expression sometimes appeared forbidding, as he was well aware, he had actually been studying her. She was a remarkable woman. Her petite stature, light and agreeable figure, and luminous eyes demanded contemplation, and he always found himself drawn to her whenever he was in her presence.

But given the way she had glanced at him, the way she had seemed to flee the sitting-room far earlier than she should have suggested she had suspected him of disapproving of her. That was something that could not stand. Far from disapproving of her, Darcy approved of her far too much.

Sighing, Darcy looked around the room, noting the lateness of the hour. It was time to retire, he decided, and he made his way to the bed.

When he was ensconced within the sheets, Darcy attempted to sleep, but his mind was too active for such a thing, and it did what it always did of late when he was at rest — it turned to contemplation of Miss Elizabeth Bennet.

She was truly a gem of a woman. Though most seemed to consider her sister to be her superior in looks, Darcy had always considered

Elizabeth Bennet to be the true beauty of the Bennet family. Her dark locks framing her angelic face, in which sat those glorious eyes, could never fail to fascinate him. But far more than that, it was her ability to laugh, her intelligence, and her tendency to state her opinions in so decided a manner which Darcy found to be the true lure. She was exceptional. Her situation in life was truly unfortunate, as she would be perfect otherwise.

Duty. At times Darcy hated that word. It had been ingrained in him by his father on many an occasion. His pride in his family estate and situation in life, his duty to the land, the people under his protection, and the ancestors who had upheld their own duty, all had been drummed into him by his father. And Darcy meant to fulfill that duty, no matter what the personal cost. And a great cost it would be, if he could not have Miss Bennet.

Darcy lay on the bed for some time, his mind oscillating from considering Miss Bennet's perfections to thoughts of duty and honor. It was some time before his mind began to quiet enough so that he could drift off to sleep.

Remember, Fitzwilliam, that true nobility is not bestowed upon a person by virtue of their situation in life or the accident of birth. True nobility shines forth from the strength of character, the ability to continue on despite hardship, the kindness one shows to others, especially those less fortunate, and the fortitude to make the right choice regardless of the cost.

Darcy's eyes snapped open as sleep fled, the words echoing through his mind, taunting him, laying his pride bare for what it was.

It took him a few moments to remember where he had heard those words spoken, but when he did, it was like a whole new world was opened up before him.

"Father," said he in a voice which was little more than a whisper of sound on the wind.

And his father it had been. Among the things Darcy's father had taught him about pride in the land and in his position, were his thoughts about the nature of man. His father had actually been a younger son, who had inherited when his elder brother had fallen from his horse and died. At the time, he had been fighting on the continent. He would confide to Darcy in his later years that he believed he had only survived because he had been called home.

His father had seen battle. He had experienced the terror, the roar of guns, the smoke of burning fields, and the sense of death stalking him like a hunter. He had also told Darcy of experiences where he had witnessed the lowliest soldiers forging ahead, heedless of their wounds, intent upon saving some comrade who was wounded and dying, while nobly born men ran at the first hint of danger. His stories had always been punctuated by the same general theme—a man was to be judged by his deeds, not by the circumstance of his birth.

By that measure, was a woman not to be judged by the content of her character? Had he not thought time and again that the latest debutant was either silly or vapid or mean of understanding? Had he not met many a woman who could not measure up to the ideal he had created in his mind? Had he not lamented over the fact that he had never met a woman who interested him as a true partner rather than an ornament to adorn his arm?

And was Miss Bennet not worth as much as the daughter of a duke in the content of her character, her kindness, her generosity, and her bright, incandescent spirit?

And if so, should he not grasp the promise of such a future with both hands? Darcy had always had his duty, and he had always striven to uphold his responsibilities. He was forced to acknowledge that his duty had never made him happy, not the way he was certain Miss Bennet could make him happy.

She was an intelligent woman—he had never doubted that fact. And if she was an intelligent woman, could she not learn quickly what was required of her as mistress of his estate? Could she not enchant London society as effortlessly as she had enchanted him? He could not imagine that she could not accomplish anything she chose to accomplish. Why then could she not learn to be as effective a mistress of Pemberley as any of his ancestors?

And finally, now that he had recalled his father's teachings, why should he not attempt to make Miss Elizabeth Bennet—a woman who was as fine as any he had ever met—his wife?

There was no reason. And in that moment Darcy decided that he would have Miss Bennet as his wife, if he could only persuade her.

He would have to proceed with caution. For one thing, he was a sober man, disposed to consider every decision carefully before he made his decision. He would need to observe her, to try to understand not only if she would enhance his life, but also if *he* would enhance *hers*.

First, he owed her an apology. It would be made tomorrow. Then he would watch and observe, speak and listen. And if she was worth his attentions—little though he doubted the matter any longer—he would attempt to woo her.

For the first time in several months, when Darcy finally succumbed to sleep that night, he was at peace with himself.

For Elizabeth, the night passed in an equally restless manner, though her reflections were of a different nature than Mr. Darcy's. For Elizabeth's mind was full of remembrances and recollections of the previous months, the changes in her life, the happy days she had spent in Caroline's company, and the new acquaintances she had made. Some were pleasant—Miss Darcy, Colonel Fitzwilliam, and Major Trent fit in that description—while some were not—Mr. Jamison and Mr. Darcy filled that role, though the later was not truly a *new* acquaintance any longer.

Elizabeth had experienced both happiness and hardship, gained a greater experience and understanding of the world, learned that she was not infallible in her judgment, and learned that men who put forth a pleasing countenance were not always possessing of a sterling character. She had truly enjoyed her time with Caroline, though the woman represented one of those errors in judgement—and one of the most egregious—but through her night of restless sleep interspersed with thoughts and feelings, she came to the understanding that her time at Hollyfield was coming to a close.

The fact of the matter was that she was a relative outsider here. She did possess a connection to the Bingleys through her sister Jane, but it paled in comparison with the connections of love and family the others possessed. The Darcys and Bingleys were intertwined with knots tight enough to last an eternity, though they were not related in a physical sense. Who was Elizabeth to intrude on such a family party, especially when she was clearly not wanted by at least one of them?

Mr. Darcy's behavior suggested that he was violently opposed to her. Mr. Darcy had been surprised to meet her here and it was clear he wished her to be anywhere else. His scowls could not be mistaken, and his pointed glares whenever Elizabeth spoke to his sister were ample evidence that he did not wish the girl to be polluted by her impertinent opinions, her lack of fashion, or even by her very presence.

Elizabeth had long known of Mr. Darcy's disapprobation, almost from the first moment of their acquaintance. What she had not truly understood until now was the level of his disgust for her. Elizabeth had never been one to shy away from trouble. She had often fancied that she could not be intimidated, that any such effort would only increase her courage and resilience.

But this situation was different. It was clear that her presence was bringing disharmony to the company, and that it would only persist if she stayed. Thus it was time to return to Longbourn to her quiet life and uncertain future. And it was all that much more barren a prospect, as she would not be comforted by Jane's steadying presence and ability to deflect her mother. But there was no help for it.

Elizabeth rose from her bed the next morning and prepared for the day, her spirits much subdued. Maria was efficient as always, and it was only a few moments before Elizabeth descended the stairs and entered the breakfast parlor. There she was greeted by Caroline, noting gratefully that there was no one else present. This would be difficult enough without witnesses.

The conversation was perfunctory, almost banal in nature, as Caroline appeared to have some matter on her mind as well. But knowing that another of the company might arrive at any moment, Elizabeth was determined to make her intentions known.

"Caroline," said she, smiling as the woman turned to look at her, "I believe it is time I took my leave and returned to Hertfordshire."

The smile fell away from Caroline's face and her dismay manifest itself in her concerned look. "But your sister has just arrived and she is to stay another month complete. I had anticipated enjoying your company for a full two months."

Elizabeth smiled, though she was certain it did not reach her eyes. "And I have enjoyed my stay with you. I thank you for your invitation, your attention, and your friendship. But . . ."

Pausing, Elizabeth considered her words. She had been about to say something to the effect that her presence was not welcome, but though she knew her friend would see through any obfuscation, she could not bring any further disharmony into her home.

"I find that I miss Hertfordshire and I miss my family, particularly my father. Rarely have I been away from home for this length of time, you see, and I wish to once again walk the paths of my youth."

It was only a small disguise—though she had often spent some months at a time with the Gardiners, Elizabeth had never been anywhere else for this length of time.

As she expected, Caroline was not fooled, nor did she appear to be particularly happy. She pursed her lips and her eyes bored into Elizabeth, recalling to Elizabeth's mind the first impression she had had of this woman. How mistaken she had been!

"I would not have you leave, Elizabeth," said Caroline after a pause of some duration.

"And yet I believe it is for the best."

"I do not see how it could be." Caroline looked at her, sympathy in her gaze, but also determination. "I understand why you feel you should leave, but I must tell you that I would much rather have you here than Mr. Darcy. His behavior yesterday was unconscionable. He should be ashamed of himself."

"That may perhaps be true," replied Elizabeth slowly. "But it is I who is the outsider. You are all bound by family ties, friendship, and love. I am merely an interloper, bound to you all by nothing more than the bonds of family with my own sister. She is the one who has been brought into the bosom of your family—not I."

Tears pricked the corners of Caroline's eyes, and she drew closer to Elizabeth, taking her hand in a comforting grasp. "You are very much mistaken," said Caroline in a voice thick with emotion, "if you believe that you are not loved. Your sister's love I know you do not doubt, but I must tell you that you are dearer now to me than my own sister. I will not have you fleeing from that man when it is he who should flee before you."

Joining her hostess in her teary-eyed state, Elizabeth reached out with her hand and grasped Caroline's between her own, marveling in the strength of affection which had built up over these past weeks and months. Indeed, other than Jane, Caroline had become closer to Elizabeth's heart than any of her sisters.

It was perhaps ironic, she thought, and surprising that such affection could spring up in such a short time. It was Elizabeth's fervent hope their friendship would weather this storm and they could once again pick up the pieces in a different time and place, one where there was not such tension to cast a pall over their felicity. For the present, Elizabeth was resolved not to cause any further problems, and that necessitated her absence.

Opening her mouth, Elizabeth started to speak to reaffirm her intention to depart, when her words were interrupted by the very man who she was certain hated her.

"Miss Bennet," said he, appearing in beside her chair as if carried on the wind.

Startled, Elizabeth gazed at him, noting the fact that the haughty displeasure of the previous evening was gone from his face. In fact, she detected no aversion to her presence which she had come to expect. He even appeared to be a little contrite, if the word could be applied to such a proud man.

"I fear I owe you an apology, Miss Bennet," said Mr. Darcy.

Had the man said the moon was made of chalk, Elizabeth would not have been more surprised.

"I confess to having been out of sorts yesterday. It was brought to my attention that you might have felt my ire to be directed toward you. For that I apologize. I never meant to offend."

Nonplused, Elizabeth found herself speaking words of forgiveness, which he received with a nod and a slight upturn of his lips. It might almost have been a smile.

"Thank you for your forgiveness. I hope that we will all be able to continue in harmony and friendship. After all, this is a joyful time—not only has your sister recently married, but Mrs. Powell, a woman who is akin to a sister to me has also married. It is time for family and friends, and I hope that our friendship can continue to increase our intimacy."

It was the single longest speech Elizabeth had ever heard from Mr. Darcy. Through her surprise she managed to express an agreement with his words. Mr. Darcy bowed to her and then he turned to the side table to collect his breakfast, Elizabeth watching him as he moved, wondering if she would ever understand such an incomprehensible and infuriating man.

A sensation of movement against her hands caught her attention, and she turned back to Caroline, noting that their hands were still joined. Gone was the woman's consternation, replaced by satisfaction and even perhaps a little mischief.

"Can I assume that there is now no question of you departing?" asked she in a low voice.

Dumbly, Elizabeth could only nod her head. Caroline smiled and turned back to her meal.

"That is good. I find I could not have parted with you just yet. I am so glad that this little misunderstanding has worked itself out."

"Misunderstanding?" said Elizabeth, her voice emerging as the croak of a frog.

"An apology has been offered and accepted. Whatever else could it be?"

Her head swimming, Elizabeth found that she could not answer Caroline's question, and her equanimity was further disturbed when a moment later Mr. Darcy brought his plate to the table and sat, not sitting apart and hiding behind a newspaper as she might have expected, but close to the ladies so that he might converse with them. And if the conversation was not the deep and thought-provoking variety, at least it was with perfect ease and friendliness. Not understanding the transformation which seemed to have taken place overnight, Elizabeth contributed little to the conversation.

She was, however, satisfied to see that when the other members of the party joined them, they appeared to be as mystified as the change in Mr. Darcy as was Elizabeth herself. Only Caroline appeared to have no confusion about the matter. She spoke of their plans for the day and a few other items, but through it all her slightly smug smile did not wane in the slightest.

Though still confused, Elizabeth was nevertheless happy that it appeared there was no need for her to depart. But she would not trust this sudden change in Mr. Darcy. She would watch the man. But should this sudden change of mood prove mercurial, she would confront him and call him out for his behavior. Now that she had been persuaded to stay, she would not allow Mr. Darcy to bother her again.

Upon reaching the decision that he owed an apology to Miss Bennet, actually offering that apology was a simple thing to accomplish. The more difficult task now awaited Darcy.

The recollection of his father's words and teachings had hit Darcy hard, bringing with it other remembrances of the counsel his father had given him over the years. And as these things came to his mind and he thought of them Darcy was forced to confess that he had strayed from what he had been taught. Though his father *had* taught him to be proud of his heritage, he had not taught him to think meanly of others. In fact, his father's words had emphasized the opposite, though Darcy had only just remembered, the sensation akin to waking after sleeping long and seeing many vivid dreams. And once these things came into his mind again, he recalled his mother, who, though she was the wife of a prominent man and daughter of an earl, had been as comfortable with a tenant's wife as with the wife of a duke.

How he had wandered from these teachings, Darcy could not state for certain, though he thought that in some measure the pressures of Pemberley's management and the responsibility for raising his young sister had exerted some influence. But he was determined not to use that to excuse his behavior. On the contrary, Darcy was well aware only he could be held accountable.

The decision to change his attitudes was again easy to determine, but difficult to execute, though he promised himself that he would be diligent.

Regarding Miss Bennet, behaving in a friendlier manner was again a simple thing to accomplish, though he was well aware that it was more because she was so easy in company than due to his own efforts. But what Darcy was not certain of was whether she was one to whom he should decide to offer his hand, despite how fascinating he found her.

And perhaps more importantly, there was no telling how she would respond to such an application, especially given what he now knew was her poor opinion of him.

So he watched her, interacting with her as much as he dared, all the while considering what his course of action should be. As he did so he considered her fine qualities, noting the fact that her manner with Georgiana was exactly as Caroline had described it. And the more he watched her, the more enchanted he became all over again. She truly was exceptional and he began to understand that he would be a fool to allow her to escape, regardless of her position and fortune.

Once he decided this, the question became how to approach her. That, he could not determine.

"I am happy you have introduced me to Elizabeth," said Georgiana one day as they walked in the gardens. "She always has such excellent advice for me."

Darcy felt an irrational surge of jealousy at the thought that his sister, who had known Miss Bennet for a fraction of the time that he had been acquainted with her, had already been given leave to address her by her given name.

"You like her?" asked Darcy, feeling a little slow of thought. He had not the power of knowing what to say.

"Very much," said Georgiana. "She has a confidence I can only wish I possessed, and yet she is kind and considerate, always making me feel at ease. I almost feel I could speak to her of anything and she will not censure or rebuke."

"I am happy you have found such a friend."

Georgiana looked toward Darcy, and he felt like he was being measured. "Are you certain? When we arrived, I almost had the impression that you did not approve of her."

Regretting that even his sister had noted his displeasure, Darcy was quick to say: "No indeed. I was out of sorts and I regret that it led you to think I do not esteem her

"The fact of the matter is quite the reverse."

Stopping, Georgiana turned and regarded him with a sort of excited interest. "What do you mean, brother?"

Darcy was not accustomed to sharing his burdens with his sister. Then again his sister would be his greatest champion in his pursuit of Elizabeth, and he could use all the help he could get.

"I have considered the possibility of courting Miss Bennet."

"Oh, that is wonderful, brother!" exclaimed Georgiana, her enthusiasm charming Darcy. "I truly think highly of her and believe that she would be the very best of sisters."

"You do?" said Darcy, feeling bemused at her eagerness.

"Can you imagine I would feel otherwise? I have the highest opinion of Elizabeth, and of Mrs. Bingley, of course. I cannot imagine that you would not be very happy with Elizabeth as a wife."

"Then it is a settled thing," said Darcy with a light-heartedness he had not felt in many years. "But you must assist me, for I have not the slightest notion of how to approach her."

Georgiana's eyes widened. "You do not know? Am I to understand that my elder brother, who is without fault, confident in any situation, cannot determine how to approach a woman?"

Laughing, Darcy could only say: "I have never wooed a woman before, Georgiana."

"Then we shall have to come up with a stratagem," said his sister. "I am certain Caroline shall be very happy to assist. She is so friendly with Miss Bennet. I am certain she would love to see Elizabeth married to you."

Privately Darcy was amused at just how close to the truth Georgian had strayed, but Caroline's assistance was not something he wished to solicit at this time. Her words to him were still fresh in his mind, and he wondered if she was not now of the opinion that Elizabeth would not be better without him. Darcy could not say that he blamed her.

"Let us keep this to ourselves for the time being," said Darcy out loud to his sister. "I am certain I can handle this matter on my own."

"I am certain Elizabeth shall make it easy on you," replied Georgiana. "I shall certainly assist. I shall give you a flaming character, I assure you."

"That is not required," murmured Darcy.

But Georgiana, who had been caught by the possibilities was well able to carry on the conversation herself, and she did so, extolling Miss Bennet's many virtues, speculating on how Darcy might go about wooing her. Darcy only made a few monosyllabic responses to his sister's raptures, allowing himself to indulge in the thoughts of what might be if he could only convince Elizabeth of his worthiness. And so they continued until they returned to the house and the rest of the party.

Darcy quickly found that there were certain subjects which would quickly draw Elizabeth's attention. Among those could be listed literature—she was exceedingly well read and always had some insight to share—her aunt and uncle, with whom she was close, her sister Jane, and the sights that she hoped to see one day.

"Pemberley is situated near the peak district?" asked she one day when they were speaking of Derbyshire.

"Indeed it is," said Darcy, content to be speaking about a subject so dear to his heart. "On a clear day, the rough crags of the nearest peaks can be seen in the distance, and the district is well within a day's carriage ride."

"I would love to see it someday," said Miss Bennet, her eyes slightly unfocused. "Hertfordshire is beautiful but the highest local hill is rather rounded and tame."

"Then you should visit Pemberley," said Georgiana, her eagerness coming out in the excitement in her voice. "I am certain brother and I would be happy to have you. And while you are there, we could tour the peaks, and maybe even go as far as the lakes!"

"That would be agreeable indeed," said Miss Bennet, smiling delightedly at Georgiana's enthusiasm. "But I might actually be able to see the lakes before you might expect. I received a letter from my aunt and uncle today. They are to journey up to the lakes this summer, and they have invited me to accompany them."

Though Darcy was a little less than excited to hear that she had plans this summer, still he decided to use the situation to his advantage. "Then you must stop at Pemberley on your way, as it is in a direct line between Hertfordshire and the lakes. Furthermore, my family has maintained a lodge in the Lake District for many years. I would be happy if you and your relatives would consider using it during your stay there."

Appearing surprised at the suggestion, Miss Bennet opened her mouth to speak, but Georgiana was already prattling by the time she had opened her mouth.

"Oh yes, what a wonderful notion! The lakes are an easy distance from Pemberley and it would be a perfect place to break your journey for a few days. Please say that you will, Elizabeth."

A tentative smile broke over Miss Benet's face and she promised that she would write her uncle to make the suggestion. Then she turned to Darcy and said:

"My aunt was actually raised in your neighborhood, Mr. Darcy. I understand the town of Lambton is very near Pemberley."

"It is not more than five miles distant," replied Darcy, surprised at such a connection. "May I ask your aunt's name?"

"Meredith Gardiner," replied Miss Bennet. "Though when she lived in Lambton her name was Meredith Plumber."

"The rector's daughter!" exclaimed Darcy. "I am astonished, Miss

Bennet. I actually remember her, though she was several years older than I."

Then a recollection of the woman in question came over Darcy and he looked down in some embarrassment.

"What is it, brother?" asked Georgiana.

Darcy looked up to see both ladies watching him with curiosity and he felt his befuddlement growing. But he knew that he would not be able to escape without informing them of what had passed over his mind, so he gathered the shreds of his courage and said:

"Miss Plumber, as I said, was several years older than I, and when she left Lambton she must have been no more than sixteen. Her leaving broke many hearts, as she was a very pretty young woman. I must own that mine was among them, as was your cousin Richard's and Bingley's, for that matter."

The ladies were silent for several moments before they turned to one another and burst into giggles. Darcy watched them as they laughed, feeling the bubble of laughter welling up in his throat as well. How times had changed — only a week earlier he likely would have been offended to be the subject of their mirth.

"I shall have to inform my aunt, Mr. Darcy," said Elizabeth between her laughter. "I am certain that she would be extremely surprised and flattered to learn that she was once the object of the heir of Pemberley's undying affections."

Darcy attempted to scowl, but he was certain that the effect was ruined by the smile tugging up at the corner of his mouth. "I beg you would not. Meredith Plumber was a very proper young woman, and I am certain she had no notion as to how she affected us."

At that moment the door opened and Caroline walked into the room followed by her husband. She stopped as she espied the three of them grinning like fools, the two girls yet suppressing snickers.

"May I be privy to the reason for your mirth?"

In consternation, Darcy shot a look of mute appeal at Elizabeth, who grinned and raised her eyebrow in his direction. Her saucy smile set his heart pounding, but she turned to Caroline and said:

"Just an amusing anecdote Mr. Darcy shared with us. It was nothing of consequence."

Caroline peered at Elizabeth and then at Georgiana who would not meet her eyes, and though it was evident that she did not believe them for an instant, she allowed the manner to drop.

A sigh of relief, though carefully hidden, escaped Darcy, and he considered the near miss he had just experienced. If Caroline ever learned of such a thing he did not doubt she would never allow him to forget it, and Bingley and Fitzwilliam would be equally within her sights. He now had another reason to appreciate Miss Bennet—she had just saved his dignity!

Chapter IX

The situation at Hollyfield had largely calmed and Elizabeth found herself once again enjoying herself. Caroline was becoming a closer friend than Elizabeth had ever dared to hope for, Georgiana was a sweet girl much in need of friends, and Jane was, as always, perfection personified. The gentlemen were also pleasant and agreeable, even Mr. Darcy, who, not long before, Elizabeth would have hesitated in allowing even one good quality.

To say that she trusted Mr. Darcy and now considered him to be an amiable man would have been stretching credulity. His moods had proven mercurial in the past, and though he now often conversed with Elizabeth with ease, she could not forget the censuring stares, the arrogance, and the outright hostility with which he had regarded her before. But she did begin to get the sense that whatever he thought of her he would not disrupt the party again by displaying his opinions again for all and sundry to witness. With that Elizabeth was content.

The second week after the arrival of the combined Bingley and Darcy families, the party prepared for an assembly to be held at the assembly hall in Brixworth. There had not been much in the way of social engagements in the week since Caroline's dinner party, and other than the visits of a few ladies of the area, followed by their return visits, Elizabeth had not seen anyone from the neighborhood.

In the final days leading up to the event, the primary subject of conversation was the participation of Georgiana Darcy in the amusement, and her guardians' reluctance to allow it. The most vocal proponent for her inclusion was Mrs. Powell who felt that a country assembly was the perfect location for her to obtain a taste of society. It was also evident that Georgiana, though shy and lacking in courage, wished to be included rather than waiting at home for the rest of the party to return.

"She can hardly come to any harm in the company of so many," argued Caroline as she pressed her case for the young girl. "Elizabeth, Jane, and I will be with her to ensure that she is surrounded by friends."

Elizabeth still was not certain that mentioning *her* name was at all conducive to convincing Mr. Darcy to agree, but he did not even glance at her.

"And if you are all standing up during the same dance?"

"Then the men will have to ensure that at least one of *you* will be available to stay with her, though I hardly think it will be necessary. Do you suggest that one of our neighbors will try to spirit her off?"

"Of course not," said Mr. Darcy, though it was with a weary sigh. "I merely wish to make certain that Georgiana is attended, so that all will know that she is *not* out. I would also not wish for her to be required to spend the evening alone with no companionship."

"Then the men will have to ensure that you are not all dancing at once since you have control over your partners. We do not."

Though Mr. Darcy still appeared to be reluctant, his cousin—who Elizabeth understood shared in the young lady's guardianship—spoke up:

"Caroline is correct, Darcy. I see little harm in it."

If Elizabeth had not been looking at Mr. Darcy she might have missed his reaction. The man seemed to consider the matter for a few moments, but then he glanced at his sister, who was watching him with an expression so hopeful it was almost pathetic. At that moment all the fight left Mr. Darcy and he relented.

"Very well, Georgiana," said he, to which Georgiana let out a childlike squeal and threw herself into his arms.

"Oh, thank you, brother! I am so excited!"

"You are very welcome," replied Mr. Darcy. "But you will be on your best behavior and you will remember you are not out. And as for your dance partners, they shall be limited to Fitzwilliam, Bingley, Powell, and me."

"I shall remember it, William," promised Georgiana with a solemn nod. "I would not wish . . . I do not believe I have the confidence to dance with someone unknown to me. I shall behave myself. You have my word."

Smiling, Mr. Darcy kissed his sister's head. "I have no doubt of your good behavior, Georgiana."

The conversation moved on to other topics, but for Elizabeth it was another insight into the man's character. Mr. Darcy had always given the appearance of cold haughtiness, and even with those intimate with him she had never seen much to indicate that he possessed any feelings at all.

Until recently, of course. The way he had readily conversed with her and the ease he now showed in company contrasted greatly with how he had behaved before, and his indulgence with his sister showed a care and concern for her wellbeing which was highly commendable. Sometimes he appeared to be every inch the authoritative guardian, but at others, it was as if he was attempting to shed that role and simply be her brother. It was complicated as he had been her guardian for some time, but for the first time Elizabeth began to believe that he was managing it with much more compassion than she had ever thought possible.

When the night of the assembly arrived, the Hollyfield party entered two separate carriages and made the short journey to the assembly hall. In addition to the dancing, Elizabeth, Caroline and Georgiana were to perform the duet they had practiced, though it had been much more difficult to obtain Mr. Darcy's permission for that than it had to get him to allow Georgiana to attend.

The hall was on a larger scale that Meryton's assembly rooms, and consequently there were more people in attendance than one would commonly find in Meryton. For Elizabeth, this would be her first time mingling with most of these people as, other than the dinner party, her exposure to the society of the area had been limited.

Still, her mood was good as she was generally of a social disposition and she was anticipating the event keenly. When they stepped in the room, a man approached them and was introduced—a Mr. Smythe, who performed the same function as Sir William did in Meryton—after which he walked them around the room, introducing him to others in attendance. During that time, two things happened, one which illuminated Elizabeth's understanding, the other which vexed her greatly.

The first was not precisely an event; it was actually nothing more than a number of conversations in the hall which Elizabeth chanced to overhear, largely because those involved could not bother to moderate their voices. One discussion in particular caught her attention.

"I have heard that he has ten thousand a year!"

"Ten thousand!" The exclamation was accompanied by a nervously waved fan. "Oh my. What a wonderful catch he must be!"

"And his uncle is an earl!" said a third voice. "Just think of the elevation in society."

"Not to mention the pin money!" said the first voice, and they all burst into excited titters.

It did not take any great insight to know of whom they spoke, and Elizabeth, without any conscious thought, found her eyes fixing on Mr. Darcy. The man was gazing straight ahead and away from the giggling ladies, but his face was set in a stone-like mask which mirrored that when she had seen when he had first arrived in Meryton.

In that moment Elizabeth was hit by a surprising insight; it was clear that Mr. Darcy endured this wherever he went, with young ladies excitedly discussing his wealth, their mothers turning covetous eyes upon him for their daughters, and likely men looking to ingratiate themselves to him without a single thought of what kind of man he was or whether he even wished to make their acquaintance. Thinking back on the evening of the assembly in Meryton where she had first laid eyes on Mr. Darcy, Elizabeth recalled a distinct instance where her mother had exclaimed about his wealth. It had likely happened more than once. The recollection was embarrassing, but of more import was the further understanding it allowed Elizabeth to gain concerning Mr. Darcy's character. His behavior had been in no way exemplary, but Elizabeth now understood the reasons for it.

The second event occurred not long after they had settled on one side of the hall. Mr. Darcy was to escort his sister to the dance floor for the first dance, while Mr. and Mrs. Powell, followed by Mr. and Mrs. Bingley were also to stand up for the set. As Colonel Fitzwilliam had fallen into conversation with Major Trent—the two men were apparently known to one another previously—Elizabeth was resigned to the idea of not dancing the first at all, though she rarely had to sit the dance out at home.

She was contemplating the room, when a shadow fell across her vision. Startled, she looked up to see the smirking visage of Gabriel Jamison.

"Miss Bennet," said Mr. Jamison, as bent in a florid fashion, "I am simply thrilled to once again meet with you. It is not often that such visions of loveliness are to be seen, and I must count myself among the most fortunate to be once again in your presence."

Before she could react, the man captured one of her hands and brought it to his lips, bestowing a kiss on the back. His leer never once diminished and his eyes never left her face.

"Mr. Jamison," said Elizabeth, finally managing to speak. She pulled her hand back from his grasp, hoping that her perfunctory greeting would induce the man to desist his attentions and depart.

She was not to have that good fortune, however, as Mr. Jamison merely released a wider smile in response. "I had hoped that I would see you here tonight, though I was not sure your party would come. I have been desolate without your company, bereft of my beating heart which has, torturously, been captivated within your hands since our meeting."

Elizabeth gazed at the man, wondering if she was truly hearing this drivel. Did he consider her to be an empty-headed flirt, one who would simper with vacant eyes and giggling laughter when a man paid compliments which sounded vaguely poetic? Surely he must have gained some measure of understanding of her character when they had met previously.

"I hardly think you have pined for me, sir," said Elizabeth. "Had you been so desirous of my company you might have visited Hollyfield at any time. I have not been anywhere else in the interim."

"A man who felt less might have. But I could not approach you with such confidence as you suggest, fearing as I did that your brilliance would scorch me, leaving nothing but an empty husk. After all, you snubbed me for that . . . for Trent, though I wondered at the singularity of such a gesture.

"And then I understood what you were about. Jealousy is indeed a powerful force, and you have succeeded in imposing your will upon me, little experience though I have with the emotion."

"I assure you I did nothing of the kind, sir."

"But you must have!" The man's expression drooped piteously, though the calculating glitter of his eyes remained. "I cannot think you cruel enough to crush me without thought, and that is the only motivation I can contemplate. I dare you to tell me it is so. If you do, I shall depart a broken man, forever bereft of my heart, which shall forever belong to you."

"Mr. Jamison—"

"Miss Bennet," said he, as the first strains of the opening set sounded from the musicians, "I implore you not to break my heart before the first dance has even begun. Instead, as I have discerned that you do not have a partner for this set, I beseech you to stand up with me. I can think of no better way for us to truly become known to one another than to spend a set, each as the sole focus of the other."

Elizabeth did not even attempt to hide her scowl. She well understood the consequences of refusing to dance with the man, but Elizabeth could not help but view the prospect with distaste.

"Ah, the fair maiden has wounded me!' exclaimed he, raising a hand to his heart with a dramatic flair. "How could I have offended thee so, my dear, when I only wish to place my heart within thy hands?"

"If we must dance, then we must," said Elizabeth. "I would ask you to cease this melodramatic farce you seem so intent upon. It serves no purpose, as it does not affect me."

"Poetic lines affect all ladies," said Mr. Jamison with perfect nonchalance, as he grasped her hand to lead her to the dance floor. "Poetry is the food of love, you know."

A grin suffused Elizabeth's face and she looked up at the man with amusement. The dance started and they began the steps, Mr. Jamison looking at her with expectation as he waited to hear the reason for her mirth.

Unfortunately for him, Elizabeth was not inclined to give him what he wanted, and after several moments his gaze darkened and he began to show the signs of impatience. Finally he appeared to lose control as he snapped, with less graciousness than he had shown before:

"Must I beg for you to tell me what has amused you so?"

"Seeing you grovel would be a novel experience indeed."

His countenance became stonier, and Elizabeth laughed, and said:

"I once told Mr. Darcy that poetry is the food of love only when that love is of a healthy variety. I dare say the roses in my mother's rose garden will flourish and bloom if they are already in a good state with the proper soil, moisture, and sunlight to encourage them. But I am convinced that one good sonnet will entirely starve a thin, meager sort of inclination until it withers and dies."

Mr. Jamison did not appear amused. "Are you accusing me of only a feigned interest in you?"

"Nothing of the sort, sir. I cannot say anything about the state of your affections. However, your poor attempts at exaggerated gallantry *cannot* be considered poetry by anyone of rational thought, and even if they were my inclination is nonexistent. Thus, you may cease your attempts."

"Nonexistent!" cried he. "I am exceedingly grieved to be thus discarded, as if I was nothing more than a worn bonnet to be jettisoned to the refuse pile."

"I am certain you shall recover anon."

"Perhaps I should shower you with lines from Shakespeare. All ladies love Shakespeare."

"'Shall I compare thee to a summer's day?'" quoted Elizabeth in a mocking tone.

"Yes, that is the one!" exclaimed Mr. Jamison. It seemed to Elizabeth like he was the child who had finally been able to persuade his playmate to part with a particularly coveted toy. "I dare say that should I regale you with Shakespeare and Donne I shall claim your affections yet!"

"Then your expectation is extraordinary given my expressed disinterest."

Mr. Jamison eyed her with an unreadable expression. They separated in the dance for a few moments, and as she moved through the steps, she saw Mr. Darcy watching her with what could only be deemed as concern. Elizabeth smiled at him to know that she was well, noting with satisfaction when he turned his attention back to his sister. For her part, Georgiana appeared to be lighting the room with nothing more than the beaming of her countenance, inducing a smile of indulgence for the girl. When the dance once again brought Elizabeth together with Mr. Jamison, he appeared to be pensive, though his eyes were still focused upon her, pressing upon her as if with a heavy weight.

"You have stated that poetry starves a tepid sort of love away. What if those feelings are . . . 'nonexistent?'"

"Come, Mr. Jamison, I do not think I even need to explain such a thing. Can a rose grow where there are no seeds? Can they grow from the top of a rock, with naught but sunlight to burn and wither them away?"

"Are you suggesting that your heart is stone, unable to feel?" countered he.

Though Elizabeth longed to tell him that in *his* case he was completely correct, she refrained, and only said:

"It is nothing but a metaphor, sir. Perhaps stating my feelings openly is more forward than I would normally speak, but I think it best that you know so that you may move on to some other, more interested woman."

"I shall take my chances and endeavor to plant those seeds," said he with what Elizabeth thought was entirely exaggerated gallantry.

"I beg you would not—"

"Nay, nay, dear lady. I have been challenged to win the heart of my lady love, and I fear I must do so or die of a broken heart. I shall hear no more of your attempts to put me off. Please allow me this chance. I promise that I shall not disappoint you."

Once again separated by the dance, Elizabeth ground her teeth together in frustration. Would nothing convince the man to leave her be? Perhaps a blow to the head with her reticule would induce him to desist!

When they came back together, Mr. Jamison did not appear inclined to speak again. Instead, he studied her, that supercilious leer still present to mock and irritate her. But since he was silent, Elizabeth took the opportunity for silence herself. When the set was complete, he led her off the floor and bowed in his grandiose manner.

"I shall take my leave of you, my lady, in order to devise the perfect strategy to touch your immovable, stony heart. I am, as always, your servant."

The man then turned and sauntered away from Elizabeth leaving her fuming by the side of the dance floor. It did not improve her mood any when Mr. Jamison directly approached another young woman and began to speak with her in the same familiar manner which he had employed with Elizabeth. The effrontery of the man was beyond measure!

"Did you have a delightful time dancing?"

Elizabeth turned and glared at Caroline, noting her amused grin.

"Personally I do not think that man should be allowed in company," said Elizabeth, her voice coming out like a growl. "His flattery is thick as molasses, and I fear the inanities which spew forth from his mouth will offend the sensibilities of maidens everywhere."

"He has been ever thus," said Mr. Powell. "Jamison has often despaired of his brother as he seems intent upon living his life as if it was some sort of Shakespearean comedy."

Elizabeth smiled. "Perhaps it would be best if he simply disappeared into the pages of *A Midsummer Night's Dream*. I have no doubt Nick Bottom could teach him a thing or two as he is unfortunately affected by a healthy dose of melodrama."

Laughing, the three proceeded to the side of the dance floor where Mr. Darcy had led his sister after the opening dance. Elizabeth soon learned that the girl was to stand up with her cousin for the second set. Elizabeth was pleased for Georgiana—she would have her share of amusement that evening, and it was clear just how much care her guardians were taking in seeing to her happiness.

"And how did you find yourself dancing with Gabriel Jamison?" asked Colonel Fitzwilliam as Elizabeth approached the gathering.

Unable to refrain from rolling her eyes at the man, Elizabeth said: "I believe it is the established custom for a lady to wait for a gentleman—though I use the term exceedingly loosely in the case of that man—to ask her to dance. She may refuse an application if she wishes, though if she is determined to avoid dancing with a man, she must forfeit the rest of the evening's entertainment."

Colonel Fitzwilliam appeared a trifle silly at Elizabeth's light admonishment, but he soon rallied. "I understand the workings of etiquette, madam, but I must inform you that the man has no good reputation. He is known to be rather loose with the ladies and a regular at the card tables. Of his level of success I cannot say, but I have heard that his skill is not commensurate with his fondness for such games."

"Of that I am not surprised," said Elizabeth. "You need not concern yourself for me, colonel, though I appreciate the sentiment. I believe that I understood Mr. Jamison's character within two minutes of hearing the first words from his mouth."

The colonel regarded her for a few moments and then burst out laughing. "I imagine you had, Miss Bennet. I do hope you will excuse my interference. I meant no disrespect to your intelligence."

"No offense taken, Colonel Fitzwilliam."

"Then I hope you will consent to dance the third with me. Had I been a little quicker, I might have spared you from dancing with the libertine at all."

"But then I would almost certainly have had to dance with the man later." Elizabeth gave the colonel an impish smile. "It is best to dispense with the unpleasantness early so that I might enjoy the rest of my evening."

"That it is, Miss Bennet. That it is."

Soon the second dance started and Elizabeth found herself paired with Mr. Powell who was as friendly as ever, and with whom Elizabeth conversed with much animation and pleasure. Unfortunately, her manner with him seemed to attract the attention of her first partner, and after the dance was complete, he once again approached her, though Elizabeth could only regard the man with exasperation.

"If your manners are anything to go by, you appeared to enjoy your dance with Powell much better than you liked your dance with me. I should warn you the man *is* already married."

"A woman does not dance with a man for the sole purpose of attaching herself to him," said Elizabeth, her frustration coming out in her clipped tones. "Surely *you* of all people should understand this, Mr. Jamison."

Rather than get a rise out of him, or another of his falsely wounded gestures, Mr. Jamison only smiled and he walked away.

That set the course for the rest of the evening. Elizabeth danced most of the sets and enjoyed herself a great deal, but a pall settled over her due to the fact that Mr. Jamison approached her frequently, always with some pithy comment or artificially embellished compliment. By the time the supper dance had arrived, Elizabeth was to the point of grinding her teeth whenever she spied the man across the room, and was contemplating the relative benefits of drenching him with a glass of wine.

As the strains of one of the later dance began to sound about the room, Elizabeth once again noticed Mr. Jamison approaching her, and she looked about desperately to see if there was any way she could avoid him. She would rather be forced to sit out for the rest of the night than have to put up with his insincere flattery for another half hour. Her salvation came from an unanticipated source.

"Miss Bennet," said a voice behind her. Elizabeth turned to see Mr. Darcy standing close behind her. "Can I prevail upon you to dance the next set with me?"

Though initially a little surprised that Mr. Darcy had requested her hand, Elizabeth eagerly accepted, thinking that he, at least, would not behave with such insouciance as Gabriel Jamison.

"Ah, I see I am too late," said Mr. Jamison with a dramatic sigh as he stepped up to Elizabeth. "Once again you wound me, fair maiden. I know not how I shall tolerate being forced to wait for another occasion to be afforded the pleasure of your hand once again."

Elizabeth turned the man and readied herself to give a stinging retort, when Mr. Darcy stepped past her and up to Mr. Jamison, who peered at him with curiosity.

"I do not believe we have been introduced," said he in a lazy drawl.

"Fitzwilliam Darcy," said Mr. Darcy. Elizabeth could hear the censure in his tone. "And who are you, sir?"

"Gabriel Jamison, at your service."

The fact that Mr. Darcy was a man did not excuse him from the same frilly bow that Mr. Jamison had been subjecting Elizabeth to all evening.

"I am acquainted with your brother. He is a good man."

"He has his own estate and a pretty young woman as his wife, though in other ways he is very dull."

Mr. Darcy peered at the man and he gave Elizabeth the impression that he was not amused. "I believe that Miss Bennet has been desiring your absence all evening, sir. Perhaps you should do the gentlemanly thing and cease bothering the lady when she wishes to be left alone."

"Wounded yet again," was Mr. Jamison's dramatic reply. "I shall leave you then, Miss Bennet, though I hope that our separation will not be of a lasting duration." And with that he turned and sauntered off.

Elizabeth watched him go, and under her breath she said, "I hope that it will be."

Apparently she did not whisper quietly enough, as Mr. Darcy turned toward her, a smile lifting the corners of his mouth. "I hope you did not find my interference officious, Miss Bennet. I divined his purpose as he approached, and seeing your interactions with him tonight I knew you would not welcome another dance with him."

Turning, Elizabeth regarded Mr. Darcy. "You were not officious in the slightest, sir. I would that he could understand that fact for himself."

Mr. Darcy bowed and gestured with a hand, and with a tentative smile Elizabeth allowed him to take her hand and guide her to the dance floor.

As the music started, Elizabeth stepped forward and grasped Mr. Darcy's hand, executing the steps of the dance without thought. Mr. Darcy was silent, though he regarded her with an intense interest, much as she had seen him do before. Their first few passes came and went without spoken words, and though Elizabeth caught snippets of conversation around her, she was focused solely upon this man and had no attention to spare for anyone else.

It was different from the dance they had shared at Netherfield. For one, Elizabeth's feelings for the man, though yet wary, had changed in the interim leaving her with a better opinion of him. She had nothing to hold against him as she had during that first ill-fated dance, and the fact that she had stood up with him eagerly — if only to escape Gabriel Jamison — altered matters between them further. This time she could almost say that she possessed a grateful feeling toward him. But even more than that, the silence between them seemed charged with some indefinable emotion. Elizabeth could not place her finger on exactly what it was; all she could state for certain was that the man had been growing in her estimation.

"I must own that I find this dance to be much more pleasant," said

Mr. Darcy.

Elizabeth knew exactly to what he referred, and she colored at the reminder of their previous performance together. But she bravely raised her head and said in a teasing tone:

"Do you suggest that I had best remain silent, Mr. Darcy?"

Mr. Darcy smiled, apparently understanding her jest. "I could certainly never suggest such a thing to a lady, Miss Bennet, especially a lady whose conversation is as lively and interesting as yours."

"Interesting? Lively?" Elizabeth raised an eyebrow at him. "Impertinent, perhaps?"

"There are some who may term it as such, but I assure you that I am not one of them."

"For that I thank you sir." Elizabeth paused for a moment, considering, and then decided that it was necessary for her to extend an apology. "In fact, I happen to agree with you about the pleasant nature of this dance when compared with the last. And for that, I can only apologize for my words. I had unfortunately given too much credence to a man's words, and was not on my best behavior."

"Neither was I, Miss Bennet. I must beg you, however, to forget that incident, though I am curious as to how you came by the knowledge of that man's falsehoods."

The dance separated them for a few moments, a blessing in Elizabeth's mind as she realized belatedly that she had no desire to discuss this subject. She had brought it up, however, and though she did not like the recollection of how easily Mr. Wickham had taken her in with his lies, it was perhaps best to speak of the matter and think of it no longer.

"My eyes were opened through the efforts of a friend," said Elizabeth when they had once again joined together. "She acquainted me with certain facts concerning Mr. Wickham's story which I later confirmed with the man himself, though by observation and insinuation rather than confrontation."

A positively anxious expression fell over Mr. Darcy's face, and he appeared to regard her with no little fear.

"Facts?" asked he, as if he feared the answer.

"Yes, Mr. Darcy," replied Elizabeth, mystified over the man's behavior. "The gambling, the unsavory habits with unsuspecting young ladies, the conditional living—all of these were made known to me. And I am glad they were, as I was able to use that knowledge in defense of my family, though my father had already done much."

Mollified, Mr. Darcy peered at her with interest, and Elizabeth wondered what she could have said to make him suffer such apprehension. She would not pry, but at the same time she could not help but be curious.

"It is well that he deceives you no longer. I understand from Mrs. Powell that he deserted his position?"

"He did," said Elizabeth. "Once I was acquainted with his behavior, I sought out my father, wishing to minimize the damage he could do to our town. I found, however, that my father and the local land owners had already taken action to prevent excesses of the militia due to a similar situation which occurred many years ago with another regiment. In time it seemed that Mr. Wickham perceived his inability to do as he would, and his flight when he discovered this was swift. I doubt we shall see him again in Meryton."

Nodding, Mr. Darcy replied: "It is well indeed that your father has protected you. Mr. Wickham is able to cause considerable damage."

Elizabeth inclined her head and then directed their conversation to some other topic, wishing to put the distasteful Mr. Wickham behind her for good. Their conversation meandered through several subjects, and though Elizabeth was not completely at ease—nor, she suspected, was Mr. Darcy—it was at least completely civil. And as it progressed, Elizabeth became more interested in what Mr. Darcy had to say. It seemed that his improved civility also improved his skills in conversation, much to Elizabeth's delight.

It was during a discussion of books that Mr. Darcy's voice trailed off and his gaze became focused on the side of the dance floor. Elizabeth, unable to account for his sudden inattention, had the opportunity due to a movement in the dance to see what had caused him concern. There, by the side of the hall, his sister Georgiana sat, and with her, speaking earnestly, also sat Gabriel Jamison.

Noting the alarm on Mr. Darcy's face, Elizabeth thought that he was about to break the formation of the dance when Caroline suddenly appeared by Georgiana's side, and after exchanging a few words, which to Elizabeth's eye seemed a little harsh, the man stood and swaggered away.

This apparently placated Mr. Darcy for the moment as he continued dancing, but he clearly wished to be off the floor and with his sister.

As the set was coming to a close, he chose to stay with Elizabeth, though he did not say much for the rest of the set. As they executed the final steps, he did turn to Elizabeth, and with regret in his eyes, said: "I am sorry that our conversation was interrupted."

"It is of no import, Mr. Darcy. I understand."

A wry smile, though somewhat of a weak one, came over his face. "I was about to observe that for someone who can never think of books in a ballroom, you seemed remarkably capable of carrying on a conversation."

Elizabeth smiled, thinking to tease him from his sudden concern. "It is impolitic for you to bring up my previous words, Mr. Darcy. Now I must find some foible of yours to laugh at, if only in retaliation."

"I am certain that I shall laugh too."

The set completed, Mr. Darcy led Elizabeth off the floor and to where his sister was sitting with Mrs. Powell, the two of them conversing softly. Mr. Darcy wasted no time in asking her concerning Mr. Jamison's actions, and was quickly put at ease.

"He was only beside me for a moment or two," said Miss Darcy.

"I apologize, Mr. Darcy," said Caroline. "I left for a moment to go retrieve some punch, thinking that Georgiana would be fine."

"And I was," said Miss Darcy. She looked up at her brother, and with a smile said: "Mr. Jamison, I think, fancies himself to be charming, but he seems to be afflicted by exaggeration."

Elizabeth laughed. "Indeed, he is. In fact, your words are remarkably similar to something I said earlier this evening."

Mr. Darcy smiled at his sister, but then his gaze turned hard again. "I am glad you think so, Georgiana, but it is not proper for him to approach a girl who is not out, without even the benefit of a previous introduction."

"Apparently Mr. Jamison's brother does not think so either," said Caroline, gesturing across the room.

It appeared she was correct, as across the room the man's elder brother was speaking in a rather pointed fashion, and it was clear from the younger brother's expression that he was not enjoying the conversation. The elder Mr. Jamison continued on for some moments, when the younger man stalked off and his brother approached the Hollyfield party, who were now all gathered, and bowed low before them.

"I apologize, Mr. Darcy, Miss Darcy, for my brother's breach in etiquette. I have spoken to him of the matter and assure you that it shall not happen again."

There were murmurs of understanding and thanks for the apology.

Later that evening as they left the hall, Elizabeth could not help but reflect on the evening. She had learned several valuable things that night which she was certain would serve her well in the future.

Chapter X

*T*here are few things so disagreeable for a young lady as to be subjected to unwanted attentions from a man she considers to be intolerable. It was a woman's lot in life, it was true, to wait for the man to express his interest, but when that interest had been extended, it was her prerogative to either accept or reject the man's advances. But when the man proved persistent, there was little she could do but to smile and attempt to convey to him with subtlety that his attentions were not welcome. Anything more would be considered forward or ungrateful, especially when the man was of much greater consequence than the woman.

It was this situation in which Elizabeth found herself. The previous evening at the assembly had been enjoyable for Elizabeth, other than the fact that it seemed like every time she turned her head Mr. Jamison was there with another of his flattering comments and flirtatious suggestions.

Unfortunately, Elizabeth could not make the man out. His flattery was in no way convincing—it was not that of a man who carries a tender regard for a woman. When Elizabeth thought of it, she thought that his words were, in a rather strange sort of way, more a means of puffing up his own vanity than Elizabeth's. A man who was attempting to know a woman would speak to her, converse of various things, all designed to bring a greater understanding. With Mr. Jamison there was nothing but flowery words, dramatic gestures, and grandiose statements of regard. Elizabeth would have thought he was courting her if she possessed a dowry, for surely a man interested in a woman only for her money might behave in such a fashion. But despite his protestations to the contrary, his actions were not those of a man in love.

There was to be no respite from Mr. Jamison as the very day after the assembly, he visited Hollyfield and specifically requested to see her. Luckily for Elizabeth's peace of mind her sister, Georgiana, and Caroline were all present, as she would not have trusted him if she was alone.

"Miss Bennet!" cried he as he was led into the room. "How I have missed you! It seems akin to a year since we last met rather than only a few hours."

"Mr. Jamison," said Elizabeth, his extravagant manners already annoying her. She did not give him the satisfaction of any further response.

Unfortunately, the man needed no such encouragement.

"May I dare hope that you have longed for my presence as much as I have for yours?"

Elizabeth was no shrinking violet. She had been out for several years, and she was well aware of the stratagems young men would use to ingratiate themselves with young women. She was not disposed to titter and answer with coquettish flirtation, even if she *had* possessed a particular interest in the man; but Elizabeth also was not one to back away from confrontation, nor would she feign feelings she did not, in fact, possess.

"I am afraid I must disappoint you, sir. For not a thought concerning you has crossed my mind since last night."

Caroline snickered and Georgiana stifled a giggle, and Jane, though she did not laugh, hid a smile behind her hand. Elizabeth, however, simply smiled sweetly at the man, wondering how he would respond to her statement, which, though untrue—she *had* thought of him, though with vexation rather than the fondness for which he professed a hope—could be considered to be rude.

"Then it appears that I must redouble my efforts."

The man swaggered forward and grasping her hand—Elizabeth idly noted that rather than taking it delicately, as a lover might hold the hand of his beloved, Mr. Jamison's act was that of a possessive man intending domination—he bowed low, bestowing a kiss on its back.

Instantly she jerked her hand away, eyes shooting daggers at the man, but he paid no notice. Rather, he turned to the rest of the room and said in a voice almost like an actor about to feign a swoon:

"And good day to you all, of course. I was momentarily stunned by the great beauty of my beloved, but truly there is such a feast for the eyes in this room, that a man entering must consider himself dead and gone to heaven, for no mere mortal realm can boast such splendor in one place."

Having said this, he stepped forward apparently intent upon kissing the hands of all the ladies, but Jane and Caroline declined to offer theirs, prompting a shrug in return. Georgiana, being slightly more naïve and a little in shock due to the man's manners, did not move quickly enough, and soon her hand was caught by the man.

He did not linger, however, and instead he chose a seat beside Elizabeth and began to converse with her to the point of almost ignoring the rest of the ladies. His conversation was much as it had been the previous night, though Elizabeth had learned the benefit of listening to only one word in three. It did not seem to make a difference, as he carried the conversation entirely by himself, his mind flitting smoothly from one topic to the next without hesitation and without any prior consideration that Elizabeth could detect. By the time the requisite half an hour had passed, Elizabeth was ready to see the back of the man if only to have a bit of quiet!

When the time for the visit had elapsed, Mr. Jamison rose and made his apologies to all of the ladies before turning to Elizabeth yet again.

"I shall meet with you once again anon, my dear Miss Bennet. Until then, let your thoughts be of me, for mine shall surely be of you."

And before Elizabeth could muster a response, he was gone in a swirl of his travelling cape, an affectation Elizabeth was certain was part of his act, as it truly was too warm for such a garment.

It was only a few moments after he left the room that the rest of the ladies burst into laughter. Elizabeth did not join them as, though she could see the humor in the situation, the man infuriated her too much for her to laugh at such a time.

"You have an admirer, Elizabeth," said Caroline with a knowing grin.

"A very handsome one." Jane's sweet smile hid her teasing, not that Elizabeth was fooled.

Elizabeth glared at them all, even Georgiana who was trying — and failing — to suppress her sniggers.

"What is the world coming to?" asked Elizabeth with a mocking glance at her sister. "When even Jane joins in the teasing the matter must be one for a court jester."

Jane only grinned, prompting another scowl from Elizabeth.

"I was a little surprised at your rudeness to him," said Caroline once the mirth had subsided, "but I suppose it will take a little rudeness to induce him to desist."

"I believe it will take *more* than a little rudeness," said Elizabeth. "He is all insolence."

"Just take care, my dear," said Caroline. "I do not trust the man. He has always behaved in such a manner, but this is beyond even his excesses. I cannot determine exactly what his game is, but whatever it is, it cannot be benign."

Elizabeth agreed, and the conversation turned, by tacit agreement, to other matters and all mention of Mr. Jamison was dropped. Though she could not divine Mr. Jamison's purpose any more than Caroline could, Elizabeth wondered at the man's audacity. Whatever he wanted, she was certain it would not be desirable for her or any other young lady to oblige him.

It was a little later that morning when Elizabeth left on her customary walk, and as she departed the house, Caroline stood in an upstairs window regarding her retreating form.

In fact, Caroline was a little peeved at what had been happening recently. She had promised herself—and had promised David—that she would do nothing more than to put Elizabeth and William in company together, and thus far she had kept to that promise. There were definite signs of improvement in the relationship between the two, but Caroline had thus far seen little to indicate that William would actually act upon his interest, though Georgiana had confided to her about what her brother had said concerning Elizabeth.

That infamous Darcy caution seemed to be holding the man back, weighing every option and proceeding with prudence rather than striking while the iron was hot. And the iron was very hot indeed, at least from William's side. From Elizabeth, it appeared like it was warming, and Caroline was certain that it only warranted a little more heat before her feelings would be sufficient.

Caroline thought that she knew what the situation needed. Mr. Jamison's behavior, though troubling and vexing, provided Caroline the weapon which just might induce William to jump where his instincts told him to go slowly. That weapon was, of course, jealousy.

What she was struggling with was whether bringing them together in company constituted a breach of her promise.

"Caroline," called a voice, and Caroline turned to see her husband approaching her, a knowing look on his face.

Greeting him warmly, Caroline nonetheless turned back to Elizabeth's retreating form which was dwindling in the distance.

"Is your matchmaking turning out to be more difficult than you had envisioned?"

Caroline rolled her eyes. "It is *not* matchmaking. I am merely putting them in company together so that they may discover for themselves how perfectly they suit."

"Then what is the problem?" asked David. "They are in company, Darcy is interested, and Miss Bennet does not appear to be ready to throw him out on his ear like she is with that fop Jamison."

"The problem is what it always is with Darcy; he moves with more caution than confidence, more hesitance than boldness."

David shrugged. "Then ensure he is in company once more with Miss Bennet when Jamison is here. That will surely induce him to proceed. Jealousy can be a powerful motivator."

Feeling as if her jaw would drop to the floor, Caroline turned and looked at her husband.

A chuckle was her answer. "You have gone this far in your schemes. What is a little manipulation to make sure they are in company?"

A slow smile crept over Caroline's face. "Then I must have your help. Rather than retreating to the billiard room or riding the estate as is your wont, you must ensure Darcy is nearby the next time Mr. Jamison visits."

"Very well," replied David. "If only to make *you* happy, my dear."

Thus it was the next time Mr. Jamison visited — which was the very next day — the gentlemen were present, though Darcy could not have known that this was by design.

One might have thought that with the owner of the estate present — he was, after all, responsible for the young lady's protection while she was present — Mr. Jamison might have been on better behavior than he had been on his previous visit. However, given what he had heard of the previous day's call, Darcy could not imagine that the man's grandiose gestures and dramatic pronouncements were in any way an improvement.

After only a few moments in company, Darcy found himself actively detesting Mr. Jamison. The man had an arrogant assurance in his own ability to woo a lady, and no matter the extent of Miss Bennet's easily observed distaste for him, he desisted not, even appearing to be spurred to greater heights of ridiculousness.

The man was attempting to pay court—though very poorly—to *his* Elizabeth. Was this to be borne?

As soon as the thought occurred to him, Darcy's thoughts were abruptly halted. He had just thought of Miss Bennet—Elizabeth—as *his*. No longer was she merely an acquaintance, a young lady he thought to be rather pretty, a bright light of intelligence, or a young woman he wanted to pay his addresses to. Now, she was to be considered *his*—his to woo, his to hold, his to eventually propose to and marry.

Darcy had thought to wait until she returned to Hertfordshire, to follow her there and stay with Bingley. Once there he would request permission for a courtship, confirm that permission with her father, and then ultimately ask for her hand in marriage. But what truly was holding him back? And what possible benefit could there be to waiting? There was no benefit that Darcy could determine, but the penance was to witness a fop lavishing attention upon her that Darcy should be bestowing on her himself.

There was no need to wait. In fact, there was every reason to proceed. Bingley, as a member of her family by marriage, may be applied to for permission in lieu of Mr. Bennet, and the man himself could be applied to when they finally did return to Meryton.

With new resolve, Darcy looked over at Elizabeth, noting her bored expression as she listened to Jamison prattle on. Caroline was looking at Darcy with exasperation, while the Colonel with amusement, no doubt wondering when his patience would snap. It just had.

Winking at them both out of the corner of his eye—and noting their sudden smiles and stifled laughter—Darcy stood and approached Elizabeth, sitting near to her position on the sofa, saying:

"Miss Bennet, I believe that we have not finished our discussion about Shakespeare, and I thought to ask you more of your opinion."

Though startled, Elizabeth immediately caught on and she turned to Darcy, leaving Jamison staring open-mouthed at them. Darcy could not help but look smugly at the man.

As their conversation began, Darcy noticed that Jamison continued to watch them, and though he was blessedly silent, his countenance took on an expression of injured vexation. It was all Darcy could do not to laugh.

"You prefer the comedies to tragedies, Mr. Darcy?" asked Elizabeth, pulling his attention back to their conversation.

"The tragedies are very dull," interjected Jamison, apparently intent upon not being left out of the conversation.

"I do indeed," replied Darcy. "The tragedies are great literary triumphs, of course, but I prefer the light-hearted variety of the bard's works to the dark. The way in which Beatrice and Benedict are led to declare their love amuses me, as do the antics of one Robin Goodfellow and the Mechanicals.

"In the tragedies, on the other hand, you witness Hamlet and his depression and Macbeth and his growing paranoia and madness — not to mention the star-crossed lovers, Romeo and Juliet. They are not exactly meant for light reading. I find that I deal with enough of the negativity life can provide in the course of daily life as I oversee the operation of my estate and the care of those people who count on Pemberley for their livelihoods. I am happy to leave such concerns out of the literature I read."

"Well said, Darcy," said Colonel Fitzwilliam. "While Shakespeare's tragedies are often accurate commentaries of life, they can be depressing."

The discussion continued, and while it was going on around him, Jamison watched them all with a faintly suspicious air. Though he injected several comments from time to time, his contributions were for the most part ignored, and Darcy could see his frustration growing. What he was about, Darcy could not say — knowing how a man courted a woman, he could not see the signs in Jamison. His interest was a mystery.

Finally, when Jamison appeared to be losing his patience, he huffed and turned to his other side, where Georgiana sat listening to the conversation, though not participating to any great degree, and addressed her:

"And you, Miss Darcy? I suppose you are also a philosopher and a connoisseur of the works of the great William Shakespeare?"

Georgiana colored and made an unintelligible response, to which the man seemed to think he was duty-bound to respond.

"I suppose you must, having such an elder brother always sitting with his nose buried in a book. As I am certain that a young girl as vibrant, intelligent, and lovely as yourself must have an opinion of what is being discussed, I must insist upon you sharing it."

Now Darcy easily perceived that Georgiana truly did not know what to say. Possessed of a shy and retiring disposition at the best of times, her confidence had been affected due to the incident with Wickham. To have a man — especially one who behaved in the manner

Jamison did—speak to her with such familiarity was disconcerting for her. He trusted that she had learned a great deal in the events of the previous summer, but still, the man was not a proper sort, and Darcy wished he would take his overdone mannerisms somewhere else.

Darcy was about to say something when Georgiana raised her eyes and said: "I am not a philosopher, sir, but I do enjoy Shakespeare. I must confess that I agree with my brother; I find the comedies to be much more enjoyable to read."

Though her words were quiet and diffident, Darcy was surprised that his sister had spoken at all. Only a few short months ago, such a response would have been beyond her capacity, and he had not known that Georgiana had progressed so much.

Then he happened to glance at Elizabeth and he noticed that she was watching his sister with a hint of a smile playing around her mouth, and he could not help but nod with satisfaction. Apparently Elizabeth's society *had* been beneficial for Georgiana.

"Oh ho!" cried Jamison. "Well said! Well said indeed! I sense that there is a similar turn of mind between us, Miss Darcy, and I salute you. Few young ladies are as sagacious as you."

Georgiana blushed and turned away, but Darcy was not amused at the man's flattery.

"You are truly like your brother then, Georgiana," said Elizabeth, looking at the girl warmly.

By the time the half hour had passed and it was time for Jamison to go, Darcy was more than ready to see him leave. For that matter, he had the distinct impression that the rest of the company felt the same way.

"Thank you, Elizabeth," said Georgiana, once Jamison had departed. "He is a strange man, and I am glad that you were able to deflect him."

"You are quite welcome, Georgiana."

"Strange is hardly the word I would use," muttered Darcy. "The man is a lunatic."

"What, do you find that any man who shows some admiration for me to be out of his wits, Mr. Darcy?"

The eyebrow raised in playful challenge told Darcy all he needed to know about her mood, and he chuckled in response.

"I think you are well aware that I meant no such thing, Miss Bennet, but I am also aware of your penchant for occasionally expressing opinions you do not in fact espouse."

Elizabeth laughed at this portrayal, but Georgiana looked a little shocked. "Brother! How can you talk of poor Elizabeth in such a way?"

"Surely you must know Elizabeth well enough now to know that she loves to play devil's advocate," said Caroline.

"Perhaps," said Georgiana with a sly smile at Darcy. "But I do not know that it is completely acceptable to state it with impunity."

"It is quite all right, Georgiana," said Elizabeth. "Your brother can say whatever he wishes. I promise that I shall have my revenge at some time or another. The best part is he will never know it is coming."

The entire party laughed, and Darcy along with them. *This* was what he would look forward to should he be fortunate enough to gain Elizabeth's hand. It was a pleasant thought indeed.

The morning obligations having been completed, Elizabeth was happy to be able to escape from company and take a little time to herself. During the late mornings and early afternoons, Charles and Jane often disappeared to indulge in each other's sole society and the Powells were the same. Mr. Darcy and Colonel Fitzwilliam could often be found in one another's company, riding or at billiards, or some other activity, and as Georgiana was still young, she spent several hours of the day in lessons. This allowed Elizabeth the opportunity for some time to herself.

On the occasion in question, Elizabeth retired to the library, intent upon finding a good book to while away the rest of her morning. The library at Hollyfield was impressive, being a large and open room with hundreds of volumes organized in shelves all about the room. It was a far cry from the few pitiful specimens Charles had displayed at Netherfield. The thought of the gentleman made Elizabeth smile; Charles was an amiable man with man fine qualities, and he had made Jane very happy indeed, but he was not a cerebral man.

With these happy memories, Elizabeth meandered about the room, perusing the shelves, running her hands across the spines, the material smooth beneath her fingers, the scents of paper and leather sharp and familiar. The room evoked memories of her father's bookroom, though it was much larger with many more volumes. That room had always been her refuge in a house where her mother, always vocal and seldom sensible, held sway with her nerves, her proclamations, and often her exasperation with her second daughter whom she could not understand. It seemed now that this particular room was another retreat for her, this time from a man who would not desist in his flowery attentions.

Instinctively shying away from thoughts of Mr. Jamison, Elizabeth focused on the books, knowing she would have to deal with the man at another time. Making her choice, she relaxed herself on a nearby sofa, soon losing herself in the pages of her book.

It was some time before she became aware of her surroundings again, and it was the opening of the door which brought her attention up from the book. There, in the doorway, stood Mr. Darcy, looking at her with an unreadable expression. For a brief moment, Elizabeth felt a sense of unease pass through her, and she wondered if the Mr. Darcy who had first arrived at Hollyfield had reappeared.

"Miss Bennet, my apologies," said Mr. Darcy, leaning forward in a bow. "I was not aware that the room was occupied."

Reassured that he was as he had been the past few days, Elizabeth stood and dropped into a curtsey. "I would not precisely call the room 'occupied' Mr. Darcy," said she. "It is quite spacious and capable to accommodate more than one person, especially since I am considered by most to be quite petite."

A grin met her declaration, which caused Elizabeth no small amount of wonder. She could not remember a time when such an expression had come so easily to the man's face.

"I am certain you are correct."

Mr. Darcy stepped forward, after making certain the door was ajar for propriety's sake, and when he caught sight of her book and read the title, his eyebrow rose in question.

"'Songs of Innocence and Experience?'" asked he, and though his tone might be considered to be severe, Elizabeth could detect a tremble at the corner of his mouth which suggested good humor.

"Yes, Mr. Darcy," replied Elizabeth with a bland expression. "I was just rereading some of my favorite poems. When you entered, I had just finished reading 'The Tyger.'"

Elizabeth turned her book around and showed Mr. Darcy the poem in question, with its grinning beast, vivid illustration, and bright, riotous colors.

After glancing at the page, Mr. Darcy turned back to Elizabeth and said: "Some consider 'Songs of Experience' inappropriate reading for a young lady of your station."

"Then it is to my good fortunate that my father does not," replied Elizabeth. She watched him, wondering what he was about, for though his words suggested censure, she was certain that he was not attempting to criticize.

"I tend to agree with your father," said Mr. Darcy, once again a smile gracing his face. "Blake's works are beautiful, and I would think it a shame should an erudite young lady as yourself be denied the pleasure of reading them.

A blush suffused Elizabeth's face, and she could only stammer a thank you for the man's words, wondering how Mr. Darcy had developed a social adeptness in such a short period of time.

"Then you enjoy Blake yourself?" asked Elizabeth when she could find her voice.

"I do indeed, Miss Bennet. I enjoy many such works, though I can also be found reading many other styles and genres."

"I do remember you saying one of the most important considerations in determining whether a woman can be deemed accomplished was whether she read extensively. Would you say that the same logic follows for a man as well?"

"I cannot say, Miss Bennet. But I can tell you that I find a well-read man to be a more interesting conversationalist."

"And yet you count Mr. Bingley your closest friend?"

Mr. Darcy chuckled and shook his head. "Bingley is indeed one of my closest companions, but you are correct that he can rarely be found with a book in his hands. But though perhaps those who read more are typically better able to converse, it does not follow that is the only quality I look for in a friend. Good character, a genuine manner, intelligence, fortitude — these are all things which are important to me."

"Another list of requirements?" said Elizabeth with eyebrow raised.

"Perhaps," replied he, "but I think that we all look for such virtues in our friends. Unless, of course, we do not possess similar qualities ourselves."

"On that, Mr. Darcy, I am sure we can agree."

"Then shall we?" asked Mr. Darcy as he gestured to a nearby sofa. "I would very much like to hear your thoughts on the work you have just read."

Elizabeth could do nothing other than accept, and the two sat and were soon engrossed in a most rewarding discussion. It was hours later before they realized how much time had passed, and they separated in order to prepare for dinner. It was one of the most interesting times Elizabeth had ever spent with a man.

From that day forward, Elizabeth saw much of Mr. Darcy. When she left to walk the grounds he would unexpectedly join her, or meet her before she had ever left the house; if she was in the sitting-room, he would seat himself nearby, and invariably engage her in conversation; on the occasions when she played the pianoforte, he would sit nearby, seemingly engrossed in her performance, and he was always the one who clapped the loudest. In company he watched her and spoke with her more than any other, and he appeared to care for her comfort and wellbeing as if it were the most important consideration in the world.

In those days, Elizabeth wondered if perhaps Caroline was not correct in her estimation of Mr. Darcy's feelings. He was certainly *acting* like a suitor. However, Elizabeth could not easily put aside those days in Hertfordshire, or perhaps more particularly the way he had regarded her with accusing eyes and harsh glares when he had first arrived at Hollyfield.

In all honesty, Elizabeth had to acknowledge that she was greatly enjoying the experience and novelty of having a suitor, if that was indeed what he was. Furthermore, she enjoyed the fact that *Mr. Darcy* was the suitor, as she had quickly determined that he was a man of sense and intelligence, of passion and discernment. There was something about his manner which appealed to Elizabeth, and she found herself greatly anticipating his appearance.

In the back of her mind, however, the memory of more difficult times in his company would not leave her. She had not been mistaken about his anger when he had come to Hollyfield, despite his present behavior. And though she knew his suit would in some respects be appealing should he ever make it, she would not spend the rest of her life wondering when Mr. Darcy would once again revert to his previous behavior. She had no indication as yet that Mr. Darcy's attentions tended toward marriage, but it would behoove her greatly to take care and understand his character in case he ever decided to propose. Furthermore, Elizabeth was determined that should he ever make his addresses to her she would have an accounting from him.

One night the Hollyfield party was invited to the Jamison estate for an evening in company, and though Elizabeth knew she would be seeing the younger brother at the elder's estate, she felt more than capable of handling the man. His constant flattery would continue to annoy her, no doubt, but it was not sufficient to induce her to wish to avoid the amusement.

The evening was everything she had expected, from the behavior of a certain gentleman to the pleasure of spending an evening in company with people she was rapidly coming to know, and amongst whom there were several she was coming to consider to be friends. But it was also a puzzling evening in some respects, and by the end of it, she was starting to suspect intrigue which concerned her.

After managing to escape from Mr. Jamison, Elizabeth had the opportunity to speak with Major Trent, whom she had not seen in company since the evening of the assembly.

"How do you do, Miss Bennet?" asked he by way of greeting.

"Very well, sir," said Elizabeth. "I am happy to see you again. I hope that nothing untoward has happened to prevent your presence at the most recent events."

"No indeed. As I am almost completely healed, I must return to my duties. My commanding officers have seen fit to ease me back into duty, and as such, I have been assisting with the training of a nearby regiment. Since they are scheduled to depart for summer encampment, I too must return to my previous assignment."

"Not to active duty on the continent, I hope."

Major Trent smiled and bobbed his head in thanks. "At present, no. It is possible that we might be deployed again, but my regiment took heavy losses in Spain, and the replacement and training of men takes some time. I doubt we will see any fighting again until at least next year."

"I am happy to hear it."

"Do not concern yourself, Miss Bennet." Major Trent regarded her with eyes expressing his appreciation of her concern. "Military men of all kinds must accept that eventually they might be pressed into battle. Should I be sent to the front again, I shall do my duty, the same as any other man. I am no different than Colonel Fitzwilliam, the lowliest soldier, or Wellesley himself."

"And that is to your credit, I am sure," said Elizabeth. "There are many who would quail before such a responsibility."

"I do not see any difference between myself and some other second son who decides his path lies as a man of God."

"Except for the fact that a parson does not face an enemy who is intent upon ensuring he never returns home."

"There is certain a difference in the level of danger, though my understanding is that some patrons can be quite demanding."

The two laughed with good-natured camaraderie.

"But be that as it may, to hear the call of God and respond to it by caring for the Lord's children is in my mind, more commendable than training in order to accomplish nothing more than to take the lives of other men."

A feeling of great deal of respect for this man welled up in Elizabeth's breast. "Then why did you not take up the cloth yourself?"

"Because I know myself. I am not suited to be a clergyman."

Their conversation continued for some time in a similar vein, and though Elizabeth's heart was not touched by Major Trent, she felt nothing but admiration for him. He was honest, interesting, and he possessed insights in many manners she might not have expected from a man of the scarlet, and he was dutiful and calm in the face of potential danger.

In fact, when Elizabeth compared him to the officers in the regiment which had been quartered in Meryton, she found that he was superior to them all. There was no comparison. There were good men in Colonel Forster's regiment, some kind, some intelligent, and some amiable, but to a man they all lacked something; thinking upon the matter further, Elizabeth decided that it was largely the simple fact that their outlooks on life were simplistic, and in many cases naïve. Lieutenant Sanderson, for example, was a pleasant young man, but his days in Meryton were consumed by flirting, laughing loudly, and boyish attention to the young ladies. And many were like him. They must attend to their duties—Colonel Forster seemed a man who would demand the best from his men—but Elizabeth could not imagine it was done with any soberness or seriousness of thought.

It was possible that it was in a large part the difference between the regulars and the militia. It was possible, and even likely that the militia did not attract the same quality of men those who inhabited the regulars. But she suspected it was more than that, more than the fact that Major Trent had seen battle, while Lieutenant Sanderson had not. It was their overall characters which were intrinsically different.

As they spoke, Elizabeth's attention was caught by Mr. Jamison's loud voice, as he made one of his typical proclamations to all the room; or more likely, to one of the ladies in attendance. Elizabeth was more often than not the target of his flattery, but he in no wise allowed the rest of the ladies to escape his attentions.

Elizabeth looked up and she noticed that he was standing in front of one of the ladies with whom Elizabeth was not at all acquainted, and as she watched him, she noticed his eyes flicker to her, toward Georgiana, who was seated a short distance away with Caroline, and away again. As he had caught her eye, Elizabeth steeled herself to once again be required to fend of his flattery, but to his surprise, he did not approach. Rather, he scowled at Major Trent and then turned away, walking away to another part of the room.

Turning to the major, Elizabeth noted that he was watching Mr. Jamison with some distaste.

"I must admit to a little surprise," said Elizabeth, thinking on the matter. "Mr. Jamison has not approached me since I have been speaking with you, and he has never cared for the fact that I am conversing with another."

Though her words were a statement, there was an implied question contained therein and Major Trent recognized it as such. "I believe that I may take responsibility for that, Miss Bennet. Jamison and I are not at all friendly. Even as boys we were different, and our interactions often ended in fisticuffs. Though I would not accuse the man of cowardice, he does tend to avoid me whenever I am present."

"But the first night we met he did not shy away from you."

"If you recall, Miss Bennet, I approached you while you were speaking with him. Had I been the one in the fortunate position by your side, I do not doubt that he would not have spoken to you at all."

Sharply, Elizabeth looked over at the man, wondering what his words could mean. The major once again showed his perception, as he immediately interpreted the meaning of her glance correctly.

"Miss Bennet, though I find you to be a fascinating conversationalist and a pretty woman, I have no intentions toward you. Even if I was inclined, at present I do not have the means to support a wife."

Abashed, Elizabeth looked down and attempted to mumble an apology, but he quickly and firmly rebuffed her.

"It was a natural reaction to my words. Please do not apologize.

"I will tell you that had I possessed the means I might have been tempted. However, I rather think that another has already all but declared his interest."

Elizabeth followed his eyes as he looked in the direction of the Darcys—Mr. Darcy had replaced Caroline as a companion to his sister—and she blushed as she caught Mr. Darcy's eye as he smiled softly at her.

"There is nothing between Mr. Darcy and me."

"Doth the lady protest overmuch?" asked the major, and he laughed when Elizabeth scowled at him, putting his hands up in surrender. "Very well then; I shall not tease. I dare say that you are far more frightening than a whole battalion of French soldiers when your ire is raised.

"But I must tell you, Miss Bennet, that between Mr. Darcy and Mr. Jamison, there is no question who is the better man. Mr. Darcy may be reticent in company and perhaps not the most amiable of gentlemen, but he is all substance. Jamison is nothing but flirtation and ostentatious manners."

"I have already ascertained that fact, major."

"I am certain you have."

The major then changed the subject and the conversation turned to other, more desultory matters, and soon after that they parted, the major turning to speak with some other members of the party, while Elizabeth went to join the Darcys. She was welcomed enthusiastically by the pair and spent some moments in their company before Mr. Darcy was called away to speak with Mr. Bingley and some men of the area.

A quiet conversation ensued and Elizabeth was happy that the girl was comfortable enough with her that she was able to talk without hesitation. It was a difficult age, caught in the cusp of womanhood while still being, in essence, a girl. Elizabeth was happy that Mr. Darcy had seen fit to allow his sister this much leeway in society; she rather thought he would prefer to continue to shelter her and deny her this activity.

"I declare I have never seen such a wonderful scene of beauty and domestic felicity!"

The nearby exclamation startled Elizabeth and she looked up, noting that Georgiana was in the same state. The outburst had come, of course, from Mr. Jamison, and he stood in front of them, gazing down at them with his typical dramatic expression. But as Elizabeth watched him, she became uncomfortable. It was nothing she could identify physically about his countenance or his manners; but in his eyes there appeared to be an almost predatory gleam, and Elizabeth did not like it one bit. It reminded her of what she had seen in Mr. Wickham's eyes the last time she had seen him.

"Miss Bennet's beauty and reputation for intelligence and insight precede her," continued Mr. Jamison, his words punctuated by a rather unctuous glance and a pretentious bow in her direction, "but I dare say that Miss Darcy will soon outshine her, both in beauty and accomplishments. I sincerely pray that you do not take my observation as a slight upon you, Miss Bennet, for as you are well aware, I consider you to be the very definition of feminine allure and loveliness."

"No offense taken, I assure you," said Elizabeth, wishing that the man would simply go away.

It was not to be, however, as Mr. Jamison took Elizabeth's lack of enthusiasm for his company as an invitation to join them, and he sat on a nearby chair.

"No man is more fortunate than I," said he, "for I believe that I hold the most coveted seat in the room." He clapped his hands together and said, "Well, what shall we speak of?"

Elizabeth exchanged a glance with Georgiana, and shooting the girl a mischievous grin, said:

"I truly enjoyed your playing the other day, Miss Darcy. The Mozart sonata you played was exquisite. You must have practiced extensively to be able to render it so beautifully."

Georgiana blushed, but she seemed to understand Elizabeth's intentions, replying:

"I *have* practiced it for some time, Elizabeth, but you know how I love to practice!"

"Then you simply must play it for me when next I visit," declared Mr. Jamison with eagerness. "You might not be aware, but I actually possess some skill on the pianoforte myself."

"Then perhaps it is *you* who should play when next you come," rejoined Elizabeth.

"Oh no, that would not do at all," said Mr. Jamison, with an—entirely affected, Elizabeth was certain—air of modesty. "I should not wish to impose my poor efforts upon you. I am quite content to listen to your own superlative efforts. Having heard Miss Bennet, I must say that I have rarely heard something so sublime, but from what I am hearing, Miss Darcy appears to have even more talent. I cannot wait!"

"Do you favor Mozart in a general sense?" asked Elizabeth, directing her attention back to her young companion.

"Mozart is wonderful," replied Georgiana, "but I find his music a little too light for my tastes at times. Beethoven is also wonderful, and his music appeals to me as being more serious."

"No doubt due to the influence of your brother," said Mr. Jamison. "I declare that I have never seen such a stern individual as Mr. Darcy. Even Trent does not glare about the room with such impunity."

Though Elizabeth bristled at the implied insult, she ignored the man.

"Yes, Beethoven is inspiring, and his melodies are intricate and beauteous. I have had the opportunity to hear his works in concert, and it was beautiful, I assure you.

"But I must say," continued Elizabeth, "that when one is in a playful or happy mood, there is nothing like Mozart. His strains are no less intricate, and when one listens to his work one cannot help but feel their cares float away."

"Personally I consider Mozart to be a jovial and happy fellow," said Mr. Jamison. "Beethoven is too much of a serious-minded man for someone of my nature."

Carefully making sure that Mr. Jamison could not see her, Elizabeth rolled her eyes, which resulted in Georgiana being required to stifle a giggle. Truly the man was senseless if he thought his inane comments were welcome

The conversation proceeded in this peculiar manner, Elizabeth and Georgiana speaking to one another with animation, their topics ranging among various subjects of mutual interest. But while Mr. Jamison was present and he interjected comments with great frequency, Elizabeth and Georgiana listened politely whenever he had something to say and then carried on speaking as if he had not opened his mouth.

Elizabeth had hoped that the man would take the hint and leave, but in this she was destined to be disappointed. It was clear that he understood what they were doing, but far from being offended, he continued on in his affected manner, and he even seemed to gain an amused smirk as the time wore on.

But Elizabeth was determined to ignore him. And though Georgiana appeared to be perplexed by his manners and from time to time even giggled at his sillier pronouncements, Elizabeth was content in the knowledge that he was not fooling her either.

Chapter XI

*L*ife for Elizabeth continued on as before. Mr. Jamison visited as was his wont, and though he continued to pay particular attention to attention to Elizabeth, often Georgiana was caught up in the man's flattery for the simple fact that she was often in company with Elizabeth. Soon he was flattering Georgiana as much as he was Elizabeth, though Elizabeth was certain the girl was becoming as exasperated with his behavior as Elizabeth was. It was not long before Georgiana began to become uncomfortable and silent whenever the man made an appearance, and at times she seemed almost fearful. The man was a rake and a flatterer, but Elizabeth could not understand why she would be frightened of him. Regardless, whenever she sensed he was becoming too much for the girl, she attempted to distract him away from her.

Mr. Darcy was also a constant presence, and though Elizabeth enjoyed the man's company much more than she enjoyed that of Mr. Jamison, she was careful to temper her expectations and remember that she still had not received a satisfactory explanation regarding his behavior. Until she was the recipient of that account, she refused to think of him as anything but a pleasant conversationalist with a mercurial temper. It was far safer for her that way.

On a fine day Elizabeth was determined to walk out, and as the warmth in the air was perhaps a little stifling, her companions laughingly allowed her the pleasure without their presence.

"You cannot blame us for not being the excellent walkers that you are," said Caroline. "I am certain you will enjoy your solitude."

"If I know Lizzy, she will relish the privacy, much more than you or I would," added Jane, though with a teasing air.

Elizabeth laughed. "Very well, I see how it will be. Since none of you can take the trouble to accompany me, I believe that I shall take your excellent suggestion and go myself."

She fooled no one with her declaration and Caroline merely waved her from the room, and Elizabeth was only happy to take her leave, reflecting on the great pleasure of good friends and happy circumstances.

Even Elizabeth had to confess that though the day was fine, it was a little too warm even for her hardy nature. However, there was also a gentle breeze which blew from the direction of the lake, and it carried with it a cooling effect which rendered the day more pleasurable than would otherwise have been the case. Elizabeth took the path out onto her favorite walk, one which looped around toward the lake and through several strands of trees situated to the north of the manor house, and for some time she was completely by herself, enjoying the trees and groves, the fine weather and the gentle scent of wildflowers floating through air.

At length, she began to make her way back, knowing that she had already been gone for some time. But rather than take the more direct path, she instead turned her steps toward the lake, which her previous path had taken her near, but not to the shore.

The water was fine that day, and as Elizabeth strode along the edge of the lake, she could see tiny fish darting in the water in search of food, and even here and there a few frogs nestled in amongst the water, cooling themselves from the heat of the day. It was as she was walking in this attitude, meandering in the general direction of the manor house, that she espied the tall form of Mr. Darcy striding toward her.

The firmness of his gait and the look in his eyes told Elizabeth that he had not come upon her by chance; rather she suspected that he had been seeking her out. She had no doubt that he had been directed hither by the efforts of Mrs. Powell who, though she had promised not to interfere, was not above giving a little nudge every so often. Before Elizabeth could think of the matter further, Mr. Darcy was standing in front of her, looking as handsome and agreeable as ever she had seen him.

"Miss Bennet," said he as he approached and sketched a bow. "I see you are enjoying a walk along the lake."

The obvious statement almost made Elizabeth laugh, but of more import, the likely *reason* for the nervousness he was betraying caused a hitch in her chest. Could he truly be contemplating what she suspected he might?

"Mr. Darcy," replied Elizabeth, but only after a pause in which she almost felt herself to be slow of thought. "Apparently I am not the only one enjoying the grounds of Mr. Powell's estate."

The man paused and Elizabeth felt sure he was going to say something of great import, but instead he settled for a smile and a gesture toward the path. "Shall we take this way together?"

Nodding, Elizabeth began walking slowly, and Mr. Darcy matched her pace, but though conversation between them did proceed, nothing of import passed between them; the day, the fineness of the season, the pleasant company — all of these things were canvassed. But Elizabeth, who was burning with curiosity as to the man's manner, was beginning to feel a little cross that it did not appear like it would be assuaged. And then he began to speak, the abrupt nature of his sudden words leaving her almost confused.

"Miss Bennet, I find myself unaccountably at a loss for words." He smiled in a self-deprecating fashion. "You are not likely to be surprised by my admission that I am not the most loquacious or eloquent of men. I often find that I am better able to say what I need when I have considered the matter and rehearsed my words in advance. But though I have thought on this moment for quite some time, still I find myself unable to say what I wish."

Giggling in spite of the situation, Elizabeth looked up at Mr. Darcy to see an expression of bemusement, one which seemed to expect a reason for her sudden mirth.

"My cousin Mr. Collins once told us that he 'arranges such elegant compliments as may be adapted to any situation.' Are you now to tell me that you have been poured from the same mold that gave us the estimable William Collins?"

Laughing openly, Mr. Darcy said: "Did he actually say that?"

"He did, sir. But I assure you that he gives them as unstudied an air as possible!"

Shoulders shaking in mirth, Mr. Darcy said: "I intend no disrespect to your cousin, but I hope that you do no find me to be so ridiculous."

"Perhaps we shall see," said Elizabeth with a laugh. "Once you have found the words to say I shall compare them against similar ones Mr.

Collins might have said, and then I can give you your answer. Will that suffice?"

Mr. Darcy shook his head, the amusement rolling off him in waves. "Being in your company is certainly not dull, Miss Bennet. I thank you for the brightness of spirit which is such a balm to us all."

"Now you take it too far, Mr. Darcy," cried Elizabeth. "That *is indeed* something Mr. Collins might have said, though I do not doubt he would have used many more words to do it."

"Miss Bennet," said Mr. Darcy, and this time his voice and demeanor were as serious as she had ever seen, "I do not speak in the manner of Mr. Collins. I do not compliment with the intent to flatter; rather, when I speak praise it is because I believe it to be warranted."

Brought up short, Elizabeth found that she could not summon a response. It appeared that here was the confirmation of all Caroline— and indeed her father—had said regarding Mr. Darcy's affections, though Elizabeth supposed that the man had been revealing the state of his regard for some time now, if she had only had the wit to see it. Or the inclination to accept what she was seeing before her very eyes.

"I can see that I have startled you," said Mr. Darcy when she did not respond. "I am exceedingly sorry if this is sudden and has caught you off guard. If you have not perceived my regard, then it is evident that my struggles to conceal my affection for you were all too effective."

The statement was like a dash of cold water, where she was feeling the warmth of his words, and Elizabeth blinked. But Mr. Darcy, apparently not observing her sudden change of attitude, continued speaking.

"When I spoke of your brightness of spirit, I was only stating what anyone with a modicum of intelligence has already seen. Perhaps you do not see it yourself, but you light up a room by nothing more than your presence. I had not been in Hertfordshire long before I became enchanted with your manners and your happy demeanor, which persisted even when confronted with my sternness."

Mr. Darcy chuckled. "I am not a man whose happiness leads to an excess of mirth, Miss Bennet. I am rather staid and sober, and there have been times that my life—especially in the past five years—when I have not been especially happy, though I have always striven to be content. You have seen the people with whom I associate—Bingley, dear chap that he is, Caroline, Colonel Fitzwilliam, David Powell; all of these people are good people, but they have a happy disposition which I cannot emulate. But being in company with them helps lighten my own spirit, when often I am unable to do so myself.

"But even if you were not of a similar temperament, I cannot imagine not being caught by your intelligence, your beauty, and your fierce loyalty to those who possess your love. Thus, I have determined to act. I wish to request a courtship of you, Miss Bennet. I believe that we could do very well together, and though I cannot be sure of your feelings toward me, I can tell you unreservedly that I love you and wish to make you the happiest of women."

A thousand thoughts all swirled in Elizabeth's head, vying for dominance. She did not feel herself capable of making an answer; one must be made, however, for the man had just bared his soul to her and deserved a response at the very least. The thought of jumping into his arms and shouting her agreement held some appeal, as did several other such options which came to mind. Now, when she had been given the opportunity to come to know the man as well as she had, Elizabeth had to confess that she felt some partiality toward him, though at this moment she could not state with any surety how far it extended.

A small voice in the back of her mind, however, told her that regardless of how strong his feelings were at present, she should be cautious. His slight the night of the assembly was forgotten—how could she still hold it against him after such beautiful words? But she still did not have an explanation from him for his behavior. And his struggles to conceal his attraction from her spoke to other considerations, ones that Elizabeth knew were valid, even as she wished that a man would be so enamored of her that none of those things would matter. The idea of being swept off her feet was a girlish fantasy that Elizabeth suspected most women dreamed of. But it was time to put such illusory matters away with all other such juvenile considerations. What Elizabeth needed to know above all else was whether Mr. Darcy respected her as much as claimed to love her, for this Elizabeth felt to be the key.

"I confess I did have some notion as to your feelings," said Elizabeth. "However, my knowledge of your intentions is the work of another."

"Mrs. Powell," said Mr. Darcy with a nod and a slight smile. "I see she has worked at you as she has worked at me."

A feeling of pique settled over Elizabeth. "She is a good friend, but I believe she may be a little officious. But be that as it may, I believe I have a few questions for you."

Mr. Darcy opened his mouth and then closed it again, and Elizabeth was certain he had meant to defend his friend. Instead, he smiled and gestured for her to proceed, though his composure appeared to have been rattled a little.

"You say you concealed your affection for me. Though I believe I apprehend the reasons for this, may I ask you to elucidate on them?"

This time Mr. Darcy was definitely uncomfortable, and he did not speak for several moments.

"Please, Mr. Darcy," said Elizabeth. "I suspect I know what you will say, but I need to hear it regardless. You have called me an intelligent creature; surely you must know then that I have apprehended the reasons for your hesitance."

"Then why canvass the matter at all?"

"Because it all speaks to the situation, both your thoughts, feelings, and intentions, but also to the prospect of future felicity between us, including both love and respect."

When Mr. Darcy was once again silent, Elizabeth huffed and said, "I assume that you did not show your regard because of my lack of connections and dowry. Perhaps you also found the behavior of some of my family to be distasteful?"

The color rose on Mr. Darcy's neck, and though he obviously wished to remain silent, he allowed it to be so. Elizabeth nodded to herself, reflecting that knowing of the matter intellectually did not blunt the fact that it was disappointing. Not so much as to prevent her from ultimately accepting his offer. The fact that a man of any sense would see such things as impediments was never in any question, and that Mr. Darcy had risen above them surely spoke in his favor.

"I do understand, Mr. Darcy," said Elizabeth out loud. "You cannot be censured for taking such matters into consideration. But this is not the reason for my hesitance. I am more interested in your behavior when you arrived at Hollyfield. My presence here was . . . distasteful to you."

"No, do not protest!" cried Elizabeth when he instantly began to refute her words. "I have eyes to see and the wit to understand what I am seeing. I know very well that my presence was unexpected and that it was not welcome. I must tell you that I had considered returning home so that my being here would not cause disharmony."

Her words were quiet, yet filled with conviction. Mr. Darcy was obviously shocked, if his look of consternation and regret were anything to go by.

"I am exceedingly sorry, Miss Bennet," said he at last, though his words almost appeared to be forced from him. He seemed to be considering his response for a moment before he sighed and looked her straight in the eye, and the remorse contained therein spoke out to her, even as the love she saw shining back at her almost undid her composure.

"The truth is that your presence *was* a surprise. I was not expecting to see you here, and as I had determined that I would not pursue you, seeing you here was almost painful."

Elizabeth gasped. "Because of your feelings?"

"Very much so." Mr. Darcy paused and smiled. "I was not using empty words when I spoke of your attractions, Miss Bennet, and to me they are manifold, I assure you. But when I had convinced myself that I could not offer for you, seeing you again was a blow to my vaunted determination.

"Surprise, as you have recognized, turned to anger quite quickly. But my anger was not directed at you — never at you. Rather I saw Mrs. Powell as the chess master behind your being here, knowing as she did the state of my affections toward you and my decision not to pursue a closer connection. I felt her meddling officious."

"I cannot disagree with you, Mr. Darcy. I hope you were not too harsh with her as she is a dear friend and I believe she acted with the best intentions."

"I was not, though I tried to be. She brought my objections up short and it was through her guidance that I began to see that my love for you might not be as hopeless as I had thought. And furthermore, her words brought back those I had heard from my father at a young age.

"My father was a good man, liberal, attentive to all his duties, nurturing, and possessed of the best of temperaments. In fact, my own temperament was inherited from my mother." Mr. Darcy laughed. "You have likely heard of Lady Catherine de Bourgh, and I assure that whatever you *have* heard, it is not an exaggeration. My mother was not as forceful or domineering as my aunt. Rather she was reserved, and if the stories I have heard are at all correct, gave offense with her reserve when she meant nothing at all.

"But my father had served in the army as a young man until my uncle's death required him to return and take up the reins of the family estate. He was witness to battle and struggle, and he always told me that true nobility is a function of a person's character and how they react to their experiences in life, not the accident of birth. And by extension, the worth of a woman is not to be measured the size of her dowry or by the fact that she may attach the appellation 'lady' to her name."

"And this is what made you change your mind toward me?"

Mr. Darcy stepped toward Elizabeth and reached out to take her hand, holding it in his own tenderly as if it were the greatest prize. Elizabeth idly thought of the way he grasped her hand contrasted with the way Mr. Jamison took it forcefully. But such thoughts could not hold her attention long, as Mr. Darcy gazed down on her, and Elizabeth could only call his expression one of the greatest love and affection.

"Nothing changed my mind, Elizabeth."

Elizabeth gasped at the intimacy of hearing him speak her Christian name for the first time.

"Nothing was changed because my opinion of you has never altered. You are a jewel among women and there is nothing which could ruin your good attributes in my estimation. What I was lacking was my fault and mine alone. I had always understood your worth as a person; what I did not understand was that your worth was far beyond what price society might apportion to you. There is nothing which is more to be desired than a woman who is genuine, caring, considerate, happy, contented—I could go on for hours and never run out of adjectives, I assure you."

Laughing at the sheer silliness of his words, Elizabeth said: "Now you are in very great danger of being branded another Mr. Collins, sir."

"And I will point out again that I mean what I say, whereas Mr. Collins simply repeats what he feels is expected.

"Now, I will have an answer from you, if you will. Have I convinced you?"

Elizabeth paused, her heart full, and looked up at Mr. Darcy, having never expected that she might feel this way. This ecstasy, this sublimity of feeling told her that she would be a fool to reject his suit. And as she thought on the matter, it was not long before she realized she had no intention of doing so. His struggles, while not precisely laudable, were understandable, and she could not hold them against him. His behavior was now better understood; had their roles been reversed Elizabeth thought that her actions might not have been much different.

"My father," said Elizabeth, "has always said that when I consider the possibility of entering the state of matrimony, that I must consult my head as well as my heart. He claims that for me to be happy in life, having my partner's respect is as important as having his love. But though I have listened to his words, I never understood that necessity as well as I understand it today."

"Are you saying then that you believe I respect you?"

"I do not think that my words can have any other meaning, sir," said Elizabeth with an impish smile. "I might not have believed it before hearing your confession, but I understand it now."

"Then may I have your answer?"

"You may. And my answer is that I accept your courtship and look forward to knowing you better."

The man's only response was to lift her hands, which he still held, and to press his lips against them both. Truly Elizabeth was not certain whether she loved this man. But she was starting to feel as if he had only to ask for her love and she would give it to him whole-heartedly.

Darcy had always thought that he was of such a sober disposition, that when he was happy, his feelings remained sober and understated. At that moment, however, he felt almost as if laughter were about to bubble up from the depths of his soul. He had finally taken the first step toward obtaining his heart's desire.

They began walking again in no particular direction, and if conversation between them was a little sparse, the silence was not awkward. In fact, Darcy thought that he had never felt so comfortable in her presence before, now that he had secured her consent.

"We must discuss the practicalities," said he with a smile. "You are still not one and twenty?"

Elizabeth giggled, and though Darcy was mystified by the reason for her laughter he was still enchanted by it.

"I assume you mean to request my father's permission, Mr. Darcy?"

"It is required," said Darcy, still wondering at her behavior.

"It is not required," said Elizabeth, who then collapsed into further laughter when he looked at her, puzzled as to her meaning.

"You see, Mr. Darcy, my father divined your interest in me before you ever left Netherfield, and he made a point of teasing me for it before I left. He also extended his blessing should you ever see fit to request my hand."

Though it was perhaps not precisely appropriate, Darcy could not help but laugh. "I have known of your father's sense of humor, but though I have not taken the trouble to know him, to my own shame, I find that I am eager to become better acquainted. He sounds like a very droll gentleman indeed."

"Thank you, Mr. Darcy. I must own that the thought of you coming to know my father is a welcome thought. This courtship will more easily lead to marriage if I can see that the two most important men in my life get on with one another."

"I can see how that would be desirable," said Darcy, now

determined to show her that he could be amiable with her family. "But your father's blessing notwithstanding, I shall still follow the proper protocols. I shall ask Bingley for permission, and then I shall write to Mr. Bennet, asking him to ratify Bingley's decision."

Elizabeth assented and they continued walking, and to Darcy, he had never thought something as simple as walking with one's beloved could be so rewarding. It was a time he would never forget.

After meandering about the grounds with Elizabeth for some time, Darcy entered the main hall at Hollyfield with a purpose. He bid Elizabeth farewell when she went to her rooms to refresh herself, and from there sought out Bingley, eager to have their courtship broadcast to all and sundry. Then, if that fop Jamison continued to lavish attention on her, Darcy would know how to act.

Bingley was discovered easily. The man rarely left his wife's side when he was not required to, which meant that they could often be found in the sitting-room attached to their suite of rooms with Mrs. Bingley for company. With a singularity of purpose, Darcy strode up to the door which led to their chambers, and knocked. A moment later permission to enter had been granted.

It was clear to see the besotted nature of the young man in front of him, and unless Darcy missed his guess, Mrs. Bingley was in a like state. He wondered that he had not seen in before. Had his infatuation with Elizabeth and conviction of her unsuitability truly blinded him to the reality? It was as plain as day!

"Bingley, Mrs. Bingley, I apologize for interrupting your solitude."

"Not at all, Darcy," said Bingley. "I believe we would have descended to join the rest of the company soon anyway."

Holding back a laugh, Darcy could only silently contradict his friend's words. Mrs. Bingley's hair was in such a state that it was clear that they had been . . . expressing their appreciation for each other before he arrived. She would need her maid to repair the damage before she would be presentable in company.

"Excellent. In that case, might I borrow your husband for a few minutes, Mrs. Bingley?"

Though Bingley himself appeared to have no inclination of what he was wanted for, the same could not be said of his wife. Pleasure shone in Mrs. Bingley's eyes and she stood with evident happiness.

"Of course, Mr. Darcy," said she. "I shall refresh myself and join the ladies downstairs. Can you tell me if my sister is with Mrs. Powell?"

Darcy almost gaped at her with astonishment. He had never considered the sisters to be similar in appearance or character, but in that moment Darcy was struck with a sense of familiarity. Mrs. Bingley did not betray her wit to the extent that her sister did, but she was certainly not bereft of it, nor was she completely lacking in Elizabeth's playfulness. While her words did not precisely indicate it, in that instant he definitely felt like he was the object of her amusement.

"I believe that she will seek out Mrs. Powell before long," said Darcy, wondering how much else had passed him by without his being aware of it.

"Thank you," said she, and after allowing her husband to kiss her hand, she entered her bedchamber. But Darcy could see the excitement which injected a little extra spring in her gait as she walked.

"Well, Darcy, what would you have of me?" asked Bingley as Darcy led him out into the hall. "I assume that this is of more import than simply a wish engage in a game of billiards."

"Much more import," said Darcy.

The two men descended the stairs and quickly found a small room toward the back of the house. Bingley was watching him with some confusion and wonder, clearly not ever having seen him in such a fashion before. Darcy smiled—at least there was one to whom he was not transparent.

"Thank you for seeing me, Bingley. I have requested you meet with me because as the only male member of Miss Bennet's family present, you have the authority to grant permission for a courtship between us."

A slow smile came over Bingley's face and he stepped forward and gasped Darcy's hand between his own, pumping it vigorously.

"Well done, Darcy. I am very happy for you. I had not the slightest notion that you were at all interested in Elizabeth, but marvelous choice indeed! I dare say she shall do you proud and you shall never regret singling her out!"

In typical Bingley fashion, his ideas proceeded forth with rapidity and without forethought, and Darcy, though he considered it to be a solemn occasion, could not help but grin at his friend. He knew that Bingley would support him in whatever course he had chosen, but to the happiness of obtaining Elizabeth for a wife, he was also happy to obtain Bingley as a brother in a closer and more binding sense.

"Thank you, Bingley. Am I to assume that I have your permission?"

"Of course, of course!" cried Bingley. "I do find myself bemused at the fact that it is *you* coming to me for permission, but I offer it without hesitation, of course." Then Bingley stopped and he looked more closely at Darcy. "I suppose I may assume that she has already agreed?"

Laughter seemed to come easier to Darcy of late, and he indulged himself and slapped his friend on the shoulder. "She did indeed, Bingley, though she required an accounting of my behavior. I am sure that I know no other lady who would do so. I consider myself the most fortunate of men."

"Wonderful!" cried Bingley. "I am certain that you shall be very happy with your chosen. She is an amazing girl."

"You will receive no argument from me on that score."

Though Bingley continued to speak of his delight, Darcy's thoughts had wandered to another part of the house where a beautiful young woman, impertinent and delightful, was almost certainly receiving the congratulations of the ladies. Darcy could not wait to be in company with her again. It was amazing to him how quickly she had become necessary for his very happiness.

Caroline waited in the sitting room barely containing her excitement. There was a sense of expectation hanging in the air, and she would not scruple to acknowledge that she fully expected an announcement to be made when the principals of the matter once again joined the company. Her knowledge had been gained by a view from one of the upper windows which had shown them to be in close company with one another. They had truly looked cozy indeed.

In fact, Caroline was feeling more than a little triumphant, vindicated, smug, happy, and expectant all at once. She had seen Mr. Darcy's attraction almost from the beginning, but she had often despaired that he would actually concede the fact that he was perfectly suited for the woman. Even his gradually thawing demeanor and growing friendliness with her had not given Caroline any surety that he would act upon his inclination. It had been a long road, and congratulations were due, most particularly, Caroline thought, to herself. The joy on her friends' faces would be enough for her, but she was not above a little crowing over the matter. She was looking forward to it immensely.

"What has gotten into you, Caroline?" asked Georgiana. "You appear to be positively giddy."

"If what I suspect is true there is reason to celebrate," replied Caroline in a teasing fashion.

It was clear that Georgiana was not able to understand her any more now than she had been the moment before, but she was saved from Caroline's teasing when the door opened and Jane stepped into the room.

Caroline stood and approached her sister, grasping her hands with excitement. "Have you seen your sister?" demanded Caroline.

"Not yet," said Jane. "But I have seen Mr. Darcy."

"And? Do not keep me in suspense, Jane!"

Jane smiled, prompting Caroline's eyes to narrow in response. The woman was actually enjoying this and was teasing her!

"I dare say that Mr. Darcy appeared as if he had something of *great import* to discuss with my husband."

A girlish squeal escaped from Caroline's lips and she caught Jane up in an enthusiastic embrace. "It is as I have always suspected!"

"What is this?" said a new voice from the direction of the door.

Caroline looked up and espied Elizabeth standing just inside the door looking on the scene with a slight smirk etched upon her features, her eyes dancing with amusement.

"I had never taken you to be so positively excitable, Caroline. It seems there was a little girl hidden inside all this time."

"You just never had the wit to see it," snapped Caroline.

Drawing Jane with her—and noting absently that Georgiana followed them, though she appeared slightly less mystified than before—Caroline approached Elizabeth and demanded:

"Well? Have you something to report to the rest of the company, Miss Bennet?"

Elizabeth affected an air of nonchalance. "Something to report? I can think of nothing which would be of any interest to you."

"Nothing to report?" asked Caroline. Then she peered at Elizabeth with some discontent. "You and your incessant teasing! We know you were out with William, and can only suspect what has happened, and still you see fit to torment us?"

"William has proposed?" cried Georgiana, though it came out more like a squeal.

"Oh, that," drawled Elizabeth. "It is nothing more than a courtship, though it shall not become official until my father's consent has been canvassed, you understand. And besides, I wonder if I am truly suited to be William's wife. It is perhaps best that this does not go beyond this house."

Watching Elizabeth with annoyance, Caroline turned to regard Jane, noting the same vexation present on the other woman's face. Such feelings could not persist in the face of this incandescent happiness however, and as Caroline turned back to Elizabeth, she noted the other woman's uncaring expression cracking.

"I have always wanted a sister!" exclaimed Georgiana, and she launched herself at Elizabeth, crying happy tears.

Soon the two girls were laughing and crying all at once, with the two older women surrounding them with their love and elation. Most of what was said bordered on incoherent, but through it all happy tears were shed, congratulations were shared, and Caroline basked in the contented smugness that only one who had been proven to be vindicated could feel. It had been an arduous task, but it had now been completed in a most satisfactory manner.

It was only a moment before the gentlemen entered the room, and they could all be seen looking at the ladies with a certain bemused indulgence.

"What do you suppose has caused this impromptu celebration?" asked David.

"Whatever it is, it must be momentous," replied Charles. "I have rarely seen them all looking so radiant."

"I believe that I have never been so happy," said William, his eyes smoldering as he looked toward Elizabeth.

Caroline chuckled. She had often seen that look in her own husband's eyes, and she knew exactly what it meant. Elizabeth, intelligent as she was, likely had some inkling as well, though Caroline knew that only experience could inform her of the true particulars.

"May I assume that you have an announcement to make?" asked David, smiling at William expectantly.

"You may. I have asked Miss Bennet for a courtship and she has accepted. Our good friend Bingley has offered his permission in Mr. Bennet's stead, and I believe that you may number me amongst the happiest of men!"

"Bingley offered his consent?" exclaimed Fitzwilliam, and though he had been heretofore silent, he was now bursting with what Caroline took as mischief. "That truly must have been a sight to see! You should have invited me."

"I shall have you know as an old married man, it is my duty to see to the needs of my sister by marriage," said Charles in an affectedly displeased voice. "I only gave my consent after careful consideration, taking into account what I have heard of Darcy's character, fortune, and situation in life. It was a near thing, I dare say!"

The colonel chortled, while Darcy tried to appear affronted. But his displeasure, such as it was, could not last in the face of such good cheer. Soon congratulations had been imparted and well wishes extended, and before long the company was ensconced in the sitting-room, speaking excitedly. But Caroline noticed that there were two of the company who were not nearly as voluble as they might normally have been. That Mr. Darcy was reserved was not a surprise, but Elizabeth seemed to have acquired some of his reticence. Or at least that is what might have seemed to be the case, had the two had eyes for anyone other than each other. And in that, Caroline was content.

Chapter XII

*F*or the next few days love and laughter continued to reign within the walls of Hollyfield, and Elizabeth found herself to be happy. The company was good and in very good humor, the location was excellent, and the presence and attentions of her now acknowledged suitor could be nothing but pleasing. Truly, Elizabeth felt blessed.

Of course, nothing changed other than Elizabeth's courtship. Life at Hollyfield continued as it had before, and the Powells were as active in the neighborhood as they had been before. But whereas Elizabeth had always conducted herself with the propriety of a young woman, her newly acquired courtship with Mr. Darcy necessitated a change in her actions toward other men. Though perhaps she might not have considered the matter consciously, she found herself less willing to give other men much of her attention, though she still attempted to be pleasant to all and sundry. The line between flirting and simple amiable behavior might have been blurred before, but now she was well aware of the difference and took care not to cross it.

When told of her courtship, Major Trent was all happy congratulations, though Elizabeth though she might have detected the smallest hint of wistfulness.

"I had often wondered if Mr. Darcy held you in such esteem," mused he as they were speaking the day after her courtship became official. "I am very happy for you both. I am sure yours will be a happy union."

"Thank you, major," said Elizabeth. "I appreciate the sentiment."

Major Trent smiled warmly at her. "I hope that you shall always consider me to be a friend, Miss Bennet. I have truly enjoyed coming to know you better."

"I am certain that I shall."

Their conversation turned to other matters, and soon the major was to depart. But before he left, he imparted one more piece of news to Elizabeth.

"Miss Bennet, I shall not see you in company again. I have received my orders to be returned to active duty, and I shall return to my regiment in Brighton upon the morrow."

Though saddened that he must leave, Elizabeth took comfort in the fact that he would not soon be sent into battle again.

"Then I wish you a speedy journey and a safe return," said Elizabeth.

The major smiled. "Thank you, Miss Bennet. I am glad that I may count upon you to convey your feelings in a simple manner without affected exclamations. I have enjoyed our friendship immensely and hope to see you again."

With those words, they parted, and after the major made the announcement, he went away. Colonel Fitzwilliam informed the company of his impending departure as well, as his leave was about to end.

The other with whom Elizabeth had been in company in recent weeks heard the news of Elizabeth's courtship in a manner similar to what Elizabeth might have expected of the man.

It came during a visit to Hollyfield, and when he began to speak in the same pretentious fashion which characterized all of his speech, William stepped in to elucidate him as to the changed facts. His words, while seemingly friendly, were also stern and left no interpretation as to what he expected of the man's behavior going forward.

"A courtship!" cried Mr. Jamison. "My dear Miss Bennet, how truly fortunate of you to have captured the attention of such an . . . illustrious gentleman as Mr. Darcy. This is a feather in your cap to be certain. I congratulate you most wholeheartedly!"

Once he had made his statement, he continued on in the same manner as he had before, chatting with Elizabeth, with occasional comments to the other ladies in the room. It was almost as if he had not just been told that for all intents and purposes Elizabeth was no longer available to be the object of his affections.

Elizabeth could see the clenching of Mr. Darcy's jaw, and the way his eyes almost seemed to spear Mr. Jamison through. But she shook her head at him, favoring him with a rueful smile, and though she knew he wanted nothing more than to take the man out and thrash him, he desisted. And if the smile he directed at her only slightly tempered the daggers which still flew from his eyes to impale Mr. Jamison, Elizabeth could not blame him in the slightest.

It was not long before an express arrived for Elizabeth, and seeing the untidy scrawl upon the outside addressed to her, knew it was from her father. In short he congratulated her for her shrewd acceptance of Mr. Darcy's hand, and in equal parts congratulated himself for discerning the gentleman's interest and teased Elizabeth that she had missed it herself. Of more import, he confirmed his previous blessing, and informed her in a sly manner that he had not informed Mrs. Bennet of the matter yet, observing that he expected his eldest unmarried daughter would prefer to take that office upon herself. When she showed William the letter he said nothing, only shaking his head and laughing. Elizabeth suspected this only furthered his interest in coming to know Mr. Bennet further.

Three days after accepting Mr. Darcy's offer of courtship, an outing to Brixworth was proposed, and Elizabeth not having had much opportunity to visit the town since her arrival, was eager to accept. But at that moment, her eye was caught by Georgiana, and the girl looked at her, a sort of wild beseeching present in her eyes. Curious as to what she was about, Elizabeth was about to speak when the girl shook her head. Understanding that she had something she wished to speak of in private, Elizabeth declined the invitation. Soon Jane and Caroline departed, and as the gentlemen were out riding around the estate, the two found themselves alone.

At first Elizabeth was merely curious, wondering why she had refused to go into town, but as she watched Georgiana, Elizabeth began to become alarmed. She almost seemed frightened over something, and Elizabeth could not determine what it was.

Knowing she had to get to the bottom of the matter immediately, Elizabeth sat beside the young girl, stating:

"What is it, Georgiana?"

Whether it was the concern in her tone or something else, Elizabeth could not tell, but Georgiana soon began crying, and she collapsed into Elizabeth's arms, wailing: "It is happening all over again and I do not know that to do!"

Shocked, Elizabeth could only look at the girl in her arms with consternation. Of what was she talking? Had this sweet young girl experienced some traumatic experience in her life at so tender an age? And if so, as difficult to comprehend as it was, they why did she believe it was about to happen again?

For the nonce all she could do was to hold the girl as she cried, imparting what comfort she could. When Georgiana finally calmed, Elizabeth, still holding her, attempted to discover what was distressing her.

"It is Mr. Jamison," said Georgiana. "He frightens me the way he looks at me."

Though taken aback, Elizabeth attempted to put her thoughts in order. "Mr. Jamison is nothing more than a fop who attempts to impress all and sundry with his nonexistent wit, Georgiana. You have nothing to fear from him."

"His eyes give him away, Elizabeth. I am convinced that he has me in his sights, most likely for my dowry." The girl sighed. "Sometime I wish I was penniless. It would be so much simpler."

"And cause other problems, like diminishing your ability to find a good husband, and putting you at risk should you decide not to marry. Not everyone can be as fortunate as I have been to find your brother, Georgiana."

Elizabeth straightened her back, pushing the girl away from her a little so that she could see her face. From the lingering fear she could see, Georgiana believed what she was saying, and though Elizabeth had seen nothing in the man's manner to give her such suspicion and thought that his attentions were largely confined to her, she could not dismiss Georgiana's fears so readily.

"Why have you not told your brother if Mr. Jamison makes you uncomfortable?"

Georgiana ducked her head. "I did not wish you all to think of me as a silly little girl afraid of her own shadow. I have felt so . . . much like an adult in everyone's company. I would not wish to lose that feeling.

"Besides," she said in a very quiet voice, "I have caused William so much trouble in the past. I do not wish to be a burden on him."

"How could you possibly have caused William trouble?" asked Elizabeth, incredulous at the mere thought that such a diffident creature could be in any way unmanageable. "Surely you overstate—"

"No, Elizabeth," said Georgiana, and she sat up a little straighter, some measure of fortitude entering her posture. "I have been at fault, and as you are to marry William, you will hear of it eventually, so I will tell you."

At first Elizabeth thought to protest—it was by no means decided that she would marry William, though her heart and her head both whispered to her that there was no other outcome. But seeing Georgiana's need to unburden herself, Elizabeth nodded, though with reluctance. She would be of use to her friend. She could always stop the conversation if it strayed into too personal areas.

"My brother had a friend," began Georgiana, "one who was very close to him as a young boy, but who strayed into habits it is best not to mention. Last summer, when I was staying near the sea as a holiday, this man came to me and persuaded me to elope."

An awful premonition welled up within Elizabeth, and without conscious design, one word escaped her mouth. "Wickham."

Georgiana recoiled at the mere mention of the name. "How did you—?"

Chastising herself for her lack of control, Elizabeth hastened to reassure the girl. "Georgiana, I know nothing of your history with Mr. Wickham. However, I have met the man, and he had some pretty tales to tell of your brother, ones which I swallowed whole without any thought as to whether there was another side to his stories."

"You know Mr. Wickham?"

"As well as I ever wish to. Suffice it to say that he is gone from my life and the lives of everyone in my family, and I cannot but say good riddance. Now, perhaps you should finish your story and explain what bearing it has on the present?"

Coloring slightly, Georgiana nevertheless seemed to gain a little confidence from Elizabeth's words.

"I knew it was wrong, Elizabeth, but I was naïve and happy to receive Mr. Wickham's attentions, and in this I was encouraged by my companion, Mrs. Younge."

"Encouraged?" exclaimed Elizabeth.

"My brother discovered a previous connection between the pair, and I can only conjecture that some of my dowry was promised to Mrs. Younge when Mr. Wickham obtained it. But I was saved, as William arrived a few days before we were scheduled to depart, and he immediately forced Mr. Wickham to leave the area. Mrs. Younge was discharged without delay."

A mirthless chuckle escaped Georgiana's lips. "I learned that day what men will do in order to gain access to money. Mr. Wickham did not care for me. He cared for my money, and if he was able to obtain his goal at William's expense, I can only think that made me especially attractive as a target."

Curious as she was, Elizabeth wished to ask more questions concerning this event. But she knew now was not the time. Elizabeth could not see anything in Mr. Jamison's demeanor which suggested that he was intending to do the same, but she readily allowed that she had been mistaken before and might be again.

"Georgiana, what has this to do with Mr. Jamison?"

"Yes, my dear Georgiana, what has this to do with me?"

As Elizabeth's eyes darted up in shock, Georgiana let out a little cry. There, just inside the door, stood the man they had just been discussing. He was watching them, a smirk affixed to his face, but with none of the affected gallantry which had been so much a part of his behavior since Elizabeth had known him.

"May inquire as to the subject of your discussion?"

The man swaggered into the room causing Elizabeth to rise in response. Though she projected an air of confidence, inside Elizabeth was a churning mass of emotions, worries, and even a little fear. Georgiana's implication, though it had seemed unlikely at the time, suddenly made sense considering the man's appearance. It would be up to her to manage the situation, as a quick glance at Georgiana showed her to be quivering with fear.

"Mr. Jamison," said Elizabeth, forcing her voice to remain calm. "I am sorry, sir, but I do not believe that I remember you being announced."

A casual shrug met her statement. "The servants seemed to be busy, so I decided not to bother them. Anything that can ease the burden on the servant class must be done, you know."

The insolence in the man's voice was obvious and Elizabeth knew that however he managed to gain entrance this deep into the house, he had not decided to spare the servants the bother of showing him in. But now was not the time to think on such things. She would need all her wits to deal with Gabriel Jamison.

"Why are you here?" asked Elizabeth, bluntness seeming to be the best option.

"Have you not already guessed?" asked Mr. Jamison. "Were you not already discussing the matter?" He regarded at Georgiana with interest, though the girl was looking anywhere but him. "And what were you talking about? I am afraid I did not enter early enough to hear your conversation. What situation has to do with me?"

Inside Elizabeth breathed a sigh of relief. Whatever the man intended by appearing at Hollyfield, it would not do for him to have any knowledge of Georgiana's experiences with George Wickham. Georgiana herself seemed to understand this, as though she paled slightly, she kept her countenance.

"That is something I would like to know myself, Mr. Jamison," said Elizabeth. "Perhaps I shall induce her to tell me once you have departed."

"Ah, but there is the rub, is it not? I do not intend to leave without securing what I came for."

"And what is that?"

An unpleasant smile spread over Mr. Jamison's face. "Come now, Miss Bennet, I am certain you have already divined the reason for my presence. Shall you not tell me?"

"I am afraid that I have no notion of why you are here, sir. Can you not elucidate?"

"Disappointing." Mr. Jamison shock his head in mock sadness. "It will do you no good whatsoever to attempt to delay, Miss Bennet. I have come for Miss Darcy as you well know."

"For what purpose?" asked Elizabeth, ignoring Georgiana's gasp.

"For the purpose of marriage, of course. I am certain that Miss Darcy and I will be very happy together."

A smug smile at Georgiana seemed to push the girl into new heights of panic. Elizabeth, however, would not be cowed. He would have to go through her to take her friend away.

"Then you mean to ask her brother's permission for a courtship? Miss Darcy is not out, as you well know, and I am certain he will require you to wait for some time before he allows a courtship to proceed."

"Antiquated rules of etiquette," said Mr. Jamison with an airy wave. "In fact, Miss Darcy and I shall proceed to Gretna Green directly where we shall be married."

"I think not," said Elizabeth firmly. "I shall not allow it. And do you think you would be able to get very far before Mr. Darcy caught up to you? To say nothing of what Colonel Fitzwilliam would do when he discovers your behavior."

An uneasy smile settled over the man's face, though he attempted to hide it. "I am certain that Mr. Darcy will understand the situation and will have no choice but to bow to the inevitable."

Elizabeth studied the man before her. Though he had always struck her as a vain man, and one who was affected in all his manners and the image he projected to the world. But she had never thought him to be a stupid man. For him to consider such an action, which seemed to have little chance of success, suggested that the man was in fact desperate. And given what Elizabeth had heard of him, she expected that it was something to do with the man's financial matters.

But none of that mattered at present, so Elizabeth merely waved her hand in a dismissive gesture. "I am certain, sir, that if you look at the girl in even a cursory manner you might find that she does not look upon the prospect with any pleasure."

"And yet it is her fate."

"I have already told you that I shall not allow it."

"How will you prevent it?" Mr. Jamison snorted in derision. "You, a woman, seek to oppose me?"

"I will."

The two stood face to face, Elizabeth projecting a calmness she did not feel, while she sensed that the man was studying her to discover her level of determination. If he was doing so, he would find her implacable, she decided. Georgiana would not be leaving in this man's company if Elizabeth could prevent it.

"Georgiana, ring the bell," said Elizabeth.

"Do not move," commanded Mr. Jamison, stepping forward.

Elizabeth neatly moved with him, keeping herself between him and Georgiana.

Throwing his hands up in the air, Mr. Jamison stalked forward, attempting to reach the girl, but Elizabeth again moved with him.

"It would be as easy for me to simply compromise her," said Mr. Jamison, though his words came out as a bit of a snarl. "If she is compromised, Darcy will have no choice but to accept me as a brother. You should not attempt to interfere, Miss Bennet, or your own reputation might suffer. If you are sullied, I doubt a man as proud as Darcy would marry you."

"And that is where you are wrong."

Elizabeth almost wilted with relief as the voice sounded from across the room, and she turned her head to see William striding forward, his face dark and stormy as he glared at Mr. Jamison. For his part, Mr. Jamison shrunk away from Elizabeth, almost seeming to collapse within himself, and Elizabeth smiled grimly; the man was nothing more than a bully, preying on those he believed to be weaker than he was himself.

As William stalked up to Mr. Jamison, Elizabeth had the image of a wolf moving for the kill. Of the two men, there was no question who was the more dangerous, and who was the better man. Watching William as he moved to protect his sister, understanding the determination and fortitude of this man, she felt the first fluttering in her midsection. Though her feelings toward him were positive and improving daily, perhaps being courted by Mr. Darcy would be something far more precious than she had even anticipated!

"What are you doing here, sir?" asked William, a hard and unforgiving look in his eye.

"I-I simply came to see the ladies," said Mr. Jamison, attempting to obfuscate. "Much as I have done . . . any other day."

"Then why have you spoken of sullying the woman I am courting?"

Clearly Mr. Jamison had no answer for that, as he hung his head and did not say anything.

Turning to the other men who had entered the room behind him, William said: "Will you take Jamison to another room where we can speak to him? I would prefer that he did not upset the ladies any further."

Nodding, Colonel Fitzwilliam stepped forward and, grasping Mr. Jamison's arm, began to propel him from the room in the company of Mr. Davidson and Charles. He made no protest—he just walked by Colonel Fitzwilliam with his head bowed.

"Elizabeth, Georgiana, are you well?"

"I am well, but we should see to Georgiana."

Turning, Elizabeth and sat beside the young girl and coaxed her to rest up against her shoulder. Georgiana did not need much persuasion. She sighed with relief, and when she spoke there was a little tremor to her voice, though it sounded stronger than Elizabeth had expected.

"I am well, brother. Elizabeth stood up to the Mr. Jamison and made sure he could do nothing to harm me."

William turned to regard Elizabeth, and the fluttering she had felt earlier increased in intensity.

"I saw enough to know that Elizabeth was masterful. I thank you again, Elizabeth, for your care for my sister."

Smiling, Elizabeth said: "Whatever I did, I could do nothing else. I shall not be intimidated by the likes of Mr. Jamison."

Georgiana sat up and smiled at Elizabeth. "I am glad you are to be my sister, Elizabeth. I would like nothing more than to emulate you."

The events of the past few minutes left Elizabeth disinclined to correct the girl and tell her it was only a courtship. Elizabeth thus only smiled and expressed her anticipation of the opportunity to provide such mentorship.

"Then if you are well, I shall leave you while I deal with Jamison," said William.

He stood, but before he departed he threw a significant glance at Elizabeth, which she received with pleasure. Elizabeth could not help but anticipate being in his company again.

Once Jamison was escorted from the estate and told never to return, Darcy allowed himself to relax and consider the matter in a rational manner. There had been several times while speaking to the man that Darcy had been required to restrain himself from striking him repeatedly. As disgusted with Wickham as Darcy had been, he almost thought the Jamison was the more despicable man. Neither Elizabeth nor Georgiana would ever been in a position to be importuned by him again, of that he was determined.

"I know not how you managed to restrain yourself, Darcy," said Fitzwilliam when they were alone. "I was almost ready to run him through with my saber."

"That is still an option," said Darcy. "If I ever see the man again it will not go well for him."

Fitzwilliam only grunted and turned to another subject. "The young lady you are courting has certainly proven to be an intrepid young woman. I am astonished by her resilience."

"As am I," replied Darcy, though he thought to himself that he really was not. He had always known Elizabeth was special. Perhaps, however, he had not known quite how special she truly was.

A sudden desire to see Elizabeth and Georgiana swept over him and Darcy leapt to his feet and strode across the room, sensing that the others were following him.

"You know, there was a time when my company was sufficient for you. I can see that is now no longer the case."

"Someday, when you have secured a good woman for yourself, I am certain you will understand."

"Mayhap I will," replied Fitzwilliam.

But Darcy paid him no more mind as he walked through the halls, stopping at the door to the music room. From the inside he could hear the sounds of the pianoforte, a few of the notes sounding in discordant chords followed by feminine laughter, voices that he would know anywhere.

Smiling to himself, he opened the door and stepped in, taking the scene in before him. Mrs. Bingley and Mrs. Powell had returned in the interim, and they now sat on the sofa near the pianoforte, laughing at the antics of Elizabeth and Georgiana, who sat side by side on the bench. Gone was the fear and distress of earlier in the day, to be replaced with happy companionship and mirth, and Darcy felt himself go warm at the sight. This was what he looked forward to in the future. This would no doubt happen frequently at Pemberley.

"William!" said Georgiana as she caught sight of him.

His sister, seemingly restored to good humor, stood from the bench and ran toward William, catching him up in an embrace. Holding her like the precious woman she was, William smiled.

"I can see you are practicing again? Is Elizabeth proving to be a talented teacher?"

"I believe Georgiana is doing more of the teaching," said Elizabeth as she rose herself. "My talents run more toward walking and reading."

"Or protecting young girls who are the targets of unscrupulous rakes," said Caroline dryly.

Elizabeth only replied with a playful frown which Caroline ignored with impunity.

"But that does bring up a good point," continued Elizabeth. "I understand that Mr. Jamison was after Georgiana's dowry, but I do not understand how he thought he could actually escape in such a manner. For that matter, why was he so desperate?"

"Because he has gambled away his estate," replied Mr. Darcy. "He is in danger of losing it, so he is looking for a woman with a large dowry to help prop up his affairs, but as his creditors were pressing him, he did not have time to actually court a woman."

"It seems that I can only attract a man who wishes to use a woman for her dowry," said Georgiana in a morose tone.

"No Georgiana," said Elizabeth. She approached Georgiana, who was still standing beside Darcy, and spoke in a firm tone which brooked no opposition. "You have been targeted by two unscrupulous men, but not all men are like that. Do you think your brother looks to a woman only to see her money?"

Georgiana shook her head. Elizabeth's posture softened slightly, and she stepped toward Georgiana and clasped her shoulders in a gentle, but stern grip.

"That is well then. Otherwise, I should have considered your brother a simpleton, for as you know, I do not possess much of a dowry."

Giggling, Georgiana, leaned forward and kissed Elizabeth's cheek, prompting a smile in return. "You are a beautiful young woman,

Georgiana, and when the time comes, some young man will see your worth and make you forget that men such as George Wickham and Gabriel Jamison even exist."

A smile and a nod met Elizabeth's declaration, and Darcy could only look at the woman he was courting with awe. He had never known quite what to say to Georgiana, especially when she had been so low after the Ramsgate incident, and yet here was Elizabeth restoring Georgiana's confidence with a smile and a positive word. Surely fortune notwithstanding Darcy was gaining a greater treasure than could be measured through a courtship with this exceptional woman!

Though it took some effort, Darcy shook his bemusement away, for there was more to tell of the story. "In fact, his first target was you, Elizabeth."

"Me?" asked Elizabeth. She chuckled and shook her head. "I hope he was not too disappointed to learn of my true circumstances."

"Disappointed yes, but he was more mystified," said the colonel. "In fact, he could not account for the fact that he was unable to impress you and earn your regard with his affected manners. In his words, he had never known them to fail him before."

"Then he must have attempted it only with the most obtuse of my sex. I cannot imagine anyone not seeing his manners for anything other than what they are."

General laughter met this statement, including, Darcy noticed, Georgiana. He saw her shoulders relax slightly, and knew that it was a little confidence returning. After all, she had seen the man's manners for what they were as well as anyone.

"Then why did he continue to focus on Elizabeth?" asked Georgiana.

"Because of me," said Darcy. "He knew that I would not take kindly to him showing any preference for you, and thought that it would catch us off our guard if he kept his focus on Elizabeth."

"Which it did," said Caroline. "I, for one, had no notion that he had focused on Georgiana."

"He was actually waiting for an opportunity to take Georgiana when she was out walking the estate, but he was forced to move his timetable up because his situation was becoming desperate."

"But how was he even able to gain access?" asked Elizabeth.

"I can answer that question," said David Powell. "It appears like he left his horse in the strands of trees to the north, and entered the house through the servants' entrance at the rear of the house. One of the under gardeners saw him walking through the gardens but did not think much of it as he has been here frequently of late."

"Which he took full advantage of," said Elizabeth.

"Once he had secured Georgiana," said Darcy, "though he was a little vague on how he planned to spirit her out of the house, he intended to ride to where his carriage was waiting and then make for Gretna Green. He *assumed* that once he had Georgiana in a compromising position in his sole company, that I would have no choice but to capitulate and allow the marriage to proceed, even if I was able to catch them before the marriage was solemnized."

"Idiot," said Fitzwilliam to no one in particular. It was understood by the entire company that matters would have gone very ill for Jamison even if he had succeeded in only a small part of his plan.

"So what shall become of him now?"

Darcy smiled—it was just like Elizabeth to be concerned for someone who had wronged them, who might have wronged *her* had the situation been a little different. It showed a greatness of character and fullness of heart which Darcy found immensely appealing.

"I expect that his brother will assist him," said Powell. "Jamison is wealthy enough that he should be able to purchase his brother's debts. But I expect that it will come with a conditions as to his future behavior. This will not be the first time he has assisted Gabriel, so he is well aware of his brother's proclivities."

"Very well," said Elizabeth. "But enough of Gabriel Jamison. I believe we may have other, more pleasant things to discuss."

And so it was that the subject was dropped and the company spent the rest of the afternoon happy in each other's company. Even Georgiana had recovered from her fright and was now speaking and laughing, as if the incident had occurred weeks ago, rather than that very day. Darcy participated, feeling as happy as he had ever felt, but for the most part he was restless, wishing to have more of Elizabeth's attention for himself. Whenever she laughed, whenever she used some witty rejoinder, whenever she made some remark that made the others laugh, he felt a surge of jealousy for whoever held her attention. It was almost maddening the need to carry her off so that her attention could be solely fixed upon him.

It was late in the afternoon before he was able to accomplish his desire, and though he thought that Caroline might have had some influence in maneuvering the rest of the company so that they were able to engage in private conversation, he was too happy to be angry with her.

"Thank you again, Elizabeth, for your great care for my sister," said Darcy in a low tone. They sat on a pair of chairs situated slightly away from the rest of the company, but their heads were close together giving them that extra illusion of privacy. "She is precious to me."

"She is precious to all of us," said Elizabeth, reaching out to touch his arm.

"Regardless, it shows to me what kind of woman you are, and I cannot help but rejoice. I dare say that you will be a fine sister to her someday, and she shall be all the better for it."

"Are you not putting the cart before the horse, Mr. Darcy?" asked Elizabeth with a raised brow.

"Not from my perspective," said William. "We shall go as slowly or as quickly as you deem necessary. But the end result will be the same unless you irrevocably decide against me. My feelings are engaged, and my purpose is clear."

A rosy hue spread from Elizabeth's cheeks to her neck, and Darcy smiled a trifle smugly at his ability to provoke such a reaction in her.

"Then I believe that we shall be well matched, Mr. Darcy. I look forward to receiving your attentions."

"Elizabeth."

Elizabeth looked up, staring into his eyes. He thought he had never seen something so fine or beautiful as her dark eyes peering into his through her long, fine lashes.

"I would prefer you to call me William. I believe it is acceptable now that we are courting."

"Very well," said Elizabeth. "William it is."

In another part of the room, one other of the company looked on with satisfaction. Though others might say that they suspected or guessed, she could always say that she *knew* that William and Elizabeth were formed for one another. The scene in front of her, the two of them sitting closely, Elizabeth laughing at something William said, left no room for interpretation. And Caroline knew they had her to thank for it, for had she not invited Elizabeth, they would not have crossed each other's paths again, much to their mutual detriment.

The family party was complete; it was true that Louisa was not present, but she had been growing more distant over the years, and they were not truly close any longer. She would likely reenter their lives, more due to Hurst's penchant for fine food and finer spirits, all of which they could provide to him, but as Caroline looked around the room, she could see the sisters of her heart she had always dreamed of, to go along with the husband she loved and the brothers who had always been there.

Jane, modest and reticent as always, but sweet and kind and one of the truly beautiful people of the world; Georgiana, so much like Jane in essentials, but shyer, quieter, and still lacking in confidence which Caroline knew she would eventually obtain with Elizabeth as a sister; and Elizabeth, beautiful, bold, intelligent, and true, an exceptional person to round out their group. Caroline could not thank Charles enough for insisting on letting an estate in an out of the way corner of the kingdom, for it had brought her so much.

"Basking in a task well done?"

Caroline turned and favored David with a delighted grin. "It seems my stratagem has been a success."

"Indeed it has, dearest. I do not doubt that you shall never let the rest of us forget it."

"Perhaps I shall stop talking of it in time," said Caroline, before a laugh burst forth from her lips. She reached forward with a soft and loving touch, and caressed her husband's cheek. "I will not burden you too much with comments of how I was correct. I am too happy to do so."

And David, dear man that he was, merely smiled and lifted his hand to caress her cheek. All was well in Caroline's world. She had everything she wanted.

Chapter XIII

Though perhaps those who knew them intimately had little doubt, in the end Elizabeth Bennet and Fitzwilliam wed, and it did not take them long to reach their happy conclusion. The wedding took place on a beautiful summer day and was celebrated by all as an excellent match made between two who truly loved and respected one another. And if Caroline Powell was unable to restrain herself from the occasional smug comment or knowing smile, and if Mr. Bennet could not help but add his own boasting of pre-knowledge of the event, Mr. Darcy and his smiling bride were well able to overlook it given how happy they were. The younger girls, of course, had been surprised at their sister's attachment to such a stern and forbidding gentleman, and perhaps even more surprised when Mr. Darcy proved that he was not all sternness and displeasure. Their mother, though thankful for her second daughter's advantageous marriage to such a wealthy man, could never understand what he saw in her most impertinent and wild daughter.

Of the rest of their families, it was not to be wondered over their reactions to the news. The Fitzwilliams, knowing of their Darcy relations' unseemly connection to those who came from trade, were resigned, and actually came to respect and esteem Elizabeth, though she was never allowed to forget that her lineage was not up to the illustrious standards of the peerage. Elizabeth chose to see humor in the situation rather than be offended, and with time they too allowed the matter to rest, only commenting on it once or twice during the course of a visit, usually in reference to how well Elizabeth coped with society despite her unfortunate descent.

Unfortunately, not all their relations were happy for the couple. Mr. and Mrs. Collins were offended on the behalf of their patroness, and made their displeasure known. But their anger was nothing compared to that expressed by the lady herself, who actually took the trouble of journeying to Hertfordshire to make her sentiments known. That her tirade had no effect on the happy couple should not come as a surprise, and she went away resentful. It was several years before a reconciliation could be accomplished between them, and though she eventually was persuaded to relent and accept Elizabeth as a niece — though ever so grudgingly! — it was more because of her incessant need to advise than for any true affection. Elizabeth chose to accept her overtures and ignore her advice.

As for Georgiana, her improvement continued with Elizabeth as an example, and when she finally entered society a year after her brother's marriage, she was able to do it with tolerable composure. She was an instant success with many admirers, and with her sister-in-law's help, along with that of Mrs. Powell and Mrs. Bingley, she grew adept at separating those who saw her from those who saw her dowry. She did not marry by the end of that season, claiming that there was no one who caught her eye. In the end, it took three seasons before she found a man who could answer all of her expectations for happiness.

But what of Charlotte Lucas? When Elizabeth returned as an engaged woman, Charlotte had added her heartfelt congratulations to those flowing in from all quarters, but Elizabeth, who knew her friend better than most, could see that Charlotte's melancholy had not abated with time. When Elizabeth married, she invited Charlotte to Pemberley, hoping that some time away from her family in new surroundings would help her friend forget her woes for a time.

Charlotte came to Pemberley and quickly settled in with the family, for not only did Elizabeth love her as a dear friend, but Georgiana soon began to look up to her as a sensible woman. It was this sense which drew the attention of Kympton's parson, the man who had been given the living in place of the unworthy George Wickham. By the time Charlotte had been there for two months, Elizabeth's unwavering hope for her friend was realized, and she was happily engaged to a good man. Charlotte forever after thanked Elizabeth for inviting her and for not losing hope. And though she was naught but the wife to a simple parson, their relationship was built upon mutual esteem, sealed with two beautiful children. Charlotte lived a simple live away from society, but as she told Elizabeth, she did not repine the loss as she was happy in her new life.

Elizabeth and Caroline, together with Georgiana and Jane, remained the closest of friends and sisters throughout their lives, and if Jane was the beloved sister of her youth, Georgiana and Caroline became as dear to Elizabeth as Jane was. Elizabeth and Darcy expanded the Darcy clan with the addition of six children, four daughters who favored their mother in both looks and temperament, to go with two sons who were much like their father. The halls of Pemberley were often filled with the sound of girlish voices raised in laughter which made their reserved father smile in contentment.

Many years after their marriages, Elizabeth and Caroline stood together, witnessing another marriage, one which was filled with joy and a further bond to tie their families together. They had both experienced all that life had to offer—the pleasures and the pain, and both now bore the countenances of women who had seen much and lived full lives, and yet were still handsome women.

As the happy couple departed the wedding breakfast, held at the bride's family estate at Hollyfield, Elizabeth turned to Caroline and with mischief in her eyes said:

"Well, it looks like you have finally achieved your life-long desire."

Though Caroline was well aware of exactly what Elizabeth referred to, she affected ignorance. "I have not the pleasure of understanding you."

"Why, you have a daughter installed as the future mistress of Pemberley, of course."

Caroline regarded Elizabeth with amusement mixed with exasperation—this had been a common form of teasing between the two women for many years.

"I will have you know that I could have been mistress of Pemberley long before William ever met you."

"Perhaps you could have," replied Elizabeth. "But you did not, and I think that the knowledge of what you lost has tormented you over the years. Now you may live vicariously through Constance."

Any feigned annoyance on Caroline's part was diffused at the mention of her daughter's marriage to Pemberley's heir, and she smiled with pleasure.

"I am very happy for her. And Bennet was looking very handsome today; in fact, I believe he is the very image of his father."

"They shall be happy together. And we shall be tied together even closer."

"My dear Elizabeth," said Caroline, linking her arm with Elizabeth's, "I do not think we require a marriage between our children to draw us closer together. We seem to have managed quite well on our own."

"I find I must agree with you," said Elizabeth, as they began to walk back into the manor. "We have indeed been blessed."

The End

Please enjoy the following excerpt from the upcoming novel *On Wings of Air*, book one of the *Earth and Sky* fantasy trilogy.

As he pulled Tierra up, Skye said, "Come with me. I'd like to show you something."

Once they were outside the palace, Skye looked about, noting with some satisfaction that it was a clear night, with none of the higher clouds visible as far as the eye could see. The sky realm, sitting as it was on the tops of various clouds, certainly received less rain than the world below, but even so, the skies above were often obscured by high, wispy sorts of clouds which made looking up into the heavens much more difficult. Their religion being dependent upon a goddess who had ascended to live among the stars meant that the Skychildren felt a special kinship with the stars, and the fact that nothing was obscuring their beauty was perfect for what Skye had in mind.

Turning to his companion, Skye raised an eyebrow, squeezing her hand and feeling an intense pleasure at the sensations engendered by the feeling of her delicate hand being ensconced in his own. "Tierra, do you trust me?" he asked, knowing already what her answer would be.

"I do, Skye," Tierra said softly, her eyes never leaving his.

Tenderly, Skye drew her into him so that she stood encircled in his arms, and then he gathered a soft wind and propelled them up into the night sky. Tierra stiffened slightly, but she soon relaxed against him, allowing him to guide them up to their destination.

Skye settled them on the top of the tallest tower in the palace. It was situated almost in the center, a little to the back, and it stood much higher than any other tower in the complex. It was so high off the base of the cloud on which the palace stood that any light from the torches and candles which burned about the courtyard remained far enough below that it did not interfere with the light from the stars. There was no clearer view of the beauty of the heavens anywhere in the sky realm.

"You Skychildren are not precisely concerned with being conventional, are you?" Tierra asked when he had settled them on the platform at the apex of the tower.

Skye waggled his eyebrows at her. "You should remember where you are, Princess. In the sky realm, what I just did was *very* conventional."

They laughed softly together, and Tierra gazed around at her surroundings with interest. "I should think that a tall tower would be superfluous for a group of people who can lift themselves up in the air any time they like."

"We can't do it indefinitely," Skye said. "We're people of the skies, but we *are* subject to gravity, the same as Groundbreathers."

"And the trap door?" Tierra said, pointing at the door in the middle platform. "Why would you need stairs if you can just float up here?"

Shrugging, Skye replied, "I had never really thought about it, to be honest. In fact, I'm not even certain exactly how the palace came to be. It's always just been here."

"A lot of things in the Groundbreather world are the same," Tierra replied softly. She was silent for a moment, and then she turned to Skye and said, "Do you think that we get so caught up in our sense of superiority that we forget to look at the things around us?"

"It's possible," he said. Then he grinned and told her, "But enough of this. I brought you up here for a specific reason—not to speak of our peoples' shortcomings."

Feeling almost giddy, like a child showing a favorite toy to another, he guided Tierra to the end of the parapet, where they could view the palace about them. The edges of the cloud were far enough away on three sides that the ground was not visible. But it was not the world below that Skye was concerned about.

"Look, Tierra," Skye said, pointing up into the heavens. "From here, you can see the skies better than anywhere else in the entire sky realm."

As she looked up, Tierra gasped, and Skye could not help the smug smile on his face.

The night was indeed as fine as any he had ever experienced. The air was warm, with the scents of midsummer eddying about Tierra and Skye, and since the firmament above was clear, the stars could be seen far more clearly and in far greater numbers would ever be witnessed on the ground. Skye could tell that Tierra was spellbound by the sight, even if her people did not hold the stars in the reverence that his did.

"I would never have imagined that there are so many," she breathed.

"The further off the ground you are, the better you can see them," Skye said. "I expect that if you could go even further up, you would see even more."

"It is magnificent as it is."

"It is at that," Skye agreed.

They remained in silence for a few moments, and then Skye pointed to a group of stars in the western sky. "Look over there," he said. "That's Celesta, the mother of all Skychildren."

Tierra turned and looked at him, a question evident on her face. "Surely the Skychildren do not believe that group of lights *is* Celesta."

"No more than you would believe that a clump of dirt is Terrain," Skye said with a smile. "It's her sign, and it's the one constellation that is visible in the sky at all times of the year. It is our constant reminder that though she left us, Celesta continues to watch over her children from afar."

They were silent as they gazed at the stars for some time, Skye reacquainting himself with the beloved sights he had been denied these past months. Tierra, he thought, was marveling in the beauty which could be found in the sky realm, and he was happy that she was able to recognize splendor when it was presented to her. He could not determine exactly why, but it was important to him that Tierra approve of his home and acknowledge the good things in the sky realm.

"Do Groundbreathers have any constellations with specific meanings?" Skye asked after a few moments of silence.

Tierra snorted. "Do you think Groundbreathers pay a lot of attention to the stars? Given that our god is an earth god who hates the sky goddess, we keep our eyes firmly toward the earth rather than fixed on the skies."

"That is a pity," Skye said. "There is much beauty in the stars."

Tierra rested her head upon his shoulder, and Skye felt his breath catch in his throat.

"You will find no dispute from me," she told him. She paused briefly before speaking again. "We do not revere beauty as you do. Terrain has never been hailed for great beauty or even benevolence. He had a great heart, but he has always been considered somewhat reserved. I often feel it is more that we respect him than love him."

Nodding, Skye reflected on the fact that he had gathered as much during his time among her people. It was not necessarily a bad thing, he decided. The Groundbreathers were different from the Skychildren, to be certain, but who was he to say that their way of life was any better or worse than his own? The mere idea that he would have had such thoughts even two months ago was laughable, but now that he thought of it, he could not say that it was wrong.

"I guess there are more differences between our peoples than simply where we live," he commented, bringing an arm to rest gently around her back. He was not sure why, but a fierce protectiveness toward this petite woman was welling up within him, and he wanted more than ever to keep her safe.

"Indeed," she said softly. "I must say, though—if I ever do return home, I will certainly miss this view."

"Maybe I'll have to bring you up here every now and then to visit," he teased.

"If you mean to bring me as a slave, then I think I will forgo the pleasure."

"It won't be as a slave," he said. "It will be as a friend."

"Good," she said, sweeping her gaze out over the stars. "Skye?"

"Hmm?"

"I want you to know . . . I never wanted a slave. The practice has never been palatable to me. And now, of course, after having met you, I like it even less. But still, I . . . I am pleased to have met you."

Skye smiled, resting his head on hers. "I'm glad I met you, too."

COMING IN 2015 FROM
ONE GOOD SONNET PUBLISHING

For updates on publications, join the OGSP mailing list:
http://eepurl.com/bol2p9

FOR READERS WHO AN UNLIKELY FRIENDSHIP

A Bevy of Suitors
When a chance remark from Mr. Darcy causes Mr. Bingley to rethink which Bennet daughter he wishes to pursue, Elizabeth Bennet finds herself forced to choose from among a bevy of suitors.

Implacable Resentment
A grudge forces Elizabeth Bennet from Longbourn, necessitating her removal to the Gardiners' home in London. Ten years later, she returns to Hertfordshire at the request of her father and learns that the prejudice has not subsided. Armed with tenacity and determination, Elizabeth must withstand her family's machinations if she is to have any hope of finding her happy ending.

Love and Laughter: A Pride and Prejudice Short Stories Anthology
Those who need a little love and laughter in their lives need look no further than this anthology, which gives a lighthearted look at beloved *Pride and Prejudice* characters in unique situations.

Open Your Eyes
Elizabeth Bennet is forced to reevaluate her opinion of Mr. Darcy when Mr. Wickham contradicts his own words. In the course of her dealings with the two men, she realizes that first impressions can be deceiving.

A Summer in Brighton
Elizabeth is invited to travel to Brighton instead of Lydia with her dear friend Mrs. Forster. But what is supposed to be a relaxing vacation turns out to be anything but. Amid intrigues and newly discovered love, Elizabeth discovers that there exists in one man an evil so vile that it will drive him to do anything to hurt his hated enemy.

Waiting for an Echo, Volumes I and II
When Mr. Darcy comes to Hertfordshire to decide between two prospective brides, he has no idea that his eye will be caught by someone so much lower in consequence than him as Elizabeth Bennet.

For more details, visit
http://rowlandandeye.com/published-works/

ALSO BY ONE GOOD SONNET PUBLISHING

THE SMOTHERED ROSE TRILOGY

BOOK 1: THORNY

In this retelling of "Beauty and the Beast," a spoiled boy who is forced to watch over a flock of sheep finds himself more interested in catching the eye of a girl with lovely ground-trailing tresses than he is in protecting his charges. But when he cries "wolf" twice, a determined fairy decides to teach him a lesson once and for all.

BOOK 2: UNSOILED

When Elle finds herself constantly belittled and practically enslaved by her stepmother, she scarcely has time to even clean the soot off her hands before she collapses in exhaustion. So when Thorny tries to convince her to go on a quest and leave her identity as Cinderbella behind her, she consents. Little does she know that she will face challenges such as a determined huntsman, hungry dwarves, and powerful curses . . . .

BOOK 3: ROSEBLOOD

Both Elle and Thorny are unhappy with the way their lives are going, and the revelations they have had about each other have only served to drive them apart. What is a mother to do? Reunite them, of course. Unfortunately, things are not quite so simple when a magical lettuce called "rapunzel" is involved.

About The Author

Jann Rowland was born in Regina, Saskatchewan, Canada. He enjoys reading, sports, and he also dabbles a little in music, taking pleasure in singing and playing the piano.

Though Jann did not start writing until his mid-twenties, writing has grown from a hobby to an all-consuming passion. His interest in Jane Austen stems from his university days when he took a class in which *Pride and Prejudice* was required reading. *Acting on Faith* is his first published novel, but he envisions many more in the coming years, both within the *Pride and Prejudice* universe and without.

He now lives in Alberta, with his wife of more than twenty years, and his three children.

Please let him know what you think or sign up for his mailing list to learn about future publications:

Website: http://rowlandandeye.com/
Facebook: https://facebook.com/OneGoodSonnetPublishing/
Twitter: @OneGoodSonnet
Mailing List: http://eepurl.com/bol2p9

CPSIA information can be obtained
at www.ICGtesting.com
Printed in the USA
LVHW021211180121
676576LV00013BA/1756